GOD OF A THOUSAND FACES

Also available from Heywood Books
by the same author

The Unholy

God of a Thousand Faces

Michael Falconer Anderson

Heywood Books

© Michael Falconer Anderson 1987

First published in Great Britain 1987
by Robert Hale Ltd

ISBN 1 85481 006 5

This edition published 1989 by
Heywood Books Limited
55 Clissold Crescent
London N16 9AR

Printed in Great Britain by
Cox & Wyman Ltd, Reading

Prologue

Natalie Field swung around when she heard the knock on the door, tutted, put down her oven gloves and strolled across the lounge. She opened the door, ready to greet her boyfriend with a smile, a kiss and a joking admonishment – 'Forgot your keys did you … and you're always saying I forget things.'

But the man facing her was not Jack Law. It was another man, slightly shorter, square-jawed, with a mole on his cheek.

He looked vaguely familiar but she couldn't place where she knew him from.

'Good evening,' he said. 'Is this Mr Law's flat?'

'Yes,' she said.

The man looked ill. His face was an odd shade of ashen grey and his lips were colourless.

'Is Mr Law in?'

'No. I …'

He looked closely at her, inclining his head, then said: 'Don't you remember me?'

'I'm not … sure.'

'Allthorp.'

'I'm sorry. Yes, I remember you. The policeman. I didn't recognise you out of uniform.'

Of course she remembered him. She remembered him from the night when reality and nightmare had become one.

'When do you expect Mr Law back?' Allthorp said. 'It's important that I talk to him.'

'Not for hours.'

Why had she lied?

Why?

Why were alarm bells ringing in her brain?

Was it because of his appearance, the sleepy, drugged look in his eyes?

'All right,' Allthorp nodded. 'Could you tell him I called. I must see him. I'll come back later.'

He nodded curtly and was gone, striding along the corridor towards the lift.

She returned to the kitchen, opened the oven door and glanced absently at a roast, still wondering why she had lied.

Probably because she was disturbed, she decided. *Yes that was it.*

Allthorp reminded her of *that* time, the time she was trying to forget.

But why did he want to see Law?

Less than a minute after Allthorp left, she heard a key grate in the front door and Jack Law entered.

'Sorry I'm a bit late. I got held up on crucial business.'

She nodded doubtfully. 'A few pints at the pub.'

'Correct first time,' he said.

He threw down his briefcase, went into the kitchen and kissed her, locking his hands behind her waist.

'Someone was just here looking for you,' she said as he drew his head back.

'Who?'

'Allthorp. You remember ... the policeman who was there ... in the warehouse. You met him the day after ...'

'Yes. What did he want?'

'I don't know. You must have passed him in the foyer.'

'I came in the back way.'

He turned away from her, strolled to the window and drew the curtains back.

His eyes picked out Allthorp immediately, getting into a car across the street.

Picked out Allthorp and something else.

He stepped away from the window, pressing his back against the wall, horror dripping into his heart like molten metal.

'What is it?' Natalie said, her face suddenly taut, afraid.

He shook his head in brief jerky motions, unable to speak.

The nightmare wasn't over.

But how?

And how the hell had all this started? Where had it started?

PART ONE

1

'Have you ever heard of the Sedali?'

That was where it all began. That was what had started the whole thing off. Those words spoken in a bar in a Delhi hotel.

It hadn't even been Law's hotel. It was one of those big, blank, touristy places that they cloned all over the world for the international traveller so that he could wake up in the morning and have no idea where he was. Not at all like the places Law was staying with its hanging plants and whispering ceiling fans.

He'd only gone into the hotel bar by chance because the suffocating heat in the street was getting too much for him. Despite all his travels in hot climates, he had never really managed to come to terms with his body and 100°F-plus going together.

'Probably not surprising,' he'd once told his girlfriend, 'considering I spent the first couple of decades of my life in Edinburgh where seventy masquerades as a heatwave and if it was ever to hit ninety people would think the jaws of hell had opened up.'

He had ordered a nice cold beer and was preparing to sip his way through it and let his body heat drop a couple of degrees when a man in his mid sixties with horn-rimmed glasses and close-cropped grey hair that made him look like a retired US Army general sat down beside him, yelled an order at the barman and said: 'Some place huh?'

Law turned and nodded weakly, his 100°F-plus nod;
when it got that hot he didn't waste his energy with grand
gestures.

In the sixty seconds which followed he had discovered
that the man's name was Richard Bromley, he was a
Canadian, married to a woman called Molly, aged
sixty-five, retired, halfway through a round-the-world trip
which had cost a small fortune, of moderately right-wing
political persuasion and that he too thought Delhi was too
damned hot.

Then Bromley had said: 'So what brings you to Delhi?
Business or pleasure?'

'Business actually,' Law told him.

'What do you do?'

'I'm the travel editor for a Sunday newspaper in
London.'

'Oh yeah, which one?'

'The Globe.'

The Canadian was impressed. 'The Globe, that's a good
paper. I read that when I was in London. That's the new
one, isn't it?'

'Ten years old this year. My editor got the brilliant idea
of writing a series of articles called Letters from India. So
here I am. I'm heading home at the end of the week.'

'I've got a good story for you,' Bromley said.

Law stiffened. Like every newspaperman he had heard
those words spoken in a thousand bars and it was usually
the prelude to a long, boring tale which would never make a
newspaper story in a hundred years.

'Oh, really,' Law said, 'I ... I ...'

'Have you ever heard of the Sedali?'

'The Sedali? No.'

'The day after tomorrow is the Festival of the Sedali. I
saw it once when I was here fifteen years ago. It's one of
those obscure festivals the tourists never see, which is
probably not surprising because it takes place in Srinwanat

which must be one of the most godforsaken holes anywhere
on this planet. Talk about primitive; you've never seen
primitive till you've seen Srinwanat.' Bromley threw back a
whisky and soda, ordered another and gestured at Law's
glass.

'I'm fine, thanks,' Law said.

'Anyway, the Sedali is a girl somewhere between the age
of five and ten. They cast a horoscope and do
god-only-knows what else to pick her, then she reigns as the
golddess of the area around Srinwanat for a thousand days.
They say she is the incarnation of the god Dacahri.'

'That's one I've never heard of.'

'He's a demon god, malevolent. The really fascinating
thing about this festival is its obscurity. The rituals are just
as they always have been. Tourists don't go and, frankly,
when I went down there fifteen years ago with a friend we
weren't exactly welcomed. But it really is an unbelievable
sight seeing all these people worshipping this kid in this
town which is straight out of the Arabian Nights.'

'Interesting,' Law said and meant it.

It sounded like the kind of thing his editor would like.
Peter Forrest was always saying things like 'Travel isn't just
about writing about what the tourists will see. It's about
strange places, odd events, weird festivals, adventure.'
There were times when he thought the editor's talents
would have been better suited to the Boy's Annual of
Astonishing Yarns.

Law took out his notepad and biro.

'Assuming I could drag myself away from Delhi, how
could I get to this Srinwanat?'

'It's not easy,' Bromley said, assuming the air of a man
entering into a conspiracy, as if he was just about to divulge
the secret of King Solomon's Mines.

Law waited, pen poised, while Bromley tried to sort out
the details in his mind.

'You can get a flight to Kokangarth,' he said at last and
Law began to write. 'Indian Airlines will give you the times.

Then you have to get a train on to Srinwanat. You could do the trip in a day easily. There's a man in Srinwanat who runs what passes for a hotel in those parts ... or did when I was there. His name is ...' He tapped his head as if trying to jar loose the memory of the hotel owner's name. 'Baisakh,' he almost yelled. 'It's a real fleapit of a place but at least you could have a place to sleep. He rented us a car too. It was a wreck but it had four wheels and when you really built up speed it would do thirty-five.'

'Tell me more about this god, Dacahri.'

Bromley shrugged: 'I don't know very much really. He's called the God of a Thousand Incarnations or the God of a Thousand Faces. Each Sedali rules for a thousand days – one day for each incarnation of Dacahri – then she goes back to being a normal girl and usually marries the most eligible guy around. On the day of the actual festival they say the incarnations of Dacahri move among the crowd. If you see some of the things these people do, you'd believe that.'

'Pretty exciting stuff, is it?'

'Some of it was a bit horrific for my taste. Seeing a man put a rusty needle through his hand is not my idea of fun. There's an old city next to Srinwanat where they used to worship Dacahri a long time ago. You might be interested in driving out and having a look. I found it boring. I've seen more exciting parking lots but it depends on your taste. All that's left now is a bit of a wall and half a statue that used to stand at one side of the main gate. Beyond the wall there's only a pile of rubble.'

Law had filled a couple of pages of his notebook when Molly Bromley arrived. Richard Bromley introduced them. She was small and sixtyish with a cute, shy smile and proud of the fact that she had been married for forty-five years. 'This trip was a present from Richard to mark our forty-fifth,' she told Law.

Bromley bought another round of drinks and they sat down at a table by the window and chatted about travel and journalism and life in Vancouver and the Bromleys' three children. Half an hour later, Law made his excuses and left.

'Do you think you'll follow up on the Sedali?' Bromley said as they shook hands.

'I think I might,' Law said. Then he strolled out of the cool airconditioned hotel into the heat of the streets and wished immediately he was anywhere but Delhi. Anchorage, Alaska, would do.

The holy man stood in the vast, burning valley of yellow sand between Srinwanat and the ancient, ruined city of Didrana, his eyes staring at the orange orb of the setting sun, his arms held aloft, one rigid hand pointing to the entrance to the old city, the other to the new. It was as if he sought to unite the past and the present and the power of the sun. He was naked except for a tiny white loincloth and his long hair and tangled grey beard and the skin of his body were stained yellow by the sand. His lips moved in a silent mantra.

A small crowd had started to gather around him, knots of people watching him, talking in whispers.

Suddenly he fell on all fours, snarled and barked like a dog, saliva dribbling from his mouth. He scrambled towards one group of people, who scattered.

Abruptly, he stopped, assumed the lotus position and sat silently for several minutes.

Then he whiplashed onto his stomach and jerked back-wards and forwards, propelling himself through the sand. Near a second group of older people his head whipped back and his tongue shot out and darted about obscenely, like that of a snake.

The older people knew what it meant.

Dacahri was among them.

Sikkim Larkin, the desk clerk at the Jahan Hotel, was a quarter English and very proud of it. He was very fond of British visitors and especially helpful to them. He liked to tell any of those polite enough to listen about the place his grandfather had come from, the city called Coventry. Jack Law had been polite enough to listen and generous enough to buy Larkin a drink on a couple of occasions and so Law was the current number one on Larkin's list of 'guests who get priority treatment.'

When he saw Jack Law entering the hotel he hurried to get his key and handed it to him with a broad smile.

'Afternoon, Mr Law.' (He had called him Jack when they had been drinking together but now he was on duty.)

'Afternoon, Sikkim.'

'A fine day.'

Law half-laughed and shrugged as he turned towards the lift.

Larkin watched him go and something that was first-cousin to a sigh passed through him. Law was tall, broad-shouldered and what people called well-made. He had a mop of reddish-brown hair which was developing greyish lines at the sides, widely spaced grey eyes and a face that could have been sculpted from granite. He looked like Larkin would have liked to look. He didn't like being small, balding and chubby. In fact, everything he imagined Law to be was everything he would have wanted to be. Handsome, sophisticated, articulate, well-travelled and rich enough to eat at any restaurant he chose. Law would have laughed at the words 'handsome,' 'sophisticated' and 'rich.' 'Like the back end of a lorry' was how he would have described his face. And he was most certainly not sophisticated in his own eyes. As for rich – how often had he tried to explain to his editor about the cost of living and how difficult it was to live on his salary nowadays?

It was cool in Law's room. He threw off his clothes, took a shower and felt much better. Towelling himself dry, he snatched his notebook out of the breast pocket of his shirt, flipped it open on the table beside his bed and began to read through the notes he had made when he was talking to Bromley. When he was dry, he sat down on the bed and rang Rajit Sandii at the National Herald.

'Hello, Rajit. It's Jack ... Jack Law.'

'I thought you'd left,' Sandii said.

'No. End of the week. What I'm calling about is a place called Srinwanat. Apparently there's some kind of festival there in a couple of days. Something to do with a young girl called the Sedali. I remembered you talking about the swarm of gods in this country and I thought you might know something about this festival. Apparently the god is called Dacahri.'

There was a pause then Sandii said: 'I don't know very much about that festival but I know enough to know it might be a good one for you to stay away from. It's a wild part of the country and from what I've heard the Sedali festival can get rather rough.'

'Sounds exciting.'

'Please yourself, Jack. But I've heard some bad things.'

'What kind of things?'

'As often as not the festival degenerates into a riot and the police have a terrible job controlling everybody. And there are stories about people doing some pretty awful things to themselves.'

'Like a man sticking a rusty needle through his hand.'

'Even worse than that. I'd steer clear of this one if I were you, Jack.'

He pumped all the information he could out of Sandii but it turned out to be little more than Bromley had told him.

Five minutes later he hung up and lay back on his bed, staring up at the ceiling.

Would he or wouldn't he?

Sedali or no Sedali, that is the question, he thought.

Then he snatched up the telephone and called Indian Airlines.

2

The next day Law managed to get some tourist leaflets about Kokangarth but he could find nothing on Srinwanat or the Sedali. He spent the pleasant one-hour flight in a Fokker F-27 from Delhi to Kokangarth reading up on that city, checking his camera and film and flicking through some notes he had made on Jaipur for an article he had not yet had time to write. He knew he would have at least a couple of hours in Kokangarth and intended to make the most of them.

It turned out to be a pleasant enough city with houses built of the local golden stone, projecting balconies, shady avenues, an immense palace which had been converted into a museum and a fascinating temple, its walls covered in time-worn erotic carvings. He took a dozen or so shots of the temple, covering all four exterior walls, although he didn't think the Globe would have much use for these pictures. *Pure pornography* would be Peter Forrest's reaction, he was sure, and in western eyes that was probably what it was. Yet India was so different, its ways and standards so alien to an outsider. Here such carvings on a temple were totally acceptable yet tourists had to be careful about wearing 'immodest' dress into temples and leather of any kind – even belts and camera cases – was often taboo.

He began to think of Natalie as he was photographing the back wall and found himself chuckling and wondering what she would make of all these carvings. He could almost hear her say: 'Mmmmmm ... I don't have the energy to try

16

that one and as for that one ... you needn't think you're
going to do that to me.'

His month in India had been fascinating but it had also
been a long, long time and he had missed Natalie. A
one-month break in an affair that had lasted only six
months was far from ideal. He had tried to rationalise the
situation by suggesting to himself that a break might not be
a bad thing. After all, hadn't she said that after two bad
marriages she didn't want to rush into anything. And
hadn't his own marriage broken up only the year before. It
wasn't as if either of them was in the first flush of youth and
didn't know the score. She was 37 and he was 39. Maybe
their future lay in bandaging each other's wounds and
parting. Who knew?

He was still thinking of her as he strode into the station.
The platform was incredibly crowded and he had trouble
forcing his way through the throng. Were they all going to
Srinwanat? When he found the long queue that led to the
ticket office, he cursed the fact that he hadn't had time to
buy a ticket in Delhi. But there was nothing for it now but
to get into the queue and be patient.

Waiting in the slowly-shuffling line, he remembered
Natalie's oh-so-long legs and the way her slender, somehow
vulnerable back tapered sharply from the neatest shoulders
he had ever seen to a trim, small waist. *Dammit, I'm sexually
frustrated*, he thought. Or was it just the effect the carvings
were having on him?

Then he found himself facing an officious-looking ticket
clerk and asked in his very poor Hindi for a first class ticket
to Srinwanat. There were no first class tickets, the clerk told
him, and no airconditioned compartments. All he could
have was second class and Law knew what that meant – a
hot, sticky compartment and hard seats. He paid for the
ticket and wished for the first time that he had never met
Bromley in that bar in Delhi.

The train journey to Srinwanat was every bit as bad as he

expected it to be. He managed to get a corner seat which was a minor blessing but men, women and children were crowded all around him, seated on the floor and crammed into the seats and standing shoulder to shoulder in the aisles.

The fetid carriage was roasting hot as they pulled out of Kokangarth and that was the easy part. Much worse was to come. The train climbed a low hill then swung down into a yellow desert, a fiery furnace of a place. He tried to read both the paperback books he had brought with him but failed. He attempted to concentrate on his notes but found that impossible too. The heat dulled his senses into a kind of stupor and half an hour out of Kokangarth he found himself drifting off into a half sleep.

The passing of time was punctuated only by the slowly increasing heat and stench of the carriage, the occasional chatter of the occupants – who talked in dialects he didn't understand – and the bouncing and jerking of the train.

He was ripped out of his dozing semi-consciousness by an excited yell and saw one man standing at the window being joined by several others. He looked past them and in the distance he saw a range of low hills hunched over in the centre of a vast plain. Down the face of one of the hills there was a chaotic confusion of two-storeyed houses, huts and hovels.

'Srinwanat?' he said to the woman seated opposite him, pointing his finger out the window.

She nodded. This was Srinwanat.

He turned his attention back to the town as they drew nearer and didn't like what he saw. It had none of the symmetry, orderliness or majesty of Kokangarth. It looked like a dirty, ugly, harsh, hot, inhospitable place.

A few moments later, the train shuddered to a halt at the bottom of the hill, beneath the town. Law climbed out the door and found himself in a slow-moving sea of dhotis and white shirts, yellow, blue and red turbans, and patterned saris of pink and purple, green and gold.

Soon he was strolling along the streets of the town itself and it was every bit as awful as it had seemed from the outside. The better houses of Srinwanat would have been the slums of Kokangarth. They were built of the same yellow stone but were rundown, ageing and decayed. The rest of the houses were simple huts and hovels as bad as anything Law had ever seen.

He approached three groups of people and asked them where he could find the hotel owned by Mr Baisakh – the name Bromley had given him in Delhi. The first group didn't understand what he was saying. The second chatted among themselves about Baisakh but finally decided they had never heard of the man. The third group glared at him with such hostility that he hurried away up the street.

All the streets led to a huge central square and when Law reached it he found a bare, treeless place without a blade of grass. In the centre of the square stood a massive, rectangular building constructed of grey stone, its walls rising to a height of about fifty feet. It was unadorned and windowless and had only one large door, made of metal.

He was studying the building, strolling among the praying pilgrims and yelling pedlars, snake charmers and murky stalls when he saw the open Land Rover draw up in a cloud of yellow dust at the end of a street away to his left.

There were two soldiers in the front seats. The driver, a private, sat ramrod straight behind the wheel, his eyes fixed straight ahead. Beside him, a major flicked his swagger stick to and fro to deter the flies which buzzed around his head. He was a lean, spare man with broad shoulders and a thick, black moustache. His eyes watched Law candidly from under his peaked cap, sizing him up.

They were sure to know where Baisakh's hotel was, Law reasoned as he started across the square.

'Ram-ram …' he began as he reached the Land Rover.

'I speak perfect English,' said Major Morarji Fariya, interrupting Law with the air of a man who was used to giving orders, to being listened to, to handling subordinates.

He flicked his swagger stick angrily at a fly which buzzed around his ear and added: 'What are you doing here? Are you a tourist?'

'No, I'm not,' Law said and briefly outlined who he was and what he was doing in Srinwanat. He concluded by saying: 'I'm looking for an hotel owned by a Mr Baisakh. Perhaps you could help me?'

'It's about two hundred yards up that street over there,' the major said, pointing with his swagger stick. 'But it won't be up to the standard you're used to.'

'I'll survive,' Law said.

The major smiled thinly as if he knew something Law didn't, understood things Law could not even begin to comprehend, but couldn't be bothered explaining himself.

'Did nobody warn you about this festival?' the major asked.

'Yes, I've heard it can get pretty rough. Coming here was a spur of the moment thing actually ...'

'Rough.' The major spat out the word. 'It's one of the smallest festivals in India yet every year we have to move troops up here from Kokangarth and every year we have trouble.'

'Why? Why is it so bad? Is it something to do with this particular sect?'

The major's shoulders moved in a hint of a shrug and he dismissed the question with a quick sniff as if to say that that wasn't his subject and he wasn't going to waste words on something he didn't understand. Loading or cleaning a rifle, instilling discipline into men, firing a Browning automatic, controlling a rioting mob – these were all his subjects. On these he would speak at length. But the Sedali and Dacahri ... they were not his field.

'What time does the festival start?' Law said.

'Midday. When the sun is at its highest.'

'Is there anyone I could talk to in Srinwanat about Dacahri and the Sedali?'

The major pursed his lips and shook his head. 'No,' he

said firmly. 'You shouldn't ask anyone any questions about the Sedali or Dacahri ... not in Srinwanat ... not during the festival. They might misunderstand, they might be offended.'

'Offended? But I ...'

'Let me put it this way, Mr Law. Let's say you were an Arab, a Moslem, and you decided to cover Easter in Jerusalem or Christmas in Bethlehem. If you started asking questions you might upset people. It's the same in Srinwanat. Here, as a Christian, *you* might upset people ... and their god is not a tolerant, understanding, forgiving god.'

Law nodded: 'I understand. I suppose you're right.'

He had never found it a good policy to argue with the police or soldiers of another country.

'I am right,' the major assured him.

Law half turned away and gestured at the massive building in the square.

'What is that?' he said.

'The temple of the Sedali,' the major said. 'She'll come out of that door at midday tomorrow.'

'I see.'

'I'd prefer you to stay away from the temple ... and stay off the streets tonight. I don't want you getting into any trouble. Trouble for you would mean trouble for me.'

'I understand.'

'I can't order you to leave ... but if you must stay you'll have to keep what you westerners call a low profile during the festival.'

Law sighed: 'OK.'

The major nodded curtly to his driver and as the Land Rover jerked forward he touched the peak of his cap with his swagger stick in a gesture of farewell.

'See you,' Law shouted at the yellow dust stirred up by the Land Rover's tyres billowed around him.

Ten minutes later he found Baisakh's hotel – although the term 'hotel' was an exaggeration. He supposed it was

the rural Indian equivalent of a workers' boarding house –
but the average boarding house in Europe or the United
States would have looked like the Taj Mahal in comparison
to this place. There was no hot water, no electricity and the
only usable lavatory was situated in a nightmarish little
hovel just outside the back door. The hotel building was
made up of two old houses with a section of the adjoining
wall knocked down. Baisakh turned out to be a short, fat,
balding man with bleak, dead-fish eyes.

The good news was he spoke some English; the bad news
was he had no rooms.

'I must have a room,' Law told him, then explained how
he had met Bromley and the Canadian had recommended
the hotel and said he could rent a car from the owner. He
made it sound as if Bromley had found his stay pleasant
and comfortable and that brought a smile to Baisakh's face.

But he still insisted he had no rooms.

The problem was there were so many pilgrims in
Srinwanat for the Sedali festival. He was sure Mr Law
would understand.

If flattery and reasoned argument failed there was
nothing left but the ancient, international, tried-and-tested
method, Law decided. He put a hundred-rupee note on the
desk in front of Baisakh then added a second. The fat man
rubbed a hand thoughtfully over the black stubble on his
chin.

'I'll just need the room for two nights ... but I must have
a room to myself, I'm not sharing,' Law said.

'I ...'

'Do you still have the car for rent? I'll pay you for that as
well.' Law added another hundred-rupee note to the pile in
front of Baisakh. Then another. That settled the deal.

Baisakh showed Law to an upstairs room which was just
about as Law had expected it to be, dingy and grimy with
scarred, scratched walls, a suffocating stench of dust, a
broken-mirrored dressing table which looked as if it had
come down from the days of the raj, and a bed which Law

feared might be home to several armies of terrible germs. He decided to look on the bright side; there *was* a sink.

'I'll need the car tomorrow,' Law told Baisakh and the Indian brought out a key ring crammed with about forty keys of all shapes and sizes, removed one and handed it to Law.

'It's at the back.' he said.

'I want to drive out to see an old city near here. Bromley told me about it …'

'Didrana,' Baisakh said, 'it's just over the valley, west of Srinwanat. You can't miss it, there's only one road.'

'Anything to eat?' Law said.

'My wife could make you a chicken curry.'

'Thank you. I'll have it in my room. Could you ask her to cook it long and thoroughly, I have a sensitive stomach.' What he really meant was cook it long enough to kill any deadly microbes.

After Baisakh left, Law washed as best he could in the sink then lay down on the bed and drank one of the bottles of beer he had brought from Delhi with him. He felt surprisingly fatigued and put it down to the train trip from Kokangarth and the heat.

Half an hour later, Baisakh returned with the chicken curry which turned out to be delicious. When he had finished eating, Law made some notes about his journey from Delhi to Srinwanat then went to bed with a paperback. He had decided to take the major's advice and stay off the streets of Srinwanat during the evening.

At nine o'clock he started to doze. He turned down the oil lamp beside his bed and fell into a deep sleep.

The sound of yelling woke him, yanking him into a sitting position.

Where … What …

His eyes snapped open, his brain fought to throw aside the clinging shrouds of sleep.

What the hell …

The chaotic tangle of blankets in which he lay told him

his sleep had not been undisturbed and yet he could not recall dreaming.

The yelling continued, voices raised in anger somewhere in the street below his window.

His mind began to clear. How long had he slept? What time was it? He glanced at the luminous dial of his watch. One minute past midnight.

He wiped a damp mat of perspiration from his face, threw back the blankets and shuffled across the room. Drawing back the heavy curtain, he looked through the open window down into the moonlit street.

There were a dozen or so dhoti-clad men below him gathered in a shouting, arguing group. Two of the men nearest him were supporting a third man between them, an older man with tangled grey hair and a long beard who convulsed and jerked as if he was having some kind of a fit.

Sleep was retreating rapidly now and Law had started to try to understand what they were shouting about when one of the men turned and hurried away down the street. The group followed him, gesticulating angrily.

That was when it happened.

In the instant that Law turned away from the window, pushing a hand up through his damp hair.

He felt *something* glide through the open window into the room; something intangible, without form. Something that was there but was not there. He couldn't see it or smell it or touch it, yet he *knew* it was there.

A chill began to run up his spine and send tiny slivers of ice radiating through the muscles of his shoulders. Then fear began to contract his throat and he swallowed.

3

This is crazy. This is bloody stupid.

The words hung in his mind, struggling to wrench him back to the rational world. He was afraid in a way he had never experienced before. A cold dread washed through him in waves.

Afraid?

But men like him didn't get scared when they were alone in their hotel rooms. That was for little kids and teenage girls with vivid imaginations. That wasn't for the Jack Laws of this world who had knocked about a bit, seen violent death close up, made love to women of almost every nationality, seen vindictiveness and love, malice and compassion; men who wore emotional overcoats of concrete to cover their scar tissue and developed an aura of healthy contempt for the world and all its possessions. This kind of thing just didn't happen to men like him.

He strode stiff-legged back to the bedside, turned up the oil lamp, and gazed around the room.

Empty.

Of course it's empty for God's sake. What did you expect to see, Law? A ghost?

It was the same room as he had entered a few hours before. The bed, the lamp, the ancient dressing table, the sink …

The sink. It's under the sink …

'Bullshit,' he said aloud as he peered at the dark space beneath the chipped white sink.

There was nothing there. *Nothing, dammit. Nothing. Nothing. Nothing.*

He dropped his full weight onto the bed and it groaned and creaked and sent up a thin cloud of dust.

It was the curry, he told himself. That was the problem. It probably wasn't cooked properly. A combination of the curry, the heat and tiredness was playing tricks on his mind. What else could it be?

They say the incarnations of Dacahri move among the people on the day of the festival.

Wasn't that what Bromley had said? Something like that?

'Oh, bullshit,' he yelled and picked up his paperback, holding it in his left hand, his right hooked behind his head. He read the same sentence four times but it might as well have been in hieroglyphics; not a single word penetrated his mind.

Suddenly, something in the room shifted. *It* wasn't under the sink any longer. *It* was at the bottom of his bed, watching him. He could feel eyes boring into him, ugly, malevolent eyes.

Then he sensed that *it* was shifting again, moving away from him. The curtain trembled very slightly (surely it was the wind?) then he had a peculiar sensation that the room was emptying. As if something was pouring out of it, like liquid from a bottle.

He felt his shoulders slacken, the tension easing away.

'Bullshit,' he said for the third time to the silent, empty room.

Major Morarji Fariya wished more than anything else that he was somewhere else, anywhere but Srinwanat. The town offended him, the people offended him and the festival of the Sedali offended him. These things belonged to the old India, backward India; they had no place in the twentieth century, no place in the new India. If he had had his way he would have abolished the festival and dragged the people screaming and kicking into the twentieth century.

'Stop,' he told his driver as the Land Rover swung into a narrow lane on the west side of the town.

As the driver braked, he studied the naked figure of a man who lay on his back in a pool of moonlight between two buildings. His hands were by his side, palms flat against his thighs, his feet together. He looked like a corpse who had been laid out for burial.

The major sighed, climbed out of the Land Rover, strode across the lane and crouched down beside the man. He searched the neck and found a pulse immediately. He also discovered that he neck muscles were abnormally hard. He grabbed the man's arm intending to shake him awake and found the arm was rigid; it felt like metal covered with skin. He examined the rest of the man's body and discovered it was all equally hard and rigid. He tried to pull the man's right hand away from his thigh but found it impossible. It was as if it was fastened in that position, as if he was a statue.

The major knew what the Sedali pilgrims would say about this man. They would say Dacahri had borrowed his soul. Of course that was nonsense. He had seen these trance states many times before. They were all part of the mass hysteria, the mass hypnosis that went with these religious festivals. It had nothing to do with ancient gods; it had to do with the part of men's minds that the scientists had not yet penetrated.

He stood up and walked slowly back to the Land Rover.

'The colonel's headquarters,' he told the driver as he slid into his seat.

He had just completed the midnight check of his patrols. Everything was in order, the town was relatively quiet. He decided he would make his final report of the night to the colonel then try to get some sleep.

They passed through the main square of the town a few moments later. Sleeping pilgrims were scattered against the front of the buildings around the square and along the blank walls of the temple. Carpets hung down in front of

the empty stalls. There was a hush about the place that
struck the major as unnatural, a hush beyond a hush. He
ordered his driver to stop and turn off the engine and sat for
a moment listening to the deep, empty silence. Then a voice
began to murmur a mantra away to their left and he told
the driver to proceed.

It was as they motored slowly out of the square that the
major caught a glimpse of a man seated at the corner of a
building, his face lit by a ragged chunk of moonlight. The
man's eyes were fixed on the moon, unblinking, his hands
held out in front of him as if in supplication. Dozens of long
needles had been thrust through his hands and neck and
cheeks and looped under the skin of his forehead, eyelids
and lower lip.

Something deep inside Major Fariya shuddered with
revulsion but his face remained impassive.

Law slept later than he had intended the next morning.
When he woke, he shaved in cold water, had a quick wash
in the sink and cleaned his teeth using water from a plastic
container he had brought with him.

It was after nine-thirty by the time he went downstairs.
He found Baisakh behind his desk, scratching at the
stubble on his face, and asked him about the route the
Sedali would take after she left her temple at midday.
Baisakh told him the girl would be carried in a litter down
the hill to the point where Law had entered Srinwanat the
day before, then she would cross the valley to Didrana,
where she would pray. After that, she would return the way
she had come.

Ten minutes later, Law was driving Baisakh's ancient
Wolseley along the road to Didrana, sounding his horn
constantly so that the crowds of pilgrims still flowing into
the town would part and let him through.

One large group seemed to resent his presence and were
reluctant to move aside. He decided the best course of
action would be to drive off the road and around them but

found there was a three-foot drop at the side of the road. The situation grew tricky as they started to gather around the car, pointing at him and yelling and arguing among themselves. Then three soldiers arrived on the scene. The crowd dispersed at once and he drove on.

The further away from Srinwanat he drove, the fewer pilgrims he encountered, and he assumed all the pilgrims were gathering at the temple.

He had no difficulty finding Didrana. The road ran right up to a line of low stones which had once formed the base of the western wall of the city. He parked the car and walked about. In places the wall had disappeared altogether while here and there it rose to a height of seven or eight feet. Beyond the wall he saw the foundation stones of what had once been major buildings and piles of rubble the meaning of which archaeologists had been trying to decipher judging by the trenches and mounds scattered about the site.

About four hundred yards from where he parked he found what had once been the main gate and the statue Bromley had mentioned.

It was about fifty feet high, an intricately carved representation of a voluptuous woman (or goddess?) with four huge breasts set in a line across her chest and four arms raised high in the air. The figure was shaven-headed and devoid of body hair and a tongue of stone shot ten feet from a gaping mouth and curved downwards. Pyramids of rock set in massive, oval eye-sockets gave the statue the impression of staring. A section of the left side was missing – about one-third of the structure – but it appeared to Law that originally it had been carved from one great, grey stone.

He strolled around the statue taking pictures then returned to the base and studied one huge foot close up. The surface was pitted and pock-marked by time and rain and sandstorms but he could still make out the magnificent detail.

He reached out a hand and touched a section of grey skin which bulged out from beneath a semi-circular toenail.

It's warm. It's alive. The words scrambled into his brain like insects scampering along hot metal.

Instantly he withdrew his hand and stepped back quickly, almost falling over. For a moment his mind was paralysed then a rasping laugh choked up from his throat.

Of course it's warm, idiot. It's standing out here in the sun. Anything would be warm in this weather. What did you expect? Ice?

He turned quickly and strode back towards the car, the *feel* of the statue staying with him, an odd prickly sensation on the palm of his right hand.

He slid into his seat and sat watching the statue for several minutes, his hands resting on the steering wheel. Why was he so jumpy? Why had he been jumpy in his room during the night? Was it something about this place or something wrong with him?

He snatched at the key and the Wolseley's engine grumbled into life.

Major Fariya waited for the Sedali to emerge from her temple with the resignation of a true professional soldier. He was standing on the seat of his Land Rover several streets down from the main square, sweeping the crowd with his binoculars.

Ten minutes before there had been pandemonium but the police and soldiers had used their lahtis mercilessly and forced the people back behind the barricades which lined the Sedali's route.

He studied the people around the temple with a thinly disguised contempt. Some were almost naked, their bodies caked in dampened yellow sand. Many had slashed their chests and legs with knives to intensify their sacrifice and passion. That morning he had seen men walking through beds of burning embers and cupping hot coals in their hands until the flesh sizzled. At that moment he had been very glad he was an atheist.

He lowered his binoculars, rubbed his eyes, then raised them again.

Suddenly a hush fell over the main square as the litter bearing the Sedali left the temple gate.

The Wolseley developed a dry cough as Law was driving away from Didrana. It didn't appear to be anything too serious at first but half a mile down the road the car began to shudder, quivering from bumper to bumper. Law eased it down a gear and nursed it along but it started to lose power steadily. Then the engine convulsed once and died away.

He kicked at the brake and as the car slowed, jerked on the handbrake. It didn't hold the first time and he hauled it on again, venomously, venting his anger on the piece of the Wolseley nearest to hand. He snapped the ignition key to the off position then on again. The engine grumbled, coughed, whined and died. He tried twice more with identical results then leaned back in his seat with a sigh and glanced at his watch. It was eleven-twenty.

I don't believe this, Law heard a voice in his head say, ice cold with anger. *I come to this stinking-hot hole of a place in a stinking-hot train and spend a night in Baisakh's stinking-hot dump. All this to see the Sedali ... And now thanks to a Wolseley with chronic bronchitis I might not get to see her at all.*

He began to swear slowly, intoning the words as if he was delivering them on stage, enunciating each one with a perfect clarity.

What the hell could be wrong with the car? he asked himself. Carburettor? Plugs? Electrical system? He knew that with a car of this age the answer could be almost anything.

He opened the bonnet, and fiddled about with leads and poked and jiggled everything in sight. Then he tried to start the Wolseley again. It grunted, shuddered, whined and died.

He searched the boot and the glovebox for tools but there weren't any. The boot contained a rolled-up carpet and the glovebox nothing but a lining of yellow sand.

He didn't have any choice, he decided, he'd have to walk. It was as he was reaching for the keys that he decided to give it one more try.

'Optimism forever,' he muttered as he flicked his wrist.

The engine growled into life like that of a car fresh from the factory.

"You must be part mule," he said to the Wolseley as he sent it shooting forward down the road to Srinwanat.

It was after midday when he reached the outskirts of Srinwanat. He headed straight for the main square but was still four hundred yards away when it became apparent he would never get through the teeming mass of pilgrims jamming the streets. He took a sharp right, drove three hundred yards up a narrow lane then swung left. He estimated when he was at a point parallel with the main square, drove another five hundred yards, then swung left again, down a steep, dusty lane. This would bring him out at the Sedali's route ... but would she have passed?

Then he saw the rows of pilgrims lining the street below him. He braked, dropped the Wolseley into third gear and peered at the crowd. They were all looking to their left – that meant the Sedali still hadn't arrived at this point.

He braked the Wolseley to a standstill on the steep, dusty slope about twenty yards from the backs of the last line of pilgrims and snatched on the handbrake. Again it didn't hold first time. He grabbed at it again and it snicked into place.

A wall of noise hit him as he jumped from the car and jogged down the hill, his cameras bouncing on his chest. People held their arms aloft and chanted prayers, women shrieked and tore their hair and scratched their faces, men yelled with voices hoarse from shouting.

He reached the crowd and jostled his way through the mass of waving, gesticulating bodies, heading uphill, towards the Sedali.

He stepped over two men who lay on their backs in the

dust, ignored by the crowd. Their bodies convulsed, their muscles twitched under the skin and foam ran from the corners of their mouths. Law spun and snapped two quick pictures, then hurried on. At the other side of the street, a man propped up on a crutch had forced his way to the front of the crowd and was slicing a long knife along his forehead and down across his cheeks. Law held the camera high above his head and got the best pictures he could.

Then he saw the Sedali.

At first he could make out only a small, black-haired figure in a blood-red robe, seated on a chair in a mound of flowers on top of a litter. He caught a glimpse of the men carrying the litter. They were wearing full-length white robes and strange white hats like skull-caps which were strapped to their heads with long white sashes which fastened under the chin.

He stepped up into the raised doorway of a house and clicked off a couple of pictures. When he lowered his camera, she was close enough for him to see her clearly. He guessed she was no more than seven. Shining, coal-black hair framed a pretty, small face. But it was her dark eyes which drew his attention. They stared straight ahead from beneath heavily-charcoaled eyelids, as if unaware of the crowd or as if it was beneath her dignity to even acknowledge their presence.

As she drew level with him she turned her head briefly and for an instant their eyes locked. He saw that hers were very large, brown and oval-shaped. He saw something else too, something that made an odd prickling sensation run up his spine.

They did not look like the eyes of a child. There was no innocence there, no un-knowing, no simplicity. They were hard, brooding and calculating. He felt a strange relief when they swept away from him.

Nonsense, he told himself. *You're getting caught up by the hysteria.*

He started to push his way through the crowd, moving

parallel to the litter, snapping pictures as he went. He saw now that the chair in which she sat was ornately carved and studded with jewels. All around him people began to fall and prostrate themselves on the ground.

He reached the lane where the Wolseley was parked about twenty feet ahead of the Sedali, sprinted up the hill and positioned himself for a high shot. Then an idea occurred to him. He hurried to the Wolseley, hoisted himself onto the bonnet and stepped up onto the roof. Perfect. From here he would get a great shot of the crowd, the bearers, the litter and the Sedali.

It was as he waited that he saw Major Fariya's Land Rover draw up in the lane opposite. He gave a quick wave but he wasn't sure if the major saw him. Fariya got out of the Land Rover, hoisted a pair of binoculars and swept them across the massed pilgrims in the street. Then the Sedali moved into view and Law raised his camera.

In that instant the car gave a brief lurch. Law staggered backwards, spreading his feet and throwing out his arms to steady himself.

The damned handbrake. It was the damned handbrake that wasn't holding properly. It had slipped down a notch.

He knelt down on the roof and was climbing onto the bonnet when the car lurched again then shot forward, pitching Law into mid-air.

His shoulder and the side of his face thudded into the ground. A spasm of pain shot across his chest and down his arm and he heard a smashing, tinkling sound as his cameras cracked wide open. He sat up groggily, spitting dust from his mouth.

Then he saw the Wolseley careering down the hill towards the pilgrims and the procession and a sense of panic stabbed into his intestines, making him feel instantly nauseous.

'Look out,' he yelled, dragging himself to his feet. But his voice was a throaty rasp and his warning was drowned in the noise from below.

He started running down the hill, yelling as loud as he could.

'Look out. Hey. Look out.'

A pink-turbanned man in the crowd turned, stared at the Wolseley then ran to one side, shouting a warning.

The Wolseley brushed the wall of a building at the far side of the lane and tore on, gathering speed with each yard.

Other faces turned now and people began to scatter.

Still Law yelled: 'Look out, for God's sake look out.'

The crowd had thinned by the time the Wolseley reached them. Law stopped dead and stood frozen with horror as it brushed aside a woman, sent three men flying into the air then punched into the line of litter bearers.

The Sedali was catapulted forward through the air.

4

For an instant the world seemed to freeze, to stand absolutely still. It was as if the faces in the street below were exhibits in a museum tableau. Dozens of eyes watched Law, uncomprehending. There was no sound, only a heavy silence. Then a woman shrieked, like a razor scraping along glass.

Law was aware that a few people had started to hurry towards the injured. His first instinct was to help and he took two quick steps down the hill. He heard some words tumble from his mouth.

'I ... I'm sorry ... it was ...'

He was addressing the small crowd of men who had started to gather at the bottom of the lane, staring up at him.

Then a man pointed at Law and yelled and the fury of the yell jolted through Law like an electric shock.

Three men broke away from the crowd and ran up the lane towards him. Instinctively he wanted to make them see sense, to reason with them. It had been an accident after all. But instantly he realised how ludicrous arguing with them would be. How could he reason with a mob like this?

As he spun and sprinted away he saw that the rest of the crowd were funnelling into the lane now, coming after him.

He dodged up a narrow alley where overhanging balconies cut out the sun, shouldered aside a handcart and spotted a door that stood slightly ajar. He kicked it open and rushed into the dim interior which had a strange stale-food smell about it. There was another door at the far side of the room and he jerked it open and found himself in a small courtyard. There were no doors exiting from the courtyard apart from the one he had come through. As his ears picked up the sounds of men shouting in the house behind him he grabbed the top of the wall and dragged himself over.

His dominant thoughts were of survival because it was obvious arrest and trial was what not what these pilgrims had in mind. But questions about the accident buzzed about in the distant corners of his mind. How badly hurt were the people the car had hit? Were any of them dead? Had the Sedali been injured?

He was in a street now and the sun burned down on him, dragging sweat from his pores, soaking his shirt and hair. He swung to his left, kicking up little puffs of dust.

Where was safety? What could he hope for? An army patrol? A place to hide? A couple of policemen?

The mob were clambering over the courtyard wall now. He could hear their frenzied yelling more clearly as they poured into the street.

Then he saw a group of men burst into the street up ahead of him, cutting off his line of escape. A thin, youngish man with a pink turban pointed at him and yelled something and they began to run towards him, jostling each other in their eagerness to get their hands on him.

Was this it? Would it all end here, beaten to death by a crowd of Indians who worshipped a god he had never heard of before he had met Bromley in that bar in Delhi?

To his left the street was bordered by a wall ten feet high. To his right there was an old house, flanked by scarred, chipped walls about six feet tall. His heart triphammered in his chest as he headed for the door. He snatched at the handle. It was locked. He shook it violently as if it was a living thing which had offended him. But it held fast. He ran to a window and pulled at it but it was useless. From both sides, the mob closed in on him.

He was beyond fear. There was no time to think about anything. It was as if something in his subconscious had taken control of him, something that would instinctively drive him towards a course of action which would give him a maximum chance of survival.

He darted to the wall adjacent to the house, drove the toe of his shoe into a hole where a brick had fallen away, grasped the top of the wall and kicked himself up.

It was as he dragged his left foot out of the hole in the wall that he felt two hands gripping his calf, pulling him back.

Major Fariya saw the Sedali die.

He saw her small body somersault in mid-air and thud into the house at the far corner of the lane.

He saw her head whip back, snapping the neck, and her skull cave in.

He saw it and reacted immediately.

As the pilgrims poured up the lane opposite in pursuit of Law, he dashed around the Land Rover.

"Move over," he yelled at his driver and slid in behind the wheel.

He wrenched the gearstick into reverse and sent the Land Rover shooting back up the lane, its wheels hacking twin trenches in the dust. He drew level with a lane that headed south, braked hard and accelerated down it, the roar of the engine deafening in the confined space between the houses.

About four hundred yards down the lane, he swung right, heading back towards the main street. Knots of pilgrims were gathered in confused, yelling, gesticulating groups, uncertain what had happened. He sounded his horn and forced a way through.

As the Land Rover climbed the slope at the other side of the main street, he flicked off the clip on his holster.

Law jerked his head around and appraised the situation instantly. The mob were still about thirty feet away. Only the pink-turbanned man and another youngish man had reached him. The first held his calf and the other dragged at the tail of his shirt then looped a hand into his belt and began to jerk at it frenziedly. Law snatched his leg free and lashed a kick at the first man. It caught him in the centre of the chest and sent his slender frame flying backwards. He sat down with a thud.

Law held onto the top of the wall with his left hand and chopped at the arms of the second man with his right. Still the man held on.

An anger like Law had never known before washed over him. He dropped from the wall, spun and hammered an awesome punch into the centre of the man's thin, young face. The blow brought blood spurting from the nose and mouth and sent the man stumbling to one side.

Law jumped at the wall again, desperately climbing with toes, knees, hands. This time he cleared it, only seconds ahead of the mob. They howled with an intensified fury as they scrambled after him.

He dropped into a garden, a cool, shady area beneath trellisses of hanging vines that seemed strangely out of place in Srinwanat, a tiny oasis of green grass, flowers, and a pond which seemed to contain some kind of fish. A woman had been seated on a bench and as Law flung himself over her wall she half rose. She stayed in that position, half-seated, half-standing, uncertain what to do, as he jumped the pond, threw open a door and ran into the house.

He entered a huge room – hanging wall-carpets, two ornamental swords, a stuffed tiger's head, hanging plants. *An open door.* He dashed through it and slammed it behind him.

He was in a long, dark hallway now but at the far end he could see what looked like another door with sunlight bleeding around the edges. There was a huge key in the door and when he reached it he fumbled the key out of the lock, stepped outside, pulled the door shut with sweating hands and locked it.

There was a lane directly opposite and he was heading for it when he heard a car horn sounding to his left and saw Major Fariya's Land Rover hurtling towards him.

'Get in,' the major shouted as the Land Rover slewed to a halt.

Law looked from the major to the lane and back again.

'Get in, hurry up,' the major bawled.

There was a loud crack then a ripping noise as the door Law had come through was torn off its hinges. Men tumbled out into the street and ran towards him.

As he threw himself into the Land Rover's back seat, he saw crowds of people running towards him from both ends of the street.

The major snatched the Land Rover's gearstick into first and accelerated forward, steering with one hand, heading for the lane.

As the mob closed in, he brought out his revolver and fired a single shot into the air. The *bam* echoed around the street.

5

Law listened to the harsh whisper of the bullet as it rocketed skywards through the clear air.

It was the last sound he heard before they plunged from sunlight into the dim, shadowy lane. The major jerked the Land Rover left, then right, then left, zig-zagging his way across Srinwanat. Law lay in the back, not bothering to sit up, just trying to catch his breath. Then he realised the yelling of the mob had become distant, subdued.

Suddenly he was thrown forward as the Land Rover slid to a halt.

He propped himself up on one elbow and listened as the major gave his driver his orders in Hindi.

'I want you to find the colonel and tell him what happened. Tell him I saw everything and that it was an accident. Tell him I am taking Mr Law to Kokangarth and I'll wait at the barracks for him to radio further orders but that in my opinion we should get Mr Law back to Delhi as soon as possible. Understand?'

The driver nodded, climbed out of the Land Rover and saluted.

'You can come up front whenever you like, Mr Law,' the major said over his shoulder as he accelerated away, nodding curtly to his driver.

Law sat up and rubbed his face. He saw now that they were leaving Srinwanat, heading along a narrow, dusty track that wound its way through low, yellow hills pock-marked with smooth grey stones.

Law nodded slowly and managed to haul himself into the front seat.

'I only picked up the gist of what you were saying,' he told the major. 'Do I understand you to mean you're going to get me out of Kokangarth immediately?'

'I think it would be best if you get out of India immediately,' the major said.

'Won't there be an inquest or something?'

'Yes, but I'll give evidence about what happened and I'd like a written statement from you before you leave.' He swung the Land Rover round a steep bend in the road then added: 'That is assuming the colonel agrees with my recommendation ... and he usually does.'

'You saved my life,' Law said slowly, studying the major's face.

'All in the line of duty.'

Law shrugged. 'I have some things at Baisakh's, some notebooks and ...'

'I'll arrange to have them forwarded to your London address.'

'Thanks.'

They reached a village – a dozen or so hovels, a herd of goats in a pen, a barking dog tethered to a stake. There were no people and Law assumed they had all gone to the festival.

'You actually saw what happened, didn't you?' Law said.

The major nodded.

Law hesitated then added: 'Was anyone killed?'

'The Sedali's dead,' Major Fariya said matter-of-factly.

'Dead,' Law almost yelled.

'Yes.'

'Are you sure?'

'I'm sure.'

'Any others.'

The major shrugged uncertainly. 'Three at least. That isn't so bad for a festival like this, believe me.'

Law sighed: 'I shouldn't have climbed up on top of the car. The handbrake gave way.' He was about to add that the handbrake had failed to work properly on two occasions during the morning and that he should never have parked the car on the hill. But he didn't.

Instead he sat in silence, examining and re-examining his memories of the day's events, aware of the idiocy of his actions and a sudden wave of guilt which washed over him. It had been stupid to park on the hill, criminally stupid. And now people were dead because of that.

The track reached the last peak in the range of hills and wound its way down into the desert.

Major Fariya broke the silence.

'It was Baisakh's car, wasn't it?'

'Yes.'

'I thought I recognised it. There aren't many cars in Srinwanat.'

'I rented it to go out to Didrana.'

The major nodded as Law began to talk about the ancient city and describe the huge statue he had seen.

'Dacahri,' the major said when Law paused.

'The statue? That was Dacahri?' Law said.

'Yes.'

'I hadn't realised Dacahri was female. I couldn't find out much about the Sedali or Dacahri before I came here ...'

'Dacahri was not always female, in some incarnations he was male. According to myth ... ' – he said the word "myth" with jagged contempt – 'Dacahri worked from his first incarnation through a thousand lifetimes until he reached a state of perfect evil. Now he moves from the body of one young girl to another ... forever.'

'The Sedali.'

'Yes. Didrana was once a great city and for a long period all the kings bore the name Dacahri.'

'Why does something like that still have a hold over the people?'

The major shrugged: 'Superstition. I've seen people stick

nails through their bodies and hold hot coals in their hands … all in the name of Dacahri. I've even seen a man who had had his leg strapped up behind his back for twenty years in honour of Dacahri.' The major half-laughed mirthlessly. 'He's not like your god, you know. He isn't a god you love. He's a god you fear, a god you must appease.'

'And what do you think?'

'Me. I think it's nonsense.'

'Are … you religious?'

'Publicly or privately?'

'I'm sorry. I didn't mean to pry.'

'That's all right. Privately I'm an atheist. What I believe in is the army and the godlike qualities of my commanding officer.'

He glanced at Law and smiled. It was the first time Law had seen a genuine smile on the major's face. It seemed to light up the hard, tanned features and give him an almost boyish look. Law realised for the first time that the major was probably no more than thirty. He had taken him for ten years older.

They were about twenty miles from Kokangarth when Law began to feel a tightening in his stomach that turned quickly to nausea. He asked the major to stop the Land Rover, got out and vomited into a ditch.

'I'm sorry about that,' he said, sliding back into his seat.

It was at that instant that he had a strange feeling they were being followed. He looked back over his shoulder. The desert was yellow and blank, unmarred by any sign of a dust cloud which would have indicated movement.

He hunched down into his seat, rested his head back and began to breathe deeply, his mouth wide open, trying to rid himself of the vile taste of his vomit.

When they reached Kokangarth, the major drove straight to the barracks. He left Law in a bare interrogation room with an ancient typewriter and the instructions: 'You're a journalist, you write your own statement. Sign the bottom of each page.'

Law outlined the reasons for his visit to Srinwanat, gave his full address in London and the address of the car's owner, and typed out a step-by-step account of everything that had happened from the moment he parked the car on the hill until he had been picked up by the major. He had just finished the third and last page of his statement when the major returned.

'There's a flight in twenty minutes,' the major said. 'You're to be on it. Colonel's orders.'

Law scribbled a signature on each sheet and handed the statement to the major, who scanned it quickly.

'Good, just one more thing. When do you plan to leave India?'

'Tomorrow or the day after.'

'Excellent. I'll forward your belongings in Baisakh's hotel to your London address. There's a driver waiting for you at the main entrance ... I'll show you the way.'

Law shook hands with the major at the front of the main barracks building.

'How can I say thanks?' he said.

'Don't say anything ... and don't blame yourself. As they say ... accidents do happen.'

'Goodbye then.'

'Goodbye, Mr Law.'

Major Fariya gave Law a half wave as the journalist was driven out the main gate. Then he turned and strode back into the cool barracks entrance hall.

An hour later, he had completed his own paperwork about the incident. He told the duty officer that he was signing off duty and would report in the morning to see if the colonel wished him to return to Srinwanat or remain in Kokangarth.

Heading home in his Ford Cortina, just as he passed through one of the city's main intersections, he had the uncanny sensation that he was not alone in the car, that something or someone was there with him. He glanced into the back seat but there was nothing there. For some reason he couldn't explain, he had expected to see Jack Law.

6

All Law felt was heat, burning heat, like he was lying in flames. A crimson fog surrounded him and he writhed about as he glided slowly through it, weightless.

Where was he?

What was happening?

The fog became denser, then thinner, then denser again. There were no definite shapes in the fog, only eddying red clouds, and he had no way of knowing what was beyond them. He struggled to make sense of it but it was as if parts of his brain were sealed off. He fought to mobilise them but failed, a horrible feeling of helplessness washing over him.

He emerged from the fog into bright sunlight with a suddenness that startled him. He was in a sea of yellow sand like the desert which surrounded Srinwanat.

He wasn't really back in the desert. He was … He was …

His mind struggled to find the answer.

A movement away to his right caught the corner of his eye and he swung his head round. At the top of a low mound he saw a bare foot, fastened to a stake by a length of rope. The foot jerked twice then quivered and lay still.

He moved towards the foot, staring at it. Then he saw two blistered legs and a triangle of pubic hair.

A woman. Staked out in the sun.

Suddenly fingers touched his shoulder and he jumped, knocking them away desperately.

Who?

What?

'Are you all right, sir?' a voice said.

A woman's voice? Yes, it was a woman.

He shot back into the crimson fog, flailing his arms about. An instant later the fog parted then disappeared altogether and he found himself looking into a pretty face, framed in fair hair.

He had seen her before. He knew that. *He knew where he was ... but couldn't quite grasp it ...*

'You were having a dream, sir.'

The woman's mouth was moving again and he heard the words as if from far away.

'Yes, I ... I'm sorry ...'

He knew now. He was on the plane, going home. She was the air hostess.

'I'm sorry,' he repeated. 'I didn't get much sleep last night. I haven't been well for a couple of days.'

He felt he ought to keep the excuses tumbling out but decided there was no point. Instead he shrugged and said: 'Could I have a whisky, a large one?'

'Certainly. Would you mind fastening your seat belt? We'll be landing shortly.'

'Landing?'

'London.'

'Yes, of course. I must have been asleep longer than I thought.'

'I'll get that drink for you.'

As she retreated along the aisle to fetch his drink, he realised how numb his face felt, like a mask of putty.

He massaged life back into it, thinking about his dream. It was whipping rapidly back into his subconscious now but he could recall the red fog and the blistered legs of the woman staked out on the low mound. Funny things, dreams, he thought. Why the red fog? Why the woman on the mound? If there had been a list of prime candidates he would have thought his subconscious likely to throw up during his nap on the plane it would have been topped by the Sedali with her brooding, brown eyes, the sight of the

Wolseley plunging into the crowd or the memory of his flight from the mob.

These were the things which had turned the last twenty-four hours of his life into a living nightmare. They had never left him since he had said goodbye to the major at the barracks in Kokangarth.

Thank God for the major. The thought of what would almost certainly have happened if the major had not intervened made him shudder.

By six o'clock the previous evening he had been back in his Delhi hotel, going over and over the events of the day, finding it difficult to believe they had actually happened, were actually real. How could he have considered parking a car with a faulty handbrake on a steep hill? How could he have been so stupid?

He had called British Airways and asked if he could get a seat on a flight the next day.

Yes, there were seats available, a woman with an attractive, sing-song voice had told him. The flight left at 6 a.m.

'I'll book one please,' Law had told her. 'What time does it arrive at Heathrow?'

'Fifteen-fifteen,' she had said.

After he had hung up, he had tried to work on some of his articles, tried to tell himself that what was done was done and the best thing to do now was to get on with the rest of his life. But the thoughts nagged away at him and eventually he flicked off the light and lay fully-clothed on the bed in the darkened room.

He hadn't slept at all during the night and he was sick twice. The first time he brought up the small salad he had had when he had first arrived back at the hotel. The second time he dry-retched over the toilet bowl for ten minutes.

He put it down to the effects of shock but when the nausea remained during his taxi ride to the airport in the morning he began to think he had picked up some bug or other – probably at Baisakh's hotel in Srinwanat. He had been sick again at the airport terminal, getting to a sink in the men's room just in time.

As he remembered it now, he could almost taste the vile vomit in his mouth and when the hostess brought his drink he took a sip immediately and swilled the whisky around his teeth.

He apologised again to the hostess and said: 'I hope I didn't startle you.'

She shook her head. 'I've seen worse things than that on aeroplanes,' she smiled.

'How long before we land?' he said.

She glanced at her watch. 'About twenty minutes,' she answered.

He nodded his thanks as she disappeared up the aisle then rested his head back and closed his eyes.

London.

Surely when he was back in London, back in his own flat, the events of India would all become remote, to be forgotten in time. India, *his* India, would be just a series of articles which would most definitely not be including a story about the festival of the Sedali. He told himself that once he was home he would be able to shut everything out.

But he wasn't absolutely certain about that.

PART TWO
7

The muffled double bump as the plane touched down were like a line drawn across Law's life.

He was home, back on British soil. Back where there were no dhotis or Sedalis, no turbans, no endless days when the heat sapped a man's strength and teased sweat from every pore. Back where people didn't put pins through their bodies or strap one of their legs up behind their back for twenty years in honour of a thoroughly nasty god. India had been a wonderful experience until he had met Bromley and gone to Srinwanat but the earlier memories had disappeared altogether now.

He got off the plane and sauntered through the terminal, letting the English accents wash over him, each word chipping away at the memories of what had happened at Srinwanat, the memories which had seemed to be forming their own breeding colony in his mind.

There was usually a sense of loss when he returned from one of his longer overseas assignments. Although it was nice to be home it was as if some pleasure he had become accustomed to had been removed from his life. This time was the exception. He wanted to soak up home, London, as quickly as possible, immerse himself in his everyday life, bury himself in the ordinary.

It was drizzling as he stepped into the cab and a keen wind lifted the back of his jacket and flapped one trouser leg. Yes, he was home all right, back in the familiar cold and rain. It was the first time he had shivered for a month.

He sat in silence in the back seat of the taxi, watching the fine rain spattering on the window. Occasionally a sufficient number of tiny drops would gather together to form one large blob of water which would hang there tantalisingly for a minute or so then roll lazily down the glass.

He decided he would like to get the last batch of articles on India finished as soon as possible and made up his mind to make a start that afternoon. He was juggling words in his mind, trying to come up with the best introductory paragraph for his article on Bangalore, when he became aware that the lingering nausea in his stomach was intensifying.

He tensed, trying to control it, hoping desperately he wouldn't have to ask the cabbie to stop and suffer the indignity of vomiting into some London gutter. It came in three waves, each lasting about five minutes. After that, it began to recede and he knew he was going to make it home all right.

Bert Miller was the porter at Lissils Mansions, in Chelsea, where Law had the flat he called home. Even at 60, he still had the erect, shoulders-back, head-up posture that 25 years in the army had produced. A one-time army middleweight boxing champion, he was strong and broad-shouldered and had a pair of hands that looked as if they had been put through a mincer and rebuilt by a plastic surgeon. As Law paid off the cabbie, Miller came through the glass front door of Lissils Mansions, wearing the blue uniform with silver buttons that always reminded Law of a chocolate-box soldier.

'Welcome home, Mr Law,' he said, taking Law's suitcase and portable typewriter.

Law nodded a greeting. 'Hello, Bert.'

'You've picked up a suntan.' Miller said. 'It was India this time, wasn't it?'

Law didn't feel suntanned. He felt as if he was a jaundiced yellow.

'Yes, India,' he said as they went through the entrance hall to the lift.

'I was in India,' the porter said. 'And Palestine and Aden and Cyprus. Joined the army and saw the world, didn't I? People think it's a joke that it can get so hot in some parts of the world that you can fry an egg on the bonnet of a car but I've actually done it ... on the bonnet of a lorry I was driving in the Punjab.'

He continued to talk as the lift arrived and carried them to the third floor. The nausea flitted about in Law's intestines.

'I liked the heat, liked the feel of the sun on my face. Brown as a berry I was. Once when I came home my wife said I looked like a Paki. What happened to the nice white boy from Camden Town she married ... that's what she wanted to know.'

He chuckled at the memory as they left the lift and walked along a red-carpeted hall to Law's flat.

'My travelling days are over now, I suppose ... and I can't stand the long, cold winters.'

Law turned the key in his lock and pushed the door open. *Home.*

He watched Miller put down his luggage.

'Every winter, I just seem to get a chill that goes deep into my bones,' Miller said, straightening up. 'Just can't seem to ever get warm enough. Getting old, I suppose.'

'I suppose,' Law said. 'Well, thanks ...'

'No trouble.'

Miller went out and Law closed his door and looked around his flat. It was just as he had left it. The packed bookshelves, his favourite chair, his desk (a damned sight tidier than it usually was), the framed sketch Natalie had done of him on the far wall ...

Yet it was different. Something was different.

The thought made his brow furrow. He was certain that

the flat was exactly as he had left it yet equally sure there
had been some subtle change. It was like dragging on a
favourite overcoat and finding that it doesn't quite fit any
more. Then it occurred to him that it wasn't the flat which
had changed, it was him; something in him was not the
same now as it had been when he had left.

He sighed and carried the suitcase and portable
typewriter into his bedroom. He threw the case down in one
corner, not bothering to pick it up when it fell onto its side,
and placed the typewriter on a broad, waist-high shelf that
ran along one wall of the room.

He began to undress, his eyes flicking along the shelf. He
had once told Natalie that as far as he was concerned home
was wherever the contents of that shelf were. Carved
bookends with the figures of men holding pens supported
three copies of his book, 'Walking in Southern Scotland.'
There was the small cup, the gold plated image of a boy
kicking a football, that he had won as a youngster in
Edinburgh and the ball with which he had scored a cup
final winner; a picture of his parents taken in the fifties
standing in front of their Morris Minor; and a couple of
dozen mementos of places he had travelled to for the Globe
– a stetson from America, an Oslo key ring, a beret from
France, a black hand-carved statue from Nigeria, a shell
from an incomparable beach in the Seychelles, an
unusually shaped piece of volcanic rock from Hawaii.

Unfastening his belt, Law caught a glimpse of his face in
the dressing table mirror, hollow-eyed and matted in
perspiration. He was cold and yet he was sweating.

He jerked his eyes away and found himself looking at the
picture of Natalie on the end of the shelf. *Natalie.* She was
grinning in the picture, a big, genuine, open grin, exposing
even white teeth. His eyes locked with the soft green eyes in
the picture which smiled out at him from beneath a fringe
of auburn hair and he stopped undressing, his hands
dangling at his sides. He felt as if someone was slowly
sliding a silver stiletto into his chest.

He turned quickly towards the lounge door, an involuntary movement as if some part of him had decided that he wanted to call Natalie now, to have her in his arms, to talk to her, to tell her everything that had happened. But the way he felt he didn't want to see anybody, particularly not Natalie. He didn't want her to see him looking like a piece of human junk.

Junk.

He laughed at the word, a mirthless expelling of air. But it *was* an appropriate word. That was what he felt like. Something that had been used up, screwed up and thrown away.

No, he decided, he'd give it twenty-four hours before he called her. Surely he would feel better in twenty-four hours.

He finished undressing, strolled naked into the lounge and crossed to his tape deck. He riffled irritably along a row of tapes, uncertain about what would be most likely to lift his mood. His fingers hesitated over a tape of military music but he decided "The British Grenadier" was hardly what he needed in his condition. He paused again at a Bruce Springsteen tape before selecting a tape of 30 Great Musical Masterpieces. He reasoned that surely one of them would strike the right note. He pushed the tape into the tape deck and turned the volume up. Instantly the room was filled with the rhythmic beat of Ravel's Bolero.

He went into the bathroom leaving the door open so that he could listen to the quickening tempo of the music, brushed his teeth vigorously and gargled with mouthwash. It was as he shaved the sweat-dampened stubble from his face that he caught sight of himself in the full-length mirror to his left and what he saw startled him. He knew that he had lost weight in India, knew that the heat had sapped away four or five pounds yet he looked fatter, heavier. His muscles had a soft, flabby appearance and his flesh seemed to hang on his bones. He flicked at the shower taps and tested the water just as Bolero reached its familiar crescendo. For about ten seconds the flat was invaded by a heavy silence punctuated only by the patter of the shower. The powerful opening to the 1812 Overture rolled over him as he stepped into the shower cubicle, holding his face up to the hot darts of water.

When he got out of the shower ten minutes later, his skin was red from the heat of the water and the vigorous scrubbing he had given himself. But the shower had failed to give him the lift he had expected. He still felt lousy. He towelled himself dry then wrapped the towel around his waist, grabbed a second towel to use on his hair and strolled back into the lounge just as the tape fell silent again then exploded into life with the Drinking Song from "La Traviata."

He turned down the volume on the tape deck and sat down at his desk. Towelling his hair dry, he grabbed the telephone and dialled the Globe's number.

'Sunday Newspapers,' a woman's voice said in his ear.

'Yes ... ah ... it's Jack Law here. I'd like to speak to Peter Forrest please?'

'One moment please,' the voice said.

There was a pause then Forrest's voice bawled down the line, sounding as exuberant as ever. People had been telling him for 30 years that he didn't have to shout into telephones but he never learned.

'Hello Jack, how was India?'

'Hot.'

'When did you get back?'

'About an hour ago.'

'Where are you now?'

'I'm at home.'

'Are you coming into the office?'

'I'll come in on Monday, Peter.'

Forrest started to say something then hesitated and said slowly: 'Your voice sounds funny, Jack. You sound tired.'

'Yeah, I'm tired.'

'Oh ... I liked your first batch of articles. We've used the first two over the past couple of weeks. Did you manage to get a copy of the Globe in India?'

'I did my first Sunday there,' Law said, 'but after that it was impossible.'

'We did you proud,' Forrest said. 'Big pictures of you looking like an intrepid adventurer.'

'Oh yeah.'

'No need to sound so impressed.'

'How were the pics I sent back?'

'A mixed bag, Jack. Some of them came out really well. I liked the Amritsar ones.'

'I ...'

'Your voice,' Forest said earnestly, cutting Law off. 'It really does sound strange. Are you sure you're all right? Are you sure you haven't got a touch of the heat or something like that? That always happens to me in hot countries. Last time I took Agnes to Greece I spent two days flat on my back feeling as sick as a dog. Doctor said it was just the heat.'

Law sighed into the receiver, debating whether or not to tell Forest about what had happened at Srinwanat. He decided against it. He would tell him in a couple of years when the wounds had healed.

'I'm not sure but I think I might have picked up some bug or other,' Law said.

'If you think that, call the doctor straight away,' Forrest told him.

That was when the whispering began, like two or three people having a secretive conversation on the very outer reaches of Law's hearing range.

He tapped the telephone's earpiece with his finger.

'I might do that,' he said.

The whispering continued. It had to be in the telephone, didn't it?

'I insist on it,' Forrest said. 'God knows what kind of filthy microbe you might have picked up in India. Call your doctor now. Have you been sick or ...'

The tiny, almost inaudible noises crowded around Forrest's words, blurring them, making him sound like an actor in an old film with a poor-quality sound-track.

'I ... I vomited a couple of times,' Law said.

Whisper, Whisper. Whisper.

'Can you hold on for a second, Peter? There seems to be a problem with the telephone.'

It was when he took the receiver away from his ear that he realised the whispering was not coming from there.

It was in the room.

8

A chill like a melting iceblock ran from the back of his neck down his spine.

Mechanically he brought the receiver back to his ear.

'Y ... yes ... yeah ... As I was saying. I've vomited a few times over a couple of days.'

Whisperwhisper.

'That settles it then ...' (*Whisperhiss*) '... Call your doctor right now ...'

The hoarse rasping rose to an audible murmur then faded again.

Law strained to make out where it was coming from, to distinguish individual words.

Forrest said: 'If the doctor thinks there is any possibility that it's more than a touch of the Bombay blues ...' (*Hissss*) '... you call me straight away.'

Law looked slowly around the lounge, then glanced into the bedroom and bathroom. Nothing. He couldn't find any obvious source for the sound. He massaged his temples with damp fingers which he noticed were trembling.

'OK,' he said. 'I've got the basis ... "(*sssSSSsss*)" ... of another half dozen stories in my notebook and ...'

'Don't worry about that now, Jack, just call the doctor.'' (*Hisswhisper. Ch-ch-ch. A laugh? Was that a laugh? Like a cackle? Only tiny faint fragments of it reached him. The rest dissolved into a long hisssss.*) 'We've still got three stories that you sent back which we haven't used yet. They'll carry us through into next month.'

'Peter, can you hear something … on the line … or …'

'Like what?'

'Sounds.'

'No. Clear as a bell to me.'

'Oh … OK … I'll see you on Monday then.'

'Yes. Bye Jack. Good to have you back.'

'Bye Peter.'

He hung up slowly.

The whispers were still there, fainter now.

Be rational, he told himself. Why was he being so irrational? Why was he trying to make sense of the sounds, trying to find words in them, or laughter? It was obvious the *whispering* had to be mechanical in origin. A wind in some pipe or a slight breeze from an open window rustling some clothing or papers or …

(*But it's not that kind of sound and you know it.*)

(*BE RATIONAL.*)

His eyes darted around the room and came to rest on the tape deck. It was playing something by Wagner now, something he couldn't name, at very low volume.

It occurred to him that a malfunctioning tape deck often had an undersound, a hiss, a whine, a steady *shshshsh* sound.

He hurried across the room and snapped it off.

The whispering did not disappear. With the sudden snatching away of the music it increased. It was as if there was a crowd of people all around him, breathing and whispering at the very lowest level.

He thrust his fingers into his ears then pulled them out with a *pop*. The whispering had diminished. It had moved away. It was a small sound somewhere else now.

He rushed into the bathroom and put his ear close to the sink top. Nothing. He stepped into the shower cubicle and listened, his ear pressed against the pipes. Nothing.

The whispering had to be mechanical.

He returned to the lounge and pulled out all the plugs then went into the bedroom. The window was firmly shut.

Nothing stirred. Nothing was switched on, nothing plugged in.

(*IT'S IN YOUR HEAD.*)

The possible answer leapt into his brain, startling him.

Could that be so? Could it?

If he had picked up something in India, could that have distended, inflamed some cluster of brain cells or affected his eardrums, making sounds buzz around in his head?

There was only one man who could answer that. Doctor Williams. He rushed back into the lounge and called the doctor.

'Can I speak to Doctor Williams please, it's Jack Law here,' he said to the receptionist.

There was a pause then she said: 'I'm transferring you now.'

'Thanks,' he said.

In that instant, the whispering ceased. It was as if a play had ended, the curtain fallen.

It was gone. The flat was silent. He heard a car driving past in the street below his window, the muffled sound of a television in another flat along the hall.

'Hello, Jack. How are you?'

It was Doctor Williams' voice.

Law quickly outlined his physical symptoms – the constant nausea, the vomiting – but held back from mentioning the whispers.

(*WHY?*)

Williams said: 'You'd better come in. I'll put you down as the first patient on evening surgery at six o'clock. We'll do some tests. It's probably just a stomach bug but it's best to be on the safe side. I thought we'd injected you for just about everything you could possibly get in India.'

'I thought you had too,' Law said, 'I felt like a human pincushion for a week. Six o'clock then?'

'Yes, I'll see you then Jack.'

He hung up and stood absolutely still, listening, waiting for the whispers to return. It was as if he knew they were out there, waiting for him.

But they didn't come back.

Bert Miller entered his small office adjacent to the front door of Lissils Mansions, threw his hat on a seat and ran his fingers through the couple of dozen strands of silver hair that were all that was left of what had once been a thick, curly, black thatch. He checked there was water in the electric kettle then switched it on, tossed three teaspoons of coffee into a large tin mug and splashed milk on top.

The water in the electric kettle boiled and it clicked off automatically. He filled his tin mug and stirred the coffee until it was an even dark brown. Then he took a sip and sat down at the table, unfastening his overcoat.

He raised his head when he heard footsteps in the foyer and the front door opening and looked out the window to see Jack Law walking between the parked cars, crossing the street.

Suddenly the mug shot six inches across the table as if sucked towards Law by some invisible force. It stopped dead and coffee splashed over the table.

He stared at it, trying to make some kind of sense of what had happened, and that was when the mug began to tremble, as if an electric shock was running through it. The tinkling of the spoon made him shift his gaze and he saw that it too was shaking violently. Then the electric kettle began to tremble, its lid clattering.

9

'That ought to do it,' Doctor Williams said, removing the needle from Law's arm and handing him a piece of cotton wool to dab on the tiny pinprick in his skin.

Law studied the vial of blood which the doctor was removing from the top of the needle. His blood. He always found it strange, fascinating, to see his own blood, the stuff that coursed through his veins and arteries, pumped around by his own thumping heart, keeping him alive.

The doctor returned to the seat behind his desk.

'We should have the results of the tests in a couple of days,' he said. 'I wouldn't worry in the meantime. It's probably just some minor stomach upset that will clear up in a few days. I'll give you something for the vomiting ...'

He began to write out a prescription.

'... and I'd like you to get plenty of rest over the next couple of days.'

'There is one other thing that I didn't mention,' Law said.

'What's that?'

'There was this whispering sound in my head. At least I think it was in my head. I'm not really sure. I suppose it could have been the wind in a pipe above my ceiling or something like that.'

'It sounded like ... what?'

'Like a couple of people whispering to each other. Very distant. Indistinct.'

'You've got a stomach upset. You're overtired. That's all.

63

A couple of days of rest and I'm sure you'll feel fine.'

'But have you ever heard of people with whispering sounds in their head?'

Williams smiled, a doctor's smile. 'I've heard of ten thousand things much more difficult to explain. It will be gone in a few days. I'm sure of it. Now ...'

He held out the prescription to Law.

'I've given you a mixture which will settle your stomach and some antibiotics which will commit mass murder on anything nasty in your blood. Take the tablets three times a day.'

Law took the prescription. 'Thanks.'

'I want you to sleep and not to worry. Call me in a couple of days and we'll see what the lab has come up with.'

Law sighed: 'OK.'

He stood up as if reluctant to leave and Williams gave him a reassuring nod.

'Tell me,' said the doctor, 'in all the time you were in India, how many days off did you have? How many days when you did absolutely nothing, or something just to relax?'

Law thought about that for a moment then shrugged.

'I can guess the answer, Jack. I've known you long enough. The answer is ... none. Not one single day.'

'My job is ... well, it's my life. I enjoy it. I don't need ...'

'You need relaxation just like everyone else. You need to paint or play squash, go boating or play golf. You need something which takes you right away from your work.'

'I'm sure you're right.'

'Think about it.'

'I will.'

Williams looked down at Law's file.

'How old are you now, Jack?'

'Thirty-nine.'

'Thirty-nine. That's not old Jack. It's young. But it's an age when a man ought to start not pushing so hard, not being so frantic. A man should have his life well organised by then. He should make sure he has time for recreation and exercise.'

'Oh Christ, I'm not a geriatric.'

'No, but you're not twenty-five either.'

Law grinned. 'That's right but don't go ordering my wheelchair just yet.'

He tugged open the door. 'I'll call you in a couple of days,' he said going out.

'Bye Jack.'

'Bye.'

Law walked three blocks from the surgery and found a chemist still open. He handed over his prescription and waited for his medicine. When the chemist brought it he asked for a spoon, explaining that he wanted to take some of the mixture straight away. There was no point in waiting – the quicker he took the medicine, the sooner it would take effect. The chemist brought a spoon and he filled it twice, throwing the oozing grey liquid to the back of his throat.

It was as he left the chemist shop that he thought he heard the whispering again.

Whispersssssssssssswhisper.

He cocked his head, listened.

Then a line of traffic rumbled along the street, drowning out all other sounds. The cars paused at traffic lights a few yards away then hurried on. By the time the din of their engines had died away the only sounds were the one hundred and one noises of a city street.

Law tried to recall the whispers but he couldn't. He wasn't sure if he had really heard anything or not.

Ben Wallace felt terrible. If there were degrees of terrible on a scale of one to ten, he was an eleven.

He stood in the pub, staring at the rows of bottles behind the bar, two lines of a poem he was working on repeating themselves over and over again in his mind.

And murky black water will gobble me up.

Hidden fingers of green-slime rock reach to caress me.

He was about five feet six and wore corduroy trousers, suede shoes, a check shirt with a maroon tie and a tweed jacket with leather elbow patches. He was forty-two but his silver hair and beard made him look ten years older. By profession, he was a teacher and poetry was his hobby but he liked to tell people he was a poet and teaching was only a hobby. His poetry had been published in some good newspapers and periodicals and he had once edited a small London poetry magazine.

He downed the last mouthful of beer in his glass, grimaced, stabbed a finger at the barman and said: 'Give me a Bells.'

And murky black water ...

The barman brought the whisky and Wallace paid him, putting a pile of change from his pocket onto the counter.

... will gobble me up.

He sipped the whisky, feeling it burn its way down into him.

Hidden fingers of green-slime rock reach to caress me.

Why could he not get beyond that line? Why?

'I've dried up,' he said to the barman who was shining a glass, occasionally holding it up to the light.

'You don't look dry to me,' the barman laughed.

Wallace knew he was slightly inebriated but he wasn't really drunk; he was just trying hard. He knew what really drunk was and this wasn't it.

'Funnyyyyyyy,' he said to the barman, sarcastically, then downed the whisky, turned carefully and walked as steadily as he could to the door.

'One thing I can't stand,' he said over his shoulder as he went into the street, 'is a smart-alec barman.'

He strode along the street, hurrying although he was going nowhere in particular. At the first corner, he turned right, his head down, not looking where he was going and that was when he walked straight into Jack Law, their shoulders colliding. Wallace almost fell but Law managed to grab his arm and pull him upright.

'Jack,' Wallace yelled. 'How are you? Fancy bumping into you like this.' He laughed briefly at his little joke then peered into Law's face. 'Jack, you look awful.'

'Thanks, Ben.'

'No, I mean it, Jack. You don't mind me saying that, do you? If a friend can't tell you the truth, who can? You really look awful … you look ill.'

'I'm not feeling well, Ben. I've just come back from India. I think I've picked up a stomach bug or something like that. I've just been to the doctor.' He paused and studied Wallace. 'Anyway, you don't look too good yourself.'

Wallace looked as if somebody had just put a large haversack of scrap iron on his back. His eyes dropped away from Law's then rose again.

'Everything's gone wrong, Jack,' he said. 'You knew Rachel had left me.'

Law nodded. 'You told me that when I met you at Martin's party last month, remember … when I told you I was going to India.'

'That's right, I remember now.' He narrowed his eyes, recalling the conversation. 'And I think I said when you came back we'd go off for a couple of days and do some fishing.'

'That's right.'

'You had your new bird with you. Natalie, isn't it? Anyway … if things weren't bad enough when Rachel left, guess what happened last week?'

'I've no idea.'

'I got the sack.'

'The sack?'

'Well, I was asked to resign.'

'Why?'

Wallace made a drinking gesture. 'I did it once too often, Jack. And please don't say I told you so even though you did.'

'What are you doing now?'

'Trying to get drunk.'

'I don't mean that. I mean, how are you living?'

'I'm unemployed. I'm living on state benefits like three million-plus other people.'

'Hell, Ben, that's terrible.'

'Yes, isn't it. Anyway let's not stand here talking when we can go into a pub and talk and drink at the same time.'

'I don't really feel like drinking,' Law said.

'Oh come on. I'm not as drunk as I look. I've just been working hard at it. Let's have one of those great nights out like we used to; those nights when we'd hit half a dozen pubs and clubs then pour ourselves into a cab.'

Nights like that were probably one of the main contributory factors in the break-up of my marriage, Law thought ruefully, but he just said: 'No thanks.'

'At least we can have a drink.'

'I …'

'How long have we been friends?' Wallace said in an accusing tone.

'About ten years.'

Wallace did his impersonation of a London Jewish tailor, gesticulating wildly, his shoulders hunched. 'After ten years you meet a close friend you haven't seen for more than a month and he won't drink with you … even when he's just been told you've lost your job. I don't believe that already.'

It was moral blackmail of course. Law knew that, but he reasoned that if he had a couple of drinks with Wallace he might be able to get him into a taxi and take him home where he could sleep it off.

Law sniffed: 'OK.'

'I know just the place,' Wallace said then spun away from Law and waved a hand frantically at a passing cab which squealed to a halt.

'Soho,' Wallace said to the cabbie as they got in.

'Not Soho,' Law sighed.

'Yeah, we'll have a drink and go and see a flesh show.'

'I'm not really in the mood, Ben.'

'Come on, be a sport.'

Law shrugged, resigned, then sat back and listened to the whole sad story of how Wallace had lost his job.

He and Law had been close friends since Law had first moved to London. They had met when Law's wife, Fiona, had started working part-time at the school where Wallace taught English. Wallace had left the school shortly after that and gone to Bonswater, a private school of the liberal, self-expression, very-little-discipline variety. 'The kind of school,' Law had told Wallace at the time with a half-smile, 'where rich kids run wild and break everything and the teachers applaud.' It seemed now that the school's liberal attitude did not include having an English teacher who liked to pour large quantities of alcohol down his throat. There had been a time when Law and Wallace and Fiona and Rachel had been inseparable. Now both marriages had broken up. Fiona was in the Isle of Man with Law's son, Todd, and Wallace had no idea where Rachel was.

Wallace directed the cabbie to the pub he wanted and he and Law drank and talked for an hour. Law realised the nausea was receding and guessed the medicine was doing its work.

Finally, Wallace banged his glass down on the counter and said: 'Right, let's go. This'll be just the thing for a red-blooded male like you.'

'Ben, I'm very tired. I'll go for one hour. After that we'll share a cab and go home.'

'I ...'

'You're pretty drunk, Ben. One hour ... then go home and sleep it off.'

'One hour ... it's a deal.'

Law followed the shorter man out into the street. Wallace was walking unsteadily, his head craned forward, eyes wide and unblinking, like a hypnotist's subject or someone peering through a snowstorm. There was a steady drizzle but Wallace seemed unaware of it. Law turned up his collar and hunched himself down into his coat. They crossed a street and plunged into another lane, striding past a sex shop, a neon-flashing topless bar and a handful of shuttered shops.

Two minutes after they left the pub they were descending the stairway into the strip club, having paid their entrance fee to a balding man in a green suit with brown teeth and nicotine-stained fingers. There were no more than twenty people in the club which appeared to have a seating capacity of about a hundred and they were congregated in the seats nearest the door as if afraid they might have to make a quick exit. Wallace led Law to a couple of front seats at the far side and they sat down just as a voice announced: 'And now ... direct from Paris ... It's Francoise.'

The girl in the black beret and leather suit didn't look much like a Francoise to Law. She looked more like a Mabel or a Gladys.

He whispered his thoughts to Wallace as he tried to wriggle his large frame into a comfortable position in the narrow chair.

'Trust you to try to destroy the illusion,' Wallace slurred.

For the next hour they watched plump women and lean, sinewy women, and everything in between; black women, white women and orientals; middle-aged women, and girls who looked as if they might have just stepped out of their school uniforms; women with fixed smiles, women with anxious eyes, and women who made it obvious they thought that next to sleeping this was just about the most boring thing a human being could do.

They weren't very good dancers, but that didn't seem to bother the patrons; they wanted a flesh show and that's what they got.

Law kept glancing at his watch, willing the hour to be up.

'Time's up,' he said at last as the curtain swung closed on a slender, disinterested redhead.

Wallace was dozing off, his chin on his chest, and Law

shook his shoulder.

'The hour is up,' he said, 'and I've seen enough female orifices to last me until I'm ninety.'

Wallace jerked his head up, suddenly wide awake.

'Just one more dance,' he said.

'No …'

'Just one more, then we'll get a taxi home.'

Law sighed. 'One more and that's it.'

'And now …' said the voice from the speaker above Law's head (it sounded as bored as the dancers looked) '… a touch of the mysterious east … from India … it's Soraya.'

'More likely to be from Bradford than Bangalore,' Law muttered as the club was filled with the sound of the sitar and the curtain swung back.

Soraya was slightly heavy for Law's taste, about twenty-five with shining black hair. What looked like half a sari was held up by her ample hips and a purple sash was tied around her breasts. In her navel was a large ruby, or a piece of glass which was meant to pass as a ruby, and she managed to gyrate it in a manner which Wallace seemed to find not unattractive.

She danced to the far end of the stage, her feet shuffling across the intricately woven carpet which had been placed there for her act, then turned … and froze, staring at Law like someone who had just found a tarantula in her bed.

For an instant he thought it was part of the act. He gave her a half-smile and raised his eyebrows. Then he felt the smile die and a frown creasing his forehead.

She was afraid. Why was she afraid?

Immobile, she tore her eyes away from Law. For a moment, she watched Wallace intently then her gaze darted beyond them and she seemed to be studying the vacant seats all around them, her eyes sweeping along the empty rows.

Why was she afraid? What …

Her lip twisted, quivered, then she tried to continue her dance, like someone coming out of a trance, but it was as if her legs and body wouldn't function properly or she had forgotten the steps.

Law turned to say something to Wallace but then whipped his head back when he heard the thump of her bare feet, running, and the urgent whisper of her sari. She crossed the stage and disappeared behind the curtain.

'What do you suppose caused that?' Wallace said as Law listened to the receding smack of the girl's bare feet on a stairway backstage.

'I've no idea,' Law said.

Suddenly Wallace giggled. 'My flies are not undone are they?'

Law smiled through his frown. 'No, it's not that. If it had been that she'd have died laughing. Anyway, I think that's our cue to get out of this joint.'

'I …'

'No arguments. I'm pouring you into a cab and I'm taking you home.'

Wallace shrugged and permitted Law to help him to his feet. With Law supporting him, he managed to make it to the door and up the stairs, but he began to crumple when the fresh air hit him. Law looped a hand under Wallace's armpit and said: 'Just hold onto me as best as you can.' They spent ten minutes stumbling along a street until Law spotted a taxi and managed to get Wallace into it without the smaller man bumping his head or cracking his shins.

As they drove through the city, Law found himself wondering about the girl but he finally dismissed the incident as just one of those things, yet another question that didn't have an answer. He'd come across a few of those in his thirty-nine years, he admitted.

Wallace had fallen asleep by the time the cab pulled up in front of the block of flats where he had lived for fifteen years.

'Wait for me,' Law told the cabbie and half-carried, half-dragged Wallace out of the taxi and across the dim, shadowy park in front of the flats. He tried the front door that led to the entrance hall but it was locked.

'Ben.' He gave Wallace a shake. 'Ben, where are your keys?'

Wallace grunted then gave a long, groaning sigh.

Law searched the smaller man's jacket pockets but came up only with a notepad, half a dozen pens and some screwed-up bus tickets.

'Ben.'

'Yeeeees,' Wallace said hoarsely, his eyes still firmly shut.

'Where are your keys?'

'Left hand ... trouser pocket.'

Wallace began to giggle loudly as Law dived a hand into his pocket and Law found the giggling contagious and began laughing too.

'What's ... so funny?' Law managed to say.

'I didn't know you cared, sweetie pie,' Wallace said and doubled up with laughter, almost falling over.

Law found the keys, hauled the still giggling Wallace into the entrance hall and managed to get him up the stairs and into his first-floor flat. Wallace's legs gave way at the front door and Law scooped him up like a child and carried him into the bedroom.

Wallace was convulsed by giggles now, tears running down his cheeks. Suddenly he kissed Law on the cheek and said through a new fit of laughter: 'You ... really do ... care, don't you ... sweetie?'

'Shut up, Ben,' he chuckled as he lowered Wallace onto the bed.

He loosened his friend's tie, flipped off his shoes and covered him with an eiderdown.

Wallace turned his face into the pillow, racked by laughter and coughing.

'Aren't you ... going to ... undress me?' he managed to say.

Law put one hand on his hip and cocked his head in an imitation of a gay mannerism. 'I wouldn't undress you if you were the nicest boy in the world,' he said.

Wallace grabbed his stomach, trying to massage away the ache of his drunken laughter.

'I'm going now, Ben. Just sleep it off,' Law said.

'See you, sweetie.'

'Bye.'

He could still hear Wallace laughing as he walked back down the hall towards the stairway.

Back in his own flat, Law studied his face in the bathroom mirror. He still looked terrible, but he didn't feel as bad as he had earlier in the day. The nausea had thinned out, receded, and he no longer felt as if he was likely to suffer an attack of vomiting at any second. He guessed a combination of the medicine and alcohol had given him a lift.

He threw off his clothes, stepped into a pair of blue pyjama bottoms and climbed into bed. It felt familiar and good. In a few moments he had fallen into a deep sleep.

And almost instantly the dream began.

In it, he felt more than a man, larger than life, stronger than he had ever felt before.

The action of the dream was repetitive and simple. He was holding a man down, kneeling across him and driving some kind of weapon into him again and again and again.

And it felt so gooooooooood.

He rolled about in his sleep, becoming entwined in the blankets, a strange kind of ecstasy raging through his veins.

Ben Wallace lay on his stomach, one knee drawn up, his face buried between the two pillows of the double bed. He was in a state of complete alcoholic oblivion, not so much asleep as unconscious, beyond dreaming, beyond stirring. He stayed like that until the first weak light of the new day began to bleed through the light-brown curtains on his window. He sighed, winced at the bad taste in his mouth and stretched a hand down to rub life back into his right leg.

That was when he heard the *badump* sound.

It was like the noise a small animal (a rat or a cat or a rabbit) might make if it jumped off a chair onto a carpeted floor.

He rolled onto his back and looked around the dim room. A pair of slippers lay in one corner ...

... and one seemed to be moving.

He did a double-take then closed his eyes, rubbed his eyelids, and looked again.

The slippers were far apart now but there was nothing there to explain why he had thought one of them had moved, actually shifted before his eyes.

He sat up, clutching at a pain in the small of his back, and that was when he heard the merest whisper of a sound, coming from the bottom of the bed.

It was as if something was pushing aside the bed cover, where it touched the floor, and moving under the bed.

He listened for a minute or so, not moving, doing nothing.

Then there was a low *hissssss* and the head of a cobra shot up at the bottom of the bed and swayed backwards and forwards, watching him.

10

The snake made no attempt to strike. It swayed backwards and forwards in a slow, weaving rhythm.

Wallace wanted to shout, to yell something that would scare the snake away but his larynx felt as if it had been forged in steel. His entire body was rigid, the only sign of life a strange fluttering in his chest. It was as if every nerve end in his body had zipped all the way up to maximum alert in one instant. For a long time his brain was on overload, incapable of rational thought.

Then a question forced its way in and others followed in a flood.

If he could get his larynx to function, should he shout? Would that make it slither away? Or would it make it strike? Where had it come from? How could there be a cobra in the middle of London?

He had to do something. Now.

Should he move? His feet were within striking distance; should he draw them away? Was there anything he could defend himself with?

Do something.

Slowly he began to pull his legs back up the bed and that was when he realised his head was beginning to sway in the same rhythm as the snake. He stopped it immediately.

What had made him do that?

As he folded his legs under him, he found that his eyes were being drawn not just to the snake's head but into its eyes, and he saw that they were not like a snake's eyes.

They were like the eyes of a human, like the eyes of a cruel and malevolent man.

The steady, unblinking gaze of the snake seemed to fold over him, cover him with a thin film. It was as if …

… he was being hypnotised.

As if it was trying to put him into a trance.

He struggled against it, drawing a pillow around in front of him to give himself some form of defence.

'Go …' a voice rasped.

He realised the word had come from his own throat. His larynx was working again, sore and raw from the night before but functioning. He cleared his throat silently and spoke again, short, sharp words.

'Go … go on. Get out.'

Could you … shoo away a snake … like you could a dog?

Thoughts were coming to him slowly now. He was becoming …

Drowsy.

It *was* mesmerising him, putting him into a trance.

He tried to draw his eyes away from the snake's but found he couldn't. It was as if they were locked together, held fast by an invisible bond.

He focussed everything in his mind on fighting it and was winning, dragging his eyes away from the cold malevolence, when the cobra dropped out of sight.

He sprang to his feet, standing in the centre of the bed, the pillow grasped in his right hand. His eyes flashed around the bed, darting from left to right, searching for the snake.

It reappeared as a blur near the bed's headboard and lashed towards him. He tried to parry the strike with the pillow but he was too late.

The fangs snatched a hole in his cords and raked down his thigh.

He kicked at it and as it flopped back from the bed he jumped, still clutching the pillow. He landed badly, his ankle twisting under him, and fell on his face.

As he rolled onto his side, pushing himself up with one hand, the snake came around the bottom of the bed, as quick as the tip of a cracking bullwhip.

Wallace swung the pillow around in front of him, jabbering now, his heart pounding in his ears.

The cobra struck once, twice, three times, ripping holes in the pillowcase, scattering lumps of rubber about the room.

'Heeeelp,' Wallace yelled, jumping to his feet, but it was not like his own voice. It did not even seem to be coming from his bedroom or his flat. It seemed to be coming from far, far away.

He stumbled away to his right, bumped into the bathroom door, scrambled to open it and had taken one step onto the cold tiles when the cobra caught up with him. He felt a pain in his calf, like a razor slicing deep into his flesh, and slapped at the snake, knocking it back out of the bathroom.

He tried to close the door but it was too quick for him and he jumped back, stepping into the bath and throwing the bath-tray blindly in the direction of the cobra.

He snatched up a foot-long scrubbing brush and spun to face it, just as it lunged at him again, streaking up towards his face. He jerked his head away but the fangs bit through his beard into his chin and held.

He screamed, grabbed the cobra with both hands and wrenched it away from him. An inch-long piece of flesh was ripped from his chin, leaving a jagged hole which spattered blood across the light-brown bathtub.

He flung the cobra's writhing body away from him …

It was warm; it felt like the arm of a muscular man with the hair shaved away.

… and jumped out of the bath.

He almost slipped on the tiles but managed to right himself and leap into the bedroom, dashing for the half-open door to the lounge. He reached it and flung it open.

It was as he crossed the threshold that he half turned and threw a glance back towards the bathroom, his eyes desperately searching for the snake in the half dark. He found it at the bathroom door, coiled into a small, quivering form.

Suddenly it sprang and flew through the air, twisting and jerking. It covered the entire width of the bedroom and hit him on the side of the chest with a force that knocked him back against the door. He flung two feeble punches at it, blows which encountered only air, then felt the long body coiling around his upper arm.

He grabbed for the darting head but missed and the cobra struck twice in quick succession, once into his eyebrow and then into his cheek.

He screamed then but heard nothing; it was as if the scream had no sound, as if it was encased in some murky vault in his subconscious.

The cobra's head lashed forward again and struck into the point of his chin ...

But this time there was no pain.

Why?

Then he realised he was on his knees and slowly sliding onto his side. He turned his head and looked down at the carpet, no longer able to comprehend what was happening to him, beyond pain now. The carpet pattern blurred and misted then became clear again, amazingly, beautifully clear.

Then the floor seemed to shoot up and thud into his face.

Srinwanat: The Seeker

The courtyard inside the temple of the Sedali was blank, empty, devoid, of all life; nothing grew there, there were no carvings or statues, just a square of yellow sand flanked by four tall grey walls.

Subhash stood in the centre of the courtyard, a tall, brown, shaven-headed man, lean and hard as an old whip.

It was the greatest day of his life and he waited patiently, his feet planted firmly in the sand. He had served seven Sedalis and now after so many years he had been chosen as The Seeker, selected from all the senior priests to walk to Porkat – with Manali and Tattap as his guards – and find a new Sedali among all the girls who had been gathered there. He knew the task was not only one of great honour but also of great simplicity – the new Sedali always showed herself quickly to The Seeker, in the old ways the priests knew so well.

He had started to try to envisage the long procession back from Porkat with the new Sedali when he heard shuffling sounds behind him and knew that Manali and Tattap had taken up their positions on either side of him.

A few moments later, the gate to the main temple building creaked open and Shoka appeared carrying The Rod. It was many hundreds of years old and had grown black because of the holy oils the priests applied to prevent it from disintegrating with age. On it a likeness of each of Dacahri's one thousand incarnations had been carved in intricate detail.

Subhash had been told by earlier Seekers that The Rod felt like a living thing, like a snake or a man's arm, and he was surprised when Shoka handed it to him because it felt like just what it was – a piece of oiled wood.

Neither Subhash nor Shoka spoke. For a moment they stood looking into each other's eyes then Subhash swung the eight-feet-long Rod over his shoulder, turned away and headed for the gate in the wall, followed by Manali and Tattap.

Law slept for fourteen hours but it felt like a thousand years. When he woke, he felt good; clear-headed, refreshed … and something else.

Elation?

Why should he feel elated, he asked himself. Was it just a good night's sleep in his own bed after being away for so long? Was it that the nausea had retreated to a distant colony in his intestines where it was no doubt fighting a rear-guard action against the antibiotics?

He shook his head slowly, thinking about it. Considering the intensity of the elation, it had to be more than that.

Then he recalled that he had had a dream in which he had been involved in some kind of physical struggle. The dream had repeated itself again and again in his mind and it occurred to him now that the dream was responsible for the feeling of elation although he couldn't say why. He had had dreams which had had that effect on him before; wonderful, pure, deep-sleep dreams about walking in quiet forests or sex or running as if he had limitless energy, as if he could run forever.

He tried to remember the details of the dream but couldn't, no matter how hard he tried. The dream had plunged back into the depths of his subconscious, sunk without trace.

"What the hell does it matter," he said aloud, throwing back the blankets and rolling out of bed.

He strode into the bathroom, brushed his teeth vigorously and shaved, humming and singing snatches of pop songs. He was amazed at how fit he felt, at the strength which seemed to course through his veins. He showered, towelled himself dry then gulped down a mouthful of the medicine that the doctor had given him and popped two of the red antibiotic tablets into his mouth, washing them down with a glass of water. The instructions on the bottle said "Take one three times a day" but he guessed a double dose now and then wouldn't do him any harm.

He went back into the bedroom, shrugged his shoulders into a dressing gown then called Natalie from the telephone on his desk.

'Hello.'

The voice at the other end of the line plucked a lot of familiar chords, all of them pleasant.

'It's me,' he said.

'Jack.' He could almost see her smiling. 'Jack, is it really you?'

Her voice had changed from the formal "hello." It altered in a very subtle way that he recognised and enjoyed. A tiny thrill sensation that he could never really put a name to ran through him.

'Yeah, it's me,' he said. 'Scoop Law. Back from the land of the turban and the sitar, back in merry England.'

She sighed an amused laugh into the telephone and seemed at a loss for words for a moment.

Then she said: 'When did you get back?'

'Yesterday afternoon.'

'Why didn't you call straight away?'

He hesitated then said: 'I didn't feel very well.'

'Why?' There was a thread of concern in her voice. 'There's nothing wrong is there?'

'No,' he assured her. 'Just some nasty version of the Bombay Blues. I went to the doctor yesterday and got some tablets. I'm fine now.'

'I've missed you,' she said.

He grinned into the telephone. 'Me too.'

'Did you behave yourself over there?' she said mock accusingly.

He held up his hand as if taking an oath to the empty room. 'I stayed as sober as a judge almost all of the time and I was as celibate and faithful as a Franciscan monk. I managed to go a whole month without making a fool of myself once.'

What about Srinwanat?

The words sliced into him but he deflected them instantly, sending them back into the darkness of his subconscious. Why tell her about that? Why worry her?

'Oh yeah,' she said as if she had grave doubts about his innocence.

'No really,' he said. 'They don't drink as much over there. They don't have a pub on every corner – they're more into temples. And I never did manage to get the hang of how to untangle a sari. Maybe that's why there are so many virgins in India.'

She chuckled down the telephone and suddenly it seemed so, so long since he had heard her laughter. Too long.

'Anyway,' he said, 'I imagine that in my absence hordes of these advertising types that you mix with have been flinging themselves at you, all pin-stripe suits and expensive aftershave.'

'Of course,' she said, 'I've been fighting them off in droves.' Suddenly her voice was serious. 'When am I going to see you, Jack?'

'How about right now?'

'Right now I'm in a mess and my flat is in a mess. I'm up to my ears in the artwork for a new advertising campaign, a big one, lots of money. I negotiated a good deal ...'

'All work and no play makes Jill a dull girl.'

'At least give me time to tidy up and have a bath.'

He looked at his watch. It was almost one o'clock.

'OK,' he said. 'I suppose I can occupy myself for a few hours. I've got plenty of work to do on these Indian articles. How about if I come over at five?'

'Perfect. I'll cook up a meal you'll never forget. I've got a giant steak in the freezer.'

'I don't know how to break this to you, Natalie,' he said, 'but it's not really your cooking I'm interested in.'

'Oh,' she said, sounding like a spinster headmistress.

Through his laughter, he said: 'I'll see you at five o'clock.'

'Bye Jack.'

'Bye.'

He strolled back into his bedroom and began to dress. It was as he drew on his trousers that he felt the heavy tug in his left-hand pocket. That was where he always carried his keys but today they seemed noticeably weightier than normal. He fastened his belt and plunged his hand into his pocket. It came out with two sets of keys.

'Damn,' he said.

He had forgotten to leave behind Ben Wallace's keys.

He went back into the lounge, dialled Wallace's number, let it ring for a long time, then hung up.

Wallace couldn't have gone out, he reasoned, because if he had he would have noticed his keys were missing and called Law. The absence of that call suggested to Law that his friend was still at home, still sleeping it off, in such a deep sleep that even the telephone couldn't wake him.

Maybe Wallace was ill? He had had a lot to drink.

Law dangled the keys on his index finger, studying them absently, then decided he would take them to Wallace's flat.

He finished dressing and took the lift down to the entrance hall. Bert Miller was in his office as Law passed and Law greeted him with a brief wave and a nod of his head.

'Morning, Bert.'

'Morning,' said Miller, unsmiling, and immediately averted his eyes and turned away abruptly.

In all the time Law had known the ex-soldier, Miller had always had something to say, a story to tell or a comment to make on a football match or a television programme or the weather or the state of the world.

So why was he so different today, Law wondered. He was still pondering the question when he reached the door and went out into the street but finally dismissed it from his mind, deciding the porter was probably just a bit off-colour or had some personal problem that was troubling him.

He debated whether or not to take his car to Wallace's, hesitating at the corner of Lissils Mansions and glancing down the lane which led to the garages at the rear. His car had lain there for a month and he knew it would probably require some coaxing to get it started. It wasn't worth the trouble, he decided. He would take the Underground.

The sun was shining, peeping down at the earth from a single jagged slit in the ceiling of dirty grey clouds. It made the wet street glisten brightly as if it had just been painted and the emulsion was still wet.

Law strode to the station at a brisk pace, enjoying the vigour that seemed to have been injected into all his muscles. He bought three newspapers and flicked through them on the train.

It was an item at the bottom of the end column on page 14 of the second newspaper that caught his eye and made him stiffen.

The 12-point heading read '37 killed' and the three-line filler paragraph said 'At least 37 people were killed and 78 injured during a riot at a religious festival in Srinwanat, India, on Wednesday, the Press Trust of India reported yesterday.'

He jerked his head up and found himself looking at his reflection in the train window. It was twisted and discoloured by the dirty glass and the black tunnel-wall beyond. He looked grey-black and gaunt, the facial bones like great ridges, the lines under his eyes and on his cheeks like trenches.

He looked away quickly, a feeling of guilt washing through him.

Had he caused that riot? Was he to blame?

There would probably have been a riot anyway, he told himself. Everybody had said the festival of the Sedali was a rough affair, almost always ending in violence.

He shrugged the worries aside. What had happened to him had been an accident and even if that accident had led to the riot there wasn't anything he could do about it now.

A moment later, he realised the train was coming into the station he wanted. Methodically, he folded the newspapers into one neat bundle. He left them on the seat beside him when he got off and, moving with the crowd, climbed the stone stairway to street level. A steady drizzle was falling now and he turned up his coat collar and hurried the three blocks to Wallace's flat.

He rapped on Wallace's door, waited, then knocked again, listening with his ear close to the door. There was no sound of activity.

He foraged in his coat pocket, brought out Wallace's keys and let himself in, flicking on the light.

Then he froze, staring into the room.

11

The flash of the bulb on the police photographer's camera made Law blink.

He took another sip of whisky from the quarter-full tumbler on the table in front of him – it had been half full fifteen minutes before – and said to Chief Inspector Martin Granger: 'I'm sorry … what did you say?'

Granger was impatient but it was the impatience of a professional who wanted to get the job done. It didn't annoy Law.

'I said … the body … it was just like that when you found it, wasn't it? You didn't move it or touch it.'

'It was just like that,' Law said and nodded to where Wallace's corpse lay, half in the bedroom, half in the lounge, the knees drawn up against the chest, the eyes staring blindly out of the bloody face which looked as if it had been ripped and torn by the point of a very sharp knife.

Who could have done that to Ben Wallace? Why?

'Did you touch anything else in the room?' the chief inspector said.

'Just the telephone to call the police and the drinks cabinet to get myself a whisky.'

Law let his eyes skip across the corpse again and it occurred to him that Wallace looked as if he had been tortured. The thought seared through Law like the pain of a branding iron on bare flesh.

Tortured. Why? By whom?

'You said you and Mr Wallace were old friends?'

'Yes.'

'How long had you known him?'

'Ten years. About that.'

'Was he married?'

'Yes ... well, recently separated.'

'He lived here alone?'

'I believe so.'

'Do you know his wife's address?'

'No.'

Law was staring out of the window, between the slats of the venetian blinds, looking into the park below but not seeing anything.

Tortured.

He swung his head round and his eyes locked with the inspector's.

'Who ... what the hell could have done that? Look at the state he's in. Have you ever seen anything like this before?'

The inspector hesitated then shook his head slowly. 'No, I can't say I have but I'm sure a post-mortem will come up with some answers. When did you last see Mr Wallace?'

'Last night. We had a drink together. I brought him home.'

'*Brought* him home?'

'He was rather drunk.'

'And you last saw him at what time?'

'I'm not sure. Nine or ten I suppose.'

'Where did Mr Wallace work?'

'He was a teacher ... but he had just lost his job.'

'What brought you over here today?'

Law explained about the keys, listening to his words as if they were spoken by someone else, as if he was absently listening to a stranger talking in a bar.

'Did Mr Wallace have any enemies that you know of?'

'None.'

'Would he have kept a large amount of money in the flat?'

'I doubt if Ben Wallace had a large amount of money.'

'The door was locked when you arrived?'

'Yes.'

'And you opened it with the keys?'

'Yes.'

'All right. Thanks for your help, Mr Law. I wonder if you'd mind waiting, then coming down to the police station to give us a full statement. I'd also like the names and addresses of any people who might be able to tell us where we can get in touch with Mrs Wallace or any other relatives.'

'OK,' Law said.

He deliberately didn't look at the corpse again, not even when a couple of ambulancemen brought in a stretcher, lifted Wallace onto it and covered him with a blanket.

The nausea had returned by the time he left the police station after giving his statement and it was accompanied by a band of pain across his stomach and the feeling that he could be violently sick at very, very short notice. Walking along the street, he considered the nausea. It seemed as bad if not worse than it had been the day before.

He guessed the shock of finding Ben Wallace's body had caused a resurgence of whatever it was he had picked up. Yet he wasn't sure if that made sense from a medical point of view.

He was still thinking about it, his face twisted into a grimace of discomfort, when he hailed a taxi and headed for Natalie's flat in Fulham.

Natalie Field hurried into the kitchen of her flat, her bare feet slapping on the pale green linoleum, turned the steak then opened the bottle of claret to let it breathe.

Going back through the lounge, she checked the table she had set for two. Yes, everything was in order. She had remembered the extra-sharp steak knives, the napkins were neatly coiled in their holders and the red candles were perfectly positioned at each end of the table in the

intricately-carved bronze candlesticks which Law had
brought back for her from Madrid.

In the bedroom, she stood in front of the full-length
mirror and studied herself. The wide-necked, clinging
orange dress looked good, she decided, then studied her
face. The dark-brown mascara had set off her green eyes
nicely but she was unhappy with her lips. A touch more
lipstick perhaps? She applied it with three quick stokes,
pressed her lips together, then pouted. Perfect.

She patted at her auburn hair until she was satisified
with it. It was styled to hang to her shoulders and curl
forward, the way Law liked it.

Then she found her eyes drawn to her nose. *That nose*. It
was slightly off-centre and it had caused her a lot of
heartache when she had been a teenager even though her
mother had assured her that hardly anyone would notice.
Her mother had been right. Although Natalie had
remained sensitive about it, if people had noticed it, very
few had mentioned it.

Law had been one of them.

'It's slightly out of symmetry with the rest of your face,'
he had said, not thinking she would be offended, wondering
if he was the first to notice it.

'I know,' she had said and he had seen her
embarrassment and apologised.

'Listen,' he had said, 'I can't stand women who yell and
break things and I can't stand female drunks but a funny
nose I can live with.'

'It's not funny, it's ...'

'In the wrong place.'

'No ...'

Then she had realised he was laughing, teasing her, and
she had laughed too. He had never mentioned it again.

She tugged at the left-hand sleeve of her dress, baring her
shoulders, wondering if that would make her look sexier. It
did. She looked at herself from different angles then pulled
the dress back over her shoulder again, afraid that Law

might make a joke of it.

She studied herself from top to bottom now and decided she looked pretty good; a good, solid, attractive seven out of ten. And if she was to rate herself against other ordinary women – leaving out really beautiful film stars and models – she decided she might even be a nine out of ten She was happy with that.

She stepped into a pair of orange shoes with very high heels and walked back to the kitchen. If it had been up to her, she would have stayed in her bare feet but she knew how much Law liked high heels – high heels with everything, even jeans. They had gone on a holiday to Devon two months before and he had even told her she should wear high heels with her bikini.

'High heels always give women that extra something,' Law had said.

So he's kinky for high heels, she had thought at the time. *Who cares? For this guy I'd swing from a trapeze wearing nothing but a top hat and an ankle bracelet.*

She glanced at her watch. It was ten past five. Law was ten minutes late.

She checked the steak then looked around for something else to do to occupy herself until he arrived. She was tense and nervous and suddenly aware of how much she had missed him.

Falling in love again …

She knew she was.

She had promised herself after her second husband had walked out that she would date lots of men but never get too emotionally involved again. That had lasted just over two years. Then one day Jack Law had walked into an advertising agency where she had been working as an artist. Everything had changed since then. Now she worked for herself and now she had Jack, the emotional involvement she had promised herself would never happen.

But she wasn't going to rush into anything this time, not after the two disastrous marriages she had had.

The three sharp raps on the door startled her, making her jump. She spun around, hurried along the hall, threw the door open and dived into Law's arms. She kissed him for a long time and the kiss felt so right, as if all the pieces of a jigsaw puzzle had just fallen into place. Something deep inside her tingled, thrilled.

Falling in love again ... Hah.

She was in love right now and she knew it with a certainty that was absolute. She was up to her eyeballs in love, on cloud nine, walking on air. Every cliché that had ever been written about love applied to her. She was in too deep to pull out, her Rubicon had been crossed.

She had never felt as she did at that moment.

She took him by the hand and led him into the lounge, words gushing out of her.

'I've got so much to tell you about this new ad campaign. You won't believe it ... it's such a break for me. And that old friend of my father that you met ... you remember ... Marcus ... he's asked me to do a portrait of him. Isn't that fantastic. Oh by the way, the Dempseys called yesterday and said they were having a party on Sunday night and would we like to come. I said you weren't back and I didn't want to go by myself but after I spoke to you today Georgina phoned and I said we'd try to make it ... God, I've missed you so much.'

She pushed him gently into the large easy chair by the window and stood back to look at him. His mouth was only halfway to a smile and there was something brooding in his eyes. It was as if he was trying to look pleased, trying to go along with her mood but not succeeding very well.

'What's wrong?' she said in a small voice.

He sighed, seeming at a loss for words, and a hundred thoughts poured into her mind. *He doesn't want me any more. He doesn't care for me. He's found somebody else, somebody in India, somebody prettier. He's decided we're getting too serious. He's ...*

'Do you remember Ben Wallace,' Law said, 'you met him ...'

'Yes, I remember him; the man with the grey beard.'

'Yeah.'

'What about him?'

'I just found his body ... at his flat.'

'His *body*.'

'Yes. It looks like he's been ... murdered ... but I'm not sure how.'

The words tumbled out of him then. He told her now he had met Wallace and they had gone for a drink and how he had found the body. Then he told her about how ill he felt. He hadn't intended to tell her any more but found himself continuing to talk, outlining the events at Srinwanat.

'The last four days of my life have been sheer hell,' he said. 'I wonder what's going to happen next.'

'Jack, I don't know what to say, I ...'

Suddenly she sniffed, shouted 'My God, the steak' and rushed into the kitchen. He listened to her clattering about for a moment then she reappeared, crossed the room and knelt down in front of him, her hands on his thighs.

'Life is sometimes like that,' she said, 'all the bad things happen at once. But sometimes all the good things happen at once too.'

He gestured to the table and said: 'I'm sorry to spoil your plans for a dinner party but I don't feel like eating anything.'

'That's OK,' she said.

'I think the shock of finding Ben's body has started off this stomach upset again.'

'Probably,' she said. 'I know just what you need. You need peace and quiet and rest. You've had some pretty bad shocks and your nerves are shattered. You're unwell and on top of that you're probably jetlagged.'

'The medicine the doctor gave me is back at the flat. I think I'll have to go home and get it. Maybe it'll make me feel a little better.'

'I'll drive you,' she said. 'We can spend a quiet night at your place. I'll just get my coat.'

She went into the bedroom and returned a moment later, tying the belt of a light-brown raincoat.

'Let's go,' she said.

They drove back to his flat, bringing each other up to date on the news of what had been happening to them. On one occasion Law tried to turn the conversation towards the subject of Ben Wallace but she steered him away from it. If it upset him, what was the point in talking about it? Law's friend was dead and no amount of words would bring him back.

'You can call the police on Monday and find out what it was that caused the wounds on his body,' she told him. 'Forget it until then.'

Once there was a lull in the conversation as she manoeuvred the green '69 Beetle, which she had had entirely rebuilt, through a heavy patch of early evening traffic. A strange sensation rushed through him, almost like a revelation. He felt as if a shadow had fallen over his life, as if he had stepped into a dark place out of the sun, as if he had turned down an emotional black alley and there was no way back. Something told him his life had changed irrevocably and would never again be the same as it had been before.

At the flat, she fussed over him, made him comfortable in a chair in front of the television, got his medicine and managed to get him to eat two boiled eggs. Then she sat on the floor at his feet, her shoulders resting against his legs, and they watched television and chatted and the sheer normality of it gradually made him feel better.

By nine-thirty she had climbed into his lap and they were kissing softly and touching, talking in whispers, murmuring intimacies. By nine-forty-five the orange dress lay in a heap on the floor and they were tangled together deep in passion.

Suddenly he pulled his head back.

'Bedroom,' he said simply.

She inclined her head, her eyes hooded, lips wet and slightly apart.

He led her into the bedroom by the hand, almost as if she was a child, stripped off her bra and panties and threw off his own clothes, watching her as she lay on the bed, one knee drawn up, the light from the lounge playing across her flesh, making it appear to glow a kind of silky yellow.

She sighed as he lowered himself onto the bed, his hands moving across her. She rolled against him.

'Skin against skin,' she said, 'I love skin against skin.'

His hands moved slowly at first then became more urgent, rougher ...

Rougher than ever before.

He gripped a fold of skin on her side between thumb and index finger and twisted it until she cried out and pushed his hand away, certain there would be a bruise there.

'Be careful,' she murmured.

He bit her shoulder violently, allowing his teeth to nip the flesh, and twisted one of her nipples.

'Jack ... Jack, you're hurting me,' she hissed.

Then he was inside her and pleasure and pain were mixed. As she felt herself moving towards an orgasm, he scratched and clawed at her.

Why?

He had always been so gentle before; almost the perfect lover.

Then she came with three quick convulsions and it was over. As they lay tangled together on the bed and the thrill of her passion receded, she felt a score of tiny pains nipping across her body, little scratches, cuts and bruises.

She was going to tell him about it, mildly rebuke him, but decided not to. He was unwell and depressed and he probably hadn't realised he was hurting her so much.

She shifted on the bed, pulling his face between her breasts and burying her face into his hair.

'I love you,' she said.

And at that moment he felt a scorching intensity of malice towards her. It was so powerful it startled him. *Malice? Why?* Why should he feel malice towards Natalie? The emotion lasted only for an instant then was gone, leaving him confused and filled with a sense of guilt and shame.

Natalie stirred and her eyes flicked open. She rolled onto her side and looked at Jack Law. He was asleep, lying on his back, his lips slightly apart, his bare chest rising and falling in a slow rhythm. The luminous dial on the clock beyond his head told her it was three a.m.

She lifted the blankets back gently and slid out of the bed, careful not to wake Law.

It was as she stood up that it occurred to her that something wasn't right in the flat, something wasn't as it should be.

She hesitated then walked on into the lounge, heading for the bathroom. A small table lamp had been left switched on and there was a valley of light between the sofa and a long occasional table. She turned on the main light and found herself scanning the room, looking for something.

But what?

What was wrong with her?

She tutted and grimaced, certain something was not right yet unable to put her finger on what it was.

As she crossed to the bathroom and went in, she was suddenly very aware of her nakedness, as if she had just realised that a curtain had blown open and people in the street could see her.

When she came back out of the bathroom, she walked very quickly across the lounge, looking neither to right nor left, a chill playing up and down the back of her neck.

There was something *in* the flat, something *unfamiliar*.

She entered the bedroom, leaving the lounge light on.

Something unclean.

She slid back under the bedclothes and cuddled up to Law, curling one of her legs over his body.

Something evil.

Evil? What had made her think such a thing? What had made that word come to her?

She shook her head slowly as if to jar the word loose then closed her eyes, trying to sleep. It was all just a mind-trick, she decided, probably caused by the sediment of a bad dream in the early part of her sleep.

That was all it could be. Wasn't it?

12

That night Law had the dream again, the dream of drifting through red fog and finding a woman's body staked out on a mound in a burning yellow desert. It was identical to the dream he had had on the flight home from India in every detail except one. When he woke he realised he had seen more of the body and it had looked somehow familiar.

Why familiar?

He decided not to dwell on it. One would have to be Freud to explain these things. A grin forced its way through a sleepy yawn as it occurred to him that a psychiatrist would probably say something about the woman representing his bullying Aunt Janet whom he had thoroughly detested as a child and would probably have enjoyed seeing staked out in the sun.

He reached an arm lazily across the bed, searching for Natalie, but found only cold sheets and a warmish trench where she had slept. His hand brushed something on the pillow and there was a crackling sound. He raised himself onto one elbow and saw a piece of notepaper with a scribbled message on it. Rubbing his eyes, he picked it up and read it.

'Dear Lazybones,
    Have gone to get Sunday newspapers. I'll get a copy of *The Globe* of course with your latest offering from India. Back soon.

                                   Natalie.'

It was as he flopped onto his back again that he noticed the odd smell. A chemical smell perhaps? Something Natalie had used in the kitchen when she was tidying up the night before? Then the smell became more pronounced. It was no chemical. It was a pungent, rotten smell. He considered for a moment that it might be some food that had gone off while he was in India that Natalie had found and put in the bin in the kitchen. Then he realised it wasn't coming from outside the room. It was in the room.

In the bed.

His brow furrowed as he drew back the blankets. Instantly the smell increased, a wave of it wafting over him. For a moment he was at a loss, his mind blank, entirely unable to hazard a guess at what it could possibly be. Then he raised his arm and smelled his flesh.

It was him.

He sniffed at his chest and his other arm and found the decayed, foul smell was all over him.

What could it be?

Suddenly he realised he felt unbelievably dirty, as if he hadn't washed or changed his clothes for a month and had been sleeping rough in cow paddocks. He swept back the blankets, hurried into the bathroom and adjusted the shower taps, making the water hotter than usual. He stepped into the gushing stream and lathered soap all over him, urgently trying to get rid of the smell and the feeling of uncleanliness. Washing the soap off, he sniffed at his arm. The smell had diminished but it was still there, mixed with the odour of the soap. He reached for the scrubbing brush and scrubbed every inch of himself. But he was still not satisfied and he repeated the process until his flesh was red and sore.

'Enough is enough,' he said aloud.

If he sniffed at his hand for a long time, he thought he could still smell it but it was very faint.

It was just being ill, he told himself. There was often a bad smell when people were ill, wasn't there?

He stepped out of the shower, towelled himself dry, returned to the bedroom and dressed.

I still feel unclean, he thought as he went back into the lounge.

He strode to the window and looked down, searching the street for Natalie. It was as he turned away from the window that he caught sight of the picture of his son Todd on the wall in front of his work desk. A surge of emotion caught him unawares, snatching at the back of his throat.

('But why do you and mum not want to live together any more? Why don't you like each other any more?'

'It's not that we don't like each other exactly, it's just that …'

'But why?'

'I know it's hard for you to understand but it's not that we don't like each other any more and it's not that we don't both love you. It's just that we've decided that being apart is best.'

'But why? Why?'

The words lashed to the very centre of his soul and a murky mixture of guilt, frustration and a sense of failure rushed through him. Fiona and Todd lived with Fiona's parents in the Isle of Man now. Law got over there whenever he could which wasn't very often, maybe once a year. There were times when he missed the boy with an almost physical ache.

He thought about Fiona then and considered ringing her and telling her about Ben Wallace but he rejected the idea almost immediately. There was no point in being the bearer of bad tidings. He reached for the radio, seeking some kind of human contact, even a stranger's voice, but withdrew his hand when he heard the door close and Natalie walking up the hall.

'You're up then?' she said, bouncing into the room.

'Yep.'

'How are you feeling?'

'Better than last night,' he conceded.

'You see,' she said in an I-told-you-so tone, 'having me around has a marvellous effect on you.'

She threw three Sunday newspapers onto the settee but kept *The Globe* tucked under her arm as she kissed him.

'The opposition's not up to much,' she said, 'but look at this.'

She unfolded *The Globe* and opened it at the centre pages. The entire spread was given over to a humorous article he had written about getting lost in Madras. A head-and-shoulders picture of Law had been superimposed on a cartoon of a man astride an elephant, which was scratching its head with its trunk. A balloon from the elephant's mouth contained the words: 'Which way now, sahib?'

He chuckled and poked a finger at the cartoon.

'I bet this was Forrest's idea.'

'I've never seen that picture of you before,' she said.

'Neither have I.'

'You even look rather confused in it.'

'Thank you very much. I admit I was confused in Madras but I assure you this picture was not taken there.' He looked at it closely. 'It's years old. Forrest must have trawled through the files to find this one. I was younger and better looking then.'

'Men,' she almost yelled, 'sometimes I think you're more vain than women.'

She spun away and headed for the kitchen. 'What do you want for breakfast,' she said over her shoulder.

'Anything you like as long as it's not bacon,' he said. 'Eggs will do.'

He sat down and leafed through *The Globe*, listening to her moving about the kitchen, the fridge door opening and closing, the click of the switches on the cooker.

'You haven't forgotten about the Dempseys' party,' she said, poking her head round the door.

'What …'

'I told you about it yesterday.'

'Yes. I vaguely remember you saying something …'

'I think we should go. I think it would do you good.'

'With Ben ... dead ... it doesn't seem right. I'm not sure the Dempseys will still be having a party after they hear about Ben. They knew him quite well, you know. I wonder if they've heard what happened to him.'

'I'll ring Georgina and see if the party's still on. There's nothing you can do for Ben. We don't have to stay at the party for long, just long enough to cheer you up.'

She gave him a big smile and he smiled back.

'I don't know.' he said.

'Have you taken your medicine?'

'No, I ...'

'Say no more,' she said with a wave of her hand. She fetched the medicine and stood over him while he took it.

'We'll have you better in no time,' she said, returning to the kitchen.

After breakfast, Natalie called Georgina Dempsey and found out that the party was still on. 'I couldn't get in touch with the people to cancel the party now even if I wanted to,' Georgina said, 'and anyway Ben would have said the show must go on.'

Natalie had hung up and looked at Law, her head cocked to one side.

'The party is definitely on and if you don't feel you are right at death's door I think we should go, even if only for a couple of hours. It'll do you good and if you start to have a bad turn we can always come home.'

'OK, we'll go,' he shrugged.

They spent a quiet day together; Law studying his notebook, collecting his thoughts and getting 500 words on paper; Natalie reading the Sundays, tidying up the flat and finally sitting in the far corner of the room, sketching Law. Late in the afternoon they both sat down to watch 'The Lavender Hill Mob' on television. Law found himself roaring with laughter even though he had seen the film so often before he knew the lines before they were delivered.

It was as he was getting ready for the party that he

realised the smell on his body was becoming stronger again. He showered, scrubbed himself and splashed aftershave on his chest and under his armpits. A feeling of being unclean lingered in his mind no matter how hard he tried to shrug it off.

He dressed in black cords, grey jacket and white roll-neck pullover then went into the lounge and said: 'I'm ready, let's go and get you spruced up and into your party gear.'

Don Singer was 68 years old and had lived in the flat next door to Jack Law for a year, ever since his wife had died. With Mary gone, the house in Hendon had been too big, too empty, too lonely. He had wanted a small place, a place he could pull around him like a comfortable, well-worn jacket, a place that had no empty spaces where nobody lived any more.

The flat suited him perfectly. It was just a short ride on the tube to his daughter's flat and to the homes of most of his friends, and the centre of the city and Hyde Park were within walking distance. It was crowded with the memorabilia of his life – pictures of Mary and the children covering the period from the war to the year before, old snaps of his parents, the two hundred first editions he had collected over the years as a hobby, the SS knife he had brought back from the war, the framed certificate he had received when he retired as chief clerk after 40 years with Wyforth Engineering and scores of ornaments worth little in themselves but each containing a fragment of some fading memory.

He was seated in a large easy chair by the window, looking down into the street, when he heard Law's door close. He had been re-reading a letter from his son, Martin, who lived in Toronto, and was holding the pages loosely in his right hand now, feeling a kind of closeness with Martin through the letter.

He heard Law's muffled voice as the journalist passed the

door, a brief woman's laugh, the subdued clatter of the lift doors – then silence.

As he dropped his eyes back towards the letter, a sharp *ping* made him jerk his head round. He studied the wall to his left, the communal wall with Law's flat, but saw nothing.

Ping.

A second sound, identical to the first.

This time his eyes picked up a tiny grey blur of movement as a small object bounced across the floor.

He had placed the letter on an occasional table in front of him and started to rise when the sound came again.

Ping.

Another object skipped across the carpet and lay still, almost invisible against the check pattern.

He took three steps across the room and knelt on one knee.

Nails.

There were three nails there – the kind used to hold down a carpet.

He picked them up and cupped them in his right hand.

Where …

Ping-ping-ping-ping-ping-ping.

Suddenly half a dozen nails flew up from the edge of the carpet and capered across the floor and the corner of the carpet began to rise lazily. As he stared at the carpet, it flicked forward and began to tumble into a roll.

Ping-ping-ping.

More nails danced through the air and he jumped back as the carpet, freed from the restraining nails, thumped towards him, rolling rapidly into itself.

What the hell …

Then a movement on the wall made him snatch his head up. Strips of wallpaper were lifting away from the wall, crackling as one section after another jumped free and nodded towards the floor.

He stepped over the roll of carpet, grabbing for the wallpaper, intending to push it back into place.

But the wall was hot, impossibly hot.

He withdrew his hands and stepped back quickly, tripping over the carpet. He stumbled, righted himself then backed away into the kitchen and snatched the telephone from the wall.

It was the instinctive gesture of a civilised man who needed help. There was always someone on the other end of the line, wasn't there? Someone with all the answers. But who could he call? The police? His daughter? The fire brigade?

And say what? 'Come quickly. My wallpaper is peeling. The nails in my carpet are popping out.' They'd think he was a senile old fool.

Odd things did happen, he told himself, things that science could not yet explain but which would have a perfectly rational explanation in fifty years. This had to be one of those cases. They happened to other people all the time. He had read about them in the newspapers. It was nothing to worry about. It was just that …

His mind darted about, seeking a rational explanation.

Perhaps a nail could become fatigued and be forced out of its socket by the pressure caused by the building as it settled?

He was a clerk, he didn't know about these things.

If one nail sprang free, the movement of the carpet could have pulled the others out. And the rising carpet could have brushed the bottom of the wallpaper. Perhaps the paste he had used on the wallpaper hadn't been strong enough.

But what about the heat?

Suddenly he realised that all movement in the flat had ceased. The roll of carpet was stationary. The wallpaper hung in crumpled strips.

How hot had the wall really been?

Slowly, uncertainly, he hung up the phone and walked back into the lounge. He stepped over the carpet, reached out and touched the wall.

It was cool. Normal. Just as it always was.

He stared at it for a long time then went into the hall, fetched his hammer and began to nail the carpet back into place.

13

'I first heard about Ben's death last night, when the police called,' Leo Dempsey told Jack Law when he and Natalie arrived at the party.

Dempsey was in his early forties, a small man, not above five feet six, with broad shoulders and shining black hair. 'My middle-aged Spanish gigolo' was how Georgina Dempsey usually referred to him despite the fact that, as far as he knew, all his ancestors came from Suffolk.

Law had first met Leo Dempsey when Leo had joined the Globe. Dempsey had been a sub-editor there, a journalist of exceptional talent with flair and imagination. He had left the year before to run a computer magazine.

Georgina was as different from Leo as it was possible to be – tall with a mop of fuzzy blonde hair.

Law had introduced Natalie to the Dempseys six months before and Natalie and Georgina had hit it off straight away and become close friends.

'Yes, my name was in Ben's address book,' Dempsey was saying. 'The police wanted to know if I knew where Rachel was … but I didn't.'

Georgina was looking sympathetically at Law. 'It must have been a shock finding him like that,' she said.

Law nodded slowly and Natalie raised her eyebrows and gave Georgina a penetrating look that Law didn't see. Georgina got the message and she and Leo dropped the subject and the four of them began to mingle with the other guests.

Law and Natalie chatted to some of Law's friends, mostly newspapermen or former newspapermen who had become information officers for government departments or public communications directors with private companies.

It was at half-past ten that Leo Dempsey cut his hand. Slightly drunk, he had reached out to put an empty wineglass on the mantelpiece. He had missed and, when the glass fell, instinctively grabbed for it.

'Shit,' he had yelled as it broke and a large fragment of glass stuck in his palm.

Law had been standing in the same group as Dempsey when the accident happened and in the instant he saw the jagged glass draw blood he felt the same intensity of malice towards Leo that he had felt towards Natalie the night before. A sense of delight at Dempsey's pain rushed through him and he realised he was grinning.

Leo jerked the glass fragment out of his hand and threw it into the fireplace. It was as he whipped a handkerchief from his pocket that he caught sight of Law.

'What the hell are you laughing at?' he said, dabbing at the wound.

'I'm not laughing,' Law said, covering up quickly, straightening his face. 'It was a grimace. I can't stand the sight of blood. Here, let me help you do that.'

He stepped forward to help Dempsey but Natalie beat him to it. She wiped the blood away, studied the cut then led Dempsey to the bathroom.

Malice. Why had he felt malice? Why had there been a surge of delight at his friend's pain?

He wandered across the room to where Georgina was pouring drinks and helped himself to a large whisky.

Law and Natalie left the party shortly after eleven. Natalie explained to Georgina that Law had been unwell and was jetlagged and needed his sleep.

When they got back to Law's flat, he showered before they went to bed – for the third time that day.

*

Leo Dempsey closed the door behind the last guest to leave, winced at the ache which had started to throb in his right temple and walked slowly back into the lounge.

'I drank too much of that Lambrusco,' he said. 'I knew I'd get a headache.'

Georgina surveyed the chaos of the lounge – heaped ashtrays spilling their contents onto tables and the arms of easy chairs, an army of glasses scattered about, half-empty bottles of wine and gin and whisky and beer crowded on tables and trays, chicken bones and half-eaten savoury biscuits on dozens of abandoned paper plates.

She ran the fingers of her left hand through her hair and said: 'My God, look at this place.'

'You'd think some down-and-outs had been using this place for a squat for the last month,' he laughed and the laugh was in danger of turning into a giggle.

She flopped down onto the settee and tutted. 'The question is, do I clear up tonight or do I leave it until the morning?'

'Leave it until the morning,' he said, finding a bottle of Lambrusco and splashing some into a glass.

'No,' she said with a note of finality, 'I'll make a start tonight. I couldn't face all this in the morning.'

'Leave it,' he said, 'let's just go to bed.'

'No, I've made up my mind.'

She stood up, pursing her lips as she caught sight of a large red stain on the carpet where somebody had dropped a glass of wine, and began to collect paper plates and empty glasses.

'Do you want me to help?' he said.

'No, I don't want you under my feet. Anyway you'd only start dropping things.'

'I'm not that drunk.'

She cocked her head to one side and gave him a wide-eyed look that seemed to suggest that perhaps he was deluding himself.

He sat down at a table, resting his weight on his

forearms, and stared into his glass of wine as if there was some secret there he hadn't discovered yet.

'Did you have a good time?' he said and noticed his words were tripping over each other.

'Yes, I thoroughly enjoyed myself.'

'So did I,' he said.

Staring into the wine was having a hypnotic effect on him and when his vision began to blur he jerked his head away.

Georgina disappeared into the kitchen with an armful of paper plates and a tray of glasses and he heard her flicking open a plastic rubbish bag.

He stood up slowly and strolled after her. When he entered the kitchen, she was running water into the sink and squirting washing-up liquid into the water.

He lifted up her hair and kissed her on the back of the neck, running his hands across her thighs, feeling her soft flesh through the flimsy dress.

'Leo, *please*, I'm trying to get some work done.'

'You're not going to be working all night, are you?' he said, running his hands up under her breasts.

'Frankly, my little Spanish gigolo, I don't think you're up to it.'

'What do you mean?' he said, drawing his head back and letting his mouth fall open in mock astonishment.

'I seem to remember you had the same idea after the last party we had ...'

'I don't remember that.'

'Yes you did ... and you fell asleep at a very, very frustrating moment.'

'You're kidding?'

'No, I'm not.'

'You're just trying to be nasty.'

'I'm not. I'm just telling you what happened. *Men*. You get a girl very interested and the next thing you pass out, snoring like a buzz-saw.'

'I do not snore.'

She threw her head back and laughed. 'You do when

you're drunk. I had to put a pillow over your head.'

'You didn't do that, did you?'

She was splashing glasses into the soapy water now.

'No, but I thought about it,' she said.

'You can be very cruel sometimes,' he said, turning away with an exaggerated expression of deep hurt.

'Want me to make you some black coffee?' she said over her shoulder as he walked slowly back into the lounge. 'It might help to sober you up.'

'Sounds like a good idea,' he said. 'I don't want you to put a pillow over my head tonight and suffocate me to death just because of a little snoring.'

He was seated at the dining table with his head in his hands when she brought him the coffee.

'Here he is, the lover of the century,' she said, putting the mug down in front of him.

'Very funny, ho ho ho.' he said, not raising his head.

'It's your own fault,' she said.

'I know, I know, don't rub it in. It's just that I was having such a good time, I forgot how much I was drinking.'

'Get the coffee inside you, you'll feel better,' she said and started to empty all the ashtrays into a cardboard box and pile them on a tray.

He raised his head, focussed his eyes on the mug, managed to grab it at the second attempt and gulped down the coffee without taking the mug from his lips.

'Everything is starting to spin,' he told her. 'I can't go to bed like this. It's worse when you lie down.' He grumbled to himself for a minute then added: 'Besides I daren't snore, otherwise it would be death by pillow.'

'Why don't you get some fresh air?' she said. 'I'll be busy here for at least fifteen minutes.'

He raised himself to his feet in stages, walked slowly to the back door and went out onto the patio.

At first the fresh air made him feel worse and he stood leaning on the cold bricks of the house, propping himself up. After a few minutes, he began to feel better. He strolled down the gravel path, through the dim garden shrubbery, lifted the latch on the wrought-iron gate in the back fence and stepped out onto the path along the riverbank.

Between the two oaks in front of him, the Thames was like a trembling dark-grey groundsheet. There was a splash of quivering yellow moonlight on the surface away to his left and two white scars far out in front of him where a log trapped near the far bank trailed out its slender branches.

He kicked his way through the knee-high weeds to the edge of the river and stood looking up at the half-moon set in a grey triangle between dark clouds and listening to the gulping and gurgling of the river.

Several minutes passed and he was about to turn away and walk back to the house when something in the river caught his eye. A large white mass, just under the surface, gliding soundlessly towards him.

Too big for a fish, he told himself, then thought *unless it's the shark from Jaws* and an uncertain half-smile creased his face.

Still the shape under the water came on. Thirty yards away, then twenty …

Suddenly he had a powerful urge to wade into the water and investigate. Now it was as if his brain was divided in two – one half urging him to go into the water, the other telling him that that was the silliest thing he had ever heard of in his life.

He felt himself take one step forward and was aware of the strange sensation that some force was drawing him into the river.

You're drunk, you idiot, go back to the house.

He tried to turn away but found it was as if an invisible web was wrapped around him, dragging him on. He felt himself take another step towards the river.

The white mass was fifteen yards away from him now, moving smoothly through the water, making no ripples at all. It was more than six feet long and three feet across, he guessed, its outline twisted by the water which flowed over it.

It had to be a fish and yet …

He felt his left foot jerk forward, heard it splash into the few inches of water at the river's edge.

… there were no fish that size in the Thames. Were there?

He felt his right foot jump forward and cold water running down into his shoe.

GO BACK, a voice in his head yelled at him. *Get away from here.*

The shape was only a few feet away from him now. It didn't look like a fish. It looked like …

a mound of human flesh.

He spun away, his feet digging desperately into the mud. He swung his right foot clear of the water but his left slithered away from him and he collapsed onto all fours.

As he tried to drag himself to his feet, something large and soft and astonishingly strong folded around his ankle and jerked at it.

'Bloody hell,' he yelled, rolling onto his back just as his left leg disappeared under the water.

He caught the briefest glimpse of what had trapped his ankle. It looked like a massive fist.

A sudden tug dragged him three feet forward so that he was sitting in six inches of water.

Instinctively he kicked down with his right leg, splashing water high into the air.

His blood chilled as he realised that that leg was trapped now too, held fast beneath the surface of the water.

He rolled onto his side, his fingers clawing grass and soil and weed-clumps in a frenzied attempt to drag himself back to the bank.

'Georgina,' he yelled.

Instantly there was a tremendous tug and he found himself in deep water, going down.

Fifteen minutes after Georgina had heard Leo's footsteps receding down the gravel path, she heard another sound in the garden, near the house.

She had managed to get all the glasses washed, put away all the bottles, wipe down the occasional tables and empty and clean all the ashtrays. Now she was on her knees, trying to get rid of the wine stain in the carpet.

She turned and looked expectantly at the back door, waiting for a sobered-up Leo to come in. When he didn't appear she returned to the carpet stain.

A minute later, just as she had decided she was happy with her work on the carpet, she heard another sound in the garden, like slow footsteps in the grass.

She stood up, went to the back window and looked out. There was no sign of her husband.

She opened the window and shouted.

'Leo … Leo, are you there?'

She thought she heard something like a heavy sigh and peered harder into the gloom.

'Leo … if this is some kind of game, it's not very funny.'

She waited, expecting him to jump out at any moment and press his nose against the window pane or do something equally silly.

When he didn't appear, she marched to the back door and threw it open.

'Stop this right now, Leo, you're frightening me,' she said, going into the garden.

14

'Leo.'

Georgina Dempsey spoke the word softly into the dark garden in front of her as she stood on the edge of the patio, her arms folded against the night chill. She wanted to shout because waves of apprehension had started to thaw out the numbness and shred the carefree feeling that had been induced by the alcohol she had consumed at the party – but she was afraid she might wake the neighbours.

'Leo,' she said again, slightly louder this time.

The word was swallowed up by the trees and shrubs and the dark night.

Suddenly her ears became attuned to the sounds of the garden – branches and leaves murmuring in the gentle breeze, the almost inaudible creak of a loose plank in the fence away to her right, a *plop-plopping* at the very outer reaches of her hearing that she knew must be coming from the river.

Could he have passed out?

She tutted and walked forward to the edge of the pool of light from the house.

'Leo. Leo, are you there?'

A pins-and-needles sensation of fear began to crawl up her spine but she shrugged it aside. Why should she be afraid in her own garden?

There were only two possibilities, she decided. Leo had either passed out or he was playing a trick on her.

'Leo,' she said once more, then she went back into the

house, fetched a torch from a drawer in the kitchen and returned to the garden.

In the torchlight, the flowers and the shrubs and the small rockery she had built were twisted grotesquely into gaunt, watching figures.

She hurried down the garden, confusion and uncertainty rekindling the pins-and-needles sensation in her spine.

'Leo,' she said gruffly, surprised at how loud her footsteps sounded on the gravel of the path.

She shone the torch to her left and right, thoroughly searching the garden, but there was no sign of her husband.

It would be a trick, she told herself. *One of his silly jokes.* She comforted herself with the thought that she would give him a tongue-lashing that he would never forget and shone the torch into the high branches of an oak tree, as if half expecting him to jump down and say: 'Had you worried that time.' But there were just dim boughs and trembling branches and leaves.

She reached the back gate and hesitated.

Would he have gone down by the river?

She lifted the latch on the gate and was irritated at how much the rasping metallic sound startled her. She stepped through the gate and shone the torch in both directions along the river path. There was no sign of Leo. She moved the beam of light slowly across the hunched trees and nodding weeds. Nothing.

Then the thought came to her, comforting her: *He's gone for a walk. It's as simple as that. He's probably gone around the block.*

She laughed, a brief expelling of air. *He was probably back in the house now. He had probably walked around the block and gone in the front door.*

She went back through the gate and hurried across the garden.

It was as she stepped onto the patio that she froze.

There were five wet footprints on the paving stones, leading from the edge of the patio to the house. She bent and stared at the first one as if mesmerised by it. It was the print of a large bare foot.

Had they been there when she came out? Had somebody taken off their shoes and socks at the party and walked about in the damp grass in the garden? Surely that had to be the answer?

She tiptoed across the patio and opened the back door.

'Leo. Leo, are you there?'

Her words echoed in the still silence of the house.

She stepped inside and closed the door behind her, wincing at the double click of the lock. As she turned away, she caught sight of her face in a mirror, a haunted, scared face, the mouth twisted down at both sides, deep trenches in her forehead.

Why was she so afraid?

It was obvious there would be a perfectly reasonable explanation for everything. Nothing that had happened justified the depth of fear that she now felt.

She stood just inside the back door, her hands on her hips, thinking it all out.

Yes, she decided, there would be a perfectly straightforward explanation in the end ... but Leo *had* disappeared and there *was* a chance he had passed out somewhere. Therefore, the best move was to get help immediately.

The decision taken, she walked to the telephone at the far side of the room, flicked open her address book at 'L' and made a mental note of Jack Law's number.

She had picked up the receiver and dialled two digits when she heard a sound behind her (*coming from the kitchen?*) like a heavy sigh or someone taking a deep, rasping breath.

She spun around, fumbled with the receiver and dropped it.

In the same instant as the receiver clunked onto the carpet she saw the figure in the kitchen, watching her, and a terrible cocktail of dread surged through her bloodstream.

The man was about seven feet tall and naked. Water

dripped from the huge folds of fat that covered him and trickled across his shaven head. A pair of oval brown eyes watched her blankly from a sagging, fleshy, impassive face. A large red stone was set in a golden ear-ring dangling from his left earlobe and a multicoloured snake was tattooed on his left forearm.

Just before her mind turned to crushed ice and instinct took over, she thought he looked like a giant eunuch guarding the harem of some Ottoman prince.

She snatched her eyes away from him, crouched and grabbed for the receiver. She missed because her hands were shaking so violently it was as if an electric current was running through them. She tried again and this time managed to scoop it up in both hands.

Her heart drummed against her ribcage and she realised she was whimpering.

Who was that man? The question lashed through her mind then was gone.

She managed to dial the third digit of Law's number by cradling the receiver between her head and her shoulder and holding her right hand steady by gripping it with her left.

Splotch.

The sound of a wet, naked foot on the linoleum in the kitchen was unmistakable.

He was coming towards her.

She turned to face him, pressing herself against the wall.

Splotch. He took a second step.

His face remained impassive, his eyes watching her steadily, unblinking.

'Wha … what … do you want? Who …'

Splotch.

Another step and he would be in the lounge.

The back door. Could she make it to the back door? Or should she try for the front door? It was closer.

The questions zipped through her mind but no answers came.

She found herself stumbling across the room and leaping up the stairs.

The bedroom telephone. She could use the bedroom telephone. There was a bolt on the bedroom door. She would have time. She would be all right.

Gasping, she reached the top of the stairs and ran along the hall. She hesitated at her bedroom door and looked back, listening. There were no sounds now. The man (*or thing? or creature?*) was not coming after her; she was certain of it. If a man of that bulk had been coming up the stairs, she would have heard the thud of his footsteps, the shifting of his weight.

She ripped her eyes back to the bedroom door, snatched it open, went in and bolted it behind her. Hurrying across the room to the bedroom telephone, she snatched up the receiver.

Who the hell was that man? What was he doing there? What did he want? WHERE WAS LEO?

The question buzzed about her brain like wasps from an upturned hive.

Jack Law. Jack Law. Ring Jack Law.

She fumbled the first four digits then stopped dead. She stood quite still now, all trembling gone, frozen by fear into a statue.

Splotch.

He was in the small bathroom that led off the bedroom. He was behind her, only a few feet away. *But how?*

She felt a massive hand slap down across her neck, ripping away her dress as if it was made of tissue paper.

Then a huge blow on her shoulder knocked her sideways onto the bed.

Law felt good when he woke the next day, strangely exhilarated and energetic. There was nothing like a good sleep, he thought, nothing in the world. He recalled it as having been dreamless and untroubled. He rubbed a hand across his stomach as if searching through the skin for any sign of the nausea which had plagued him. It was still there, but distant now, a light sediment lingering in his system. He sniffed at his skin. The smell was much fainter, almost undetectable unless he took a really deep breath through his nostrils.

He glanced over at Natalie, her face peaceful and tranquil in sleep, then looked at the clock. Two minutes and the shrill clatter of the alarm would ravage the silence of the room. He reached over and stabbed the alarm button down then climbed out of bed, careful not to wake Natalie, and walked into the bathroom.

The medicine the doctor had given him was on a shelf above the sink. He studied it for a moment then decided it was better to be safe than sorry. He popped two of the tablets into his mouth and gulped them down with a swig of the foul-tasting stomach medicine.

He showered and returned to the bedroom to dress. Natalie was still asleep, her breathing sounding like deep sighs. He decided not to wake her and went into the kitchen to cook his breakfast. He found he was ravenously hungry and made himself bacon and eggs.

Natalie came into the kitchen just as he had sat down at the table and started flicking low-sodium salt onto his food. She was wearing a silk dressing gown he had brought back for her from Japan.

'Morning,' she said, stifling a yawn.

'You slept well,' he said, smiling.

She frowned as if suddenly remembering something which had been troubling her. Just as he was about to comment on it, she suddenly smiled, hurried across the room and put her arms around his shoulders.

'You must be feeling better, you've got your appetite back,' she said.

'Yes, I think I'm on the mend,' he said.

She ran her fingers through his hair. 'You should still take your medicine,' she said. 'You should always finish the course.'

'I've already taken my medicine,' he said, 'and just for you I will finish the whole course.'

He turned to face her, parted his knees and pulled her up against him.

'Well, that's our weekend over,' he said. 'For me, it's back to the office today.'

'It's a hard life,' she said impishly.

'How about meeting me at about five-thirty at the Dragon's Tongue.'

'OK.'

He ran his right hand up her thigh and she jerked away from him instantly.

'What's wrong?' he said.

'Nothing. It's all right.'

'No, I ...'

She held his face in her hands and looked into his eyes. 'It's nothing, just a bruise, that's all.'

'Let me see.'

'It's nothing. I bruise easily, you know that.'

He unfastened the belt on the dressing gown and lifted it open. The bruise on her hip was an ugly mottled black and blue lump, about three inches long and two inches wide.

'How did you do that?'

She hesitated then said: 'There are more.'

He stared at her, incredulous, and said: 'More? More what? More bruises?'

She drew the front of the dressing gown wide open and he saw that there was an inch-square bruise on the inside of her right breast. Then she pointed to the inside of her thigh, just below the triangle of pubic hair. The bruise there was a dark blue tinged with red.

'How did you get these?' he said, his voice high-pitched with shock and surprise.

'Don't you remember?' she said.

'Remember? Remember what? What are you talking about?'

'Don't you remember last night when we ... made love?'

He half smiled with disbelief. 'Natalie, we didn't make love last night. We got back here and I was so tired I threw my clothes off had a quick shower, got into bed and went straight to sleep.'

'And you don't remember waking up in the middle of the night?'

He shook his head slowly. 'No.'

She sighed. 'It was probably because you were drinking on top of the medicine you're taking. That can have a funny effect on the brain.'

'I don't remember a thing. Are you saying we made love and I left you with all those bruises?'

She nodded and her lower lip twitched at one corner.

'It wasn't very nice, Jack,' she said, dropping her eyes away from his. 'You threw me out of the bed. You were like a crazy man. It was ... it was like rape, Jack.'

He stood up and folded his arms around her. 'Oh, Natalie, I'm so sorry. I must have had some kind of blackout. Nothing like this has ever happened to me before.'

Porkat: The Ritual

Tattap strode into the dimness of the small temple that stood on a low mound in the centre of Porkat and found the naked, blood-spattered figure of Subhash seated on the steps that led to an ancient stone statue of Dacahri in his half-man half-tiger incarnation. The Seeker heard the whisper of Tattap's sandals but did not look up. He remained where he was, as still as the statue behind him, his face buried in his hands, muttering The Seeker's mantra over and over again.

When he had arrived at the village four hours before, Subhash had found the three maiden priestesses awaiting him in the darkness of the temple's altar room, their bodies annointed by the *clepengui* fungus, as the ritual of The Finding demanded.

He had stood naked on the altar as they stripped him and rubbed the fungus into his body. Then he had had sexual intercourse with each – to symbolise the rebirth of Dacahri, as it was set down in The Book. At each climax he had felt the warm blood of The Sacrifice spattering over him; first the blood from a dog's throat – sliced open by Tattap – then the blood of a snake and finally the blood from the decapitated head of a goat.

Then as he lay exhausted on the altar the priestesses had drawn on his body in the blood of the animals and their maidenhood the ritual diagrams which Dacahri would recognise – the forms of the divine snake, the head of the goat, the paws of the dog, the secret symbols of death and rebirth, the huge circles of the endless cycle.

'Is there anything you wish?' Tattap said in a whisper.

Subhash raised his head slowly.

'No,' he said.

Everything had been done. There was only the waiting now. When the sun reached its highest point the next day, the girl children would be brought to him – the prettiest, the most perfect, the unblemished – and among these he would find the new Sedali.

15

'It was great stuff, tremendous stuff. I really thought you managed to capture the essence of India,' Peter Forrest told Jack Law after he had shaken Law's hand vigorously, sat down and thrown his feet up on his desk. It was two in the afternoon and the Globe's editor had just returned from his weekly briefing at Briars, the home of Sir Rhodes Bentley, the Globe's owner.

'I really think it's the best writing you've ever done for this newspaper,' Forrest said, 'and so does Sir Rhodes.'

It was typical of Forrest. He had a reputation for being generous with compliments and advice but not so generous with money, a spendthrift with words, a miser with cash – his own or the company's. He was a small, neat, impeccably-dressed man with the quick gestures of a tiny animal and a rapid-fire way of talking. His face was lean and watchful and he was as fit and tough as he looked, fit enough to beat Jack Law at squash whenever he really wanted to and that was on most occasions when they played. He was in his early fifties, bald on top, and the hair that he had left at back and sides was cut as short as a soldier's.

Law had spent the morning at his typewriter and managed to finish two more of the Indian articles. The words had come easily to him, almost as if they were programmed on a tape in the typewriter and came out as soon as his fingers fell on the keys. He never had to pause to think about the right word or the best phrase – everything just came in a steady relentless flow. It was like that sometimes, he knew. When it happened, you just accepted it gratefully.

It had been a couple of minutes after noon when he had called the police. And asked about Ben Wallace.

'Oh, by the way,' Forrest was saying now. 'I've decided to include your stuff in a survey we're doing, just to see how popular it really is.'

Suddenly Law was only half listening. He found himself thinking about his phone call to the police and what the policeman had told him about Ben Wallace.

A cobra. How could Ben have been killed by a cobra in the centre of London?

'If your stuff is as popular as I think it is,' Forrest was saying, 'I think we should do something big.' He waved his hands through the air as if trying to grab an answer. 'Maybe we could send you to China. We could get some fabulous pictures of you standing on the Great Wall.'

Wallace had had enough venom in him to kill three men. He had been attacked by a snake which had struck again and again and again.

Forrest continued to talk and Law nodded and gestured automatically as if the words were sinking in.

'Maybe you could go on some expedition climbing K2. You could go as far as the base camp. Or you could go with some army group going up the Nile in a hovercraft ... or on some epic raft journey. Travel writing shouldn't be just about the tourist stuff.'

A cobra. How was it possible?

Over a drink at the Dragon's Tongue pub that evening, Law told Natalie what had happened to Ben Wallace.

'A cobra,' she said, quizzically, then sat in silence for a long time, sipping her drink, deep in thought, as if unable to comprehend what he had said.

He broke the silence by saying: 'I called the doctor this afternoon, about my blood tests.'

'And?'

'They came up negative. They can't find anything wrong with me.'

'That's a relief,' she said. 'At least we know now that it was just a passing thing.'

'Well what do you want to do tonight?'

'I'd rather have a quiet night at home,' she said.

'Your place or mine?'

'Mine,' she said and realised she had spoken the word too quickly.

In that instant she was aware for the first time just how much she was afraid of his flat. A jumble of emotions swarmed into her brain. She remembered waking on Saturday night and the feeling that there was something unclean, something ugly in the flat. She recalled his violent lovemaking the night before. And she remembered what had happened in the flat that morning when Jack had gone up to the newsagent to get the morning papers. She had been alone for no more than ten minutes and although she was entirely incapable of putting into words exactly what had happened to her she had never felt such an intensity of fear. It was a fear that cut so deep she hadn't even been able to tell Jack about it.

The incident had started the moment she had heard the door clunk shut behind Law.

Immediately it had been as if all the energy had been sucked out of the flat, as if it had been emptied, become a void. The feeling was so intense that she had stopped washing the breakfast dishes for a moment and looked around the kitchen. Everything had been physically the same but she had felt somehow that the flat had been drained emotionally. There had been no way to explain it or understand it but the change in the flat could not have been more dramatic if she had been magically transported from a wild party in London to the Gobi Desert or a blank grey cell where nothing happened, nothing moved. There is an aura about all places habited by humans – it is as if each house or flat, office or factory is the keeper of fragments of a thousand past images. This flat had always been a happy place, filled with a kind of lingering sediment of laughter and shared rememberings and memories of lovemaking. Now it had become ...

Nothing.

A vacuum.

The feeling of emptiness had lasted for about five minutes. She had tried to ignore it, tried to shrug aside the growing apprehension. She had finished the dishes, poured herself a glass of milk and stood at the window looking down into the street, waiting for Jack Law to come into view.

Then, abruptly, she had become hot. It had been as if the temperature in the room had shot up to one hundred and ten. And more than that. Suddenly she had felt oddly uncertain about who she was. She had felt as if she wanted to get into her own car or hold Jack's hand or get to her sketchbook or do something, anything, to grasp at her identity, her personality.

'Natalie,' she had said aloud and even her voice had sounded strange.

She had looked down at the hand which held the glass of milk and seen a bead of perspiration running through the hairs on her wrist.

She wasn't just hot. She was burning. The flesh of her arm was red.

Panic had started to sprint through her but it was a distant panic, a panic that seemed to belong to a faraway Natalie (*the Natalie she had been before Jack left the flat?*).

Why was she thinking such things? There was only one Natalie.

Why was she so hot?

Then the room had started to fill again, not with the emotions and memories that belonged there but with something else altogether, something horrible and loathsome. It had been as if the room was being occupied by ugliness, an ugliness that had eyes and was watching her.

Fear had hacksawed at the nerve-ends on the back of her

neck and she had had the strange sensation that acid was being dribbled across her shoulders.

Then the heat had disappeared abruptly to be replaced by dank chill and she had dropped the glass and watched it smash in the sink, milk geysering up across the drying dishes and window sill. The beads of perspiration running down her back were ice cold then and she had started shivering violently, gripping the edge of the sink.

As she had raised her eyes to look out the window again, she had become aware with a searing certainty that there was something in the corner of the room away to her left.

Something she dare not look at.

WHAT?

Don't look, don't look, don't look, a voice in her head had shrieked.

Then she had heard the thud of the door and Law shouting 'I'm back' and instantly the horror in the room and the events (or *illusions?*) of the previous ten minutes had started to slip away, to melt like ice on a hotplate.

'You're thinking about Ben, aren't you?' Law said and his voice brought her back to the present, back to the Dragon's Tongue.

'Yes,' she said and wished instantly she hadn't lied.

'There's no point in dwelling on it,' he said. 'Drink up and let's go.'

Agnes Forrest was house-proud and it showed. Everything in the five-bedroom Forrest home in Surbiton was immaculate. As she stood at the lounge window waiting for her husband to come home, she surveyed the room. Each intricately-stitched cushion was balanced perfectly in position on a chair or settee. The wooden furniture shone. The dazzling white lace curtains swayed gently in a breeze from the half-open windows. Awards and certificates Peter Forrest had received were lined up on a wall in perfect symmetry alongside framed copies of some of the Globe's front pages. Each day they were dusted and cleaned and each day she checked that they were lined up with the precision of parade-ground soldiers.

She parted the curtains and waved when she saw Forrest's Jaguar coming up the gravel path. He smiled and winked as he drew the car to a halt, jerking on the handbrake.

Straightening her dress, she hurried to the front door, calling Henry, their Golden Labrador, from his basket in the kitchen. The dog padded slowly after her as she went out the front door. Henry was very much a one-man dog and Forrest was the master. Henry would pine and become sluggish and lazy whenever Forrest was away from the house for more than a few days. His affection was reciprocated – Forrest was very fond of his dog even though now, at fourteen, Henry was something of a slow, creaking veteran.

Forrest was lifting his briefcase out of the car when Agnes reached him.

'Hi,' he said, giving her a kiss on the cheek.

Then he shifted his attention to Henry. 'Hello, boy.' He bent forward to fondle the dog's ears as he had a thousand times before but this time Henry bared his teeth and a low growl rumbled from his throat.

'What's wrong, boy?' Forrest said.

Then the dog leapt at him, snarling and biting for the throat.

16

Peter Forrest had very fast hands, as anyone who had ever played squash with him would have been more than willing to testify. But his serving hand had never moved as fast on the squash court as it did now.

Instinctively he snatched it across the front of his face, swiping aside Henry's muzzle.

The full bulk of the dog's powerful body crashed into him, one paw ripping the front of his shirt, raking a long ugly weal across his chest.

Forrest stumbled backwards, aware that Agnes was screaming. The dog fell perfectly balanced on its four paws and came at him again, snarling, dribbling saliva. He swung a hand in front of him as it jumped for the second time, but this time he was not so successful. The dog's teeth flashed and snapped at his arm, biting through suit, shirt and flesh. He yelled as a burning pain scorched up his arm.

'Get off, Henry. Let go.' His own voice, distant and shrill.

The dog held on as he swung it around, its hind legs skittering across the ground, pushing it up, enabling it to hold on, dig its teeth deeper.

'Henryyyyyyyy.'

He caught a blurred glimpse of Agnes, eyes staring from a red face, hands clenched into little fists under her chin. She was still screaming.

The pain was terrible, searing up his arms in waves and disappearing into the side of his neck. The rest of his body felt numb.

'Henryyyyyyy.'

He clubbed at the dog's head with his briefcase, once, twice, three times The teeth were loosening, shifting out of the holes they had made, he was sure of it. He continued to club at the dog frenziedly. Suddenly it fell back, rolling onto its side.

'Peter, what's happening?' Agnes shrieked.

Forrest regained his balance, aware that the arm that had been bitten was twitching violently, and turned to face the dog. It scrambled to its feet, snarling, watching him.

'Henry, good boy. Henry …'

Then it leapt at him again. He managed to bang its head aside with his briefcase and there was a horrible snap as its teeth came together. It fell on all fours, but awkwardly this time, its feet skidding in the deep gravel.

Instinctively (later he couldn't remember what had made him think of doing it), Forrest clouted the dog on the back of the neck with the briefcase, grabbed its collar and slung its fifty-pound bulk through the open door of the car. He shouldered the door shut and fell to his knees, staring at the dog as it snapped and snarled and bit at the window in a futile attempt to get at him. In a moment the glass was covered in frothy, white saliva.

'I'm all right,' he mumbled, shifting his gaze to Agnes. 'I'm OK.'

He realised he was gripping the wounds on his right forearm with his left hand and looked down to see blood oozing between his fingers.

'I'll call the doctor,' Agnes said, her voice shaking.

'And the vet,' he shouted after her as she headed for the house in a stumbling run.

'The police,' Natalie said, looking at the ID card the taller of the two men at the door held under her nose.

'Yes,' the man said. 'I believe you knew Leo and Georgina Dempsey, I understand that you were at a party at their house last night.'

'That's right.'

'We have some questions we'd like to ask you. May we come in?'

'Well … yes, of course.'

Natalie and Law had spent a quiet night together with a couple of TV dinners, the Channel 4 News, a bottle of chablis, a half an hour of Mozart, and a video of a documentary about El Salvador which Natalie had recorded for Law when he was in India. They hadn't talked as much as they usually did and when conversations had started they had usually been about what had happened during the course of the day. They had neither strayed into anything deep nor taken part in any light-hearted banter.

'There's nothing wrong is there?' Natalie said over her shoulder as she led the policemen down the hall.

'We'll explain everything.'

Law stood up when he saw the two men, looking from them to Natalie.

'It's the police, Jack, something about Leo and Georgina.'

'You're Jack Law?' the taller policeman said.

'Yes.'

'I'm Sergeant Coates, this is Detective Constable Smith. I believe you were at the Dempseys' party as well.'

'Yes, what …'

Natalie gestured to two chairs, cutting Law off: 'Please, sit down.'

The policeman took their seats and Smith opened a notebook.

'Were you close friends of the Dempseys?' Coates said.

Law nodded, lowering himself back into his seat.

'Yes, very good friends …'

'What's happened? Have they been burgled?' Natalie said.

'I'm sorry about this. There's no easy way I can tell you … they're both dead.'

'Dead,' Law said slowly, heavily.

Natalie's face crumpled and she took a small red handkerchief from her sleeve and held it up in front of her mouth, crushing it ino a tiny ball in her fist. She stared at the policeman, her eyes filling with tears of shock.

'How?' Law said.

'Mrs Dempsey was beaten to death and possibly raped beforehand. Mr Dempsey drowned.'

'Drowned?'

'Yes, in the river. We found his body late this afternoon.'

Natalie began to sob quietly, her shoulders shaking.

'What happened?' Law said.

'We'd like all the people who were at the party to help us find out.'

Leo was dead. Clever-tongued Leo. Georgina's little Spanish gigolo. Laughing Leo. He wouldn't ever laugh again. His face would be slack now, an expression that would last forever. He was gone, out of it. Shiiiiiiit.

Something that was first cousin to a sob caught in Law's throat but he coughed it away.

'We'll help,' he said, his voice leaden.

'Thank you. Can you tell me if Mr and Mrs Dempsey argued or had any differences at the party?'

'Argued.' Law spat the word out. 'No, I don't think so.'

'Were they a happy couple?'

Law looked quizzically at Natalie and then said: 'Yes.'

'I know this is a hard question to answer … but were there any other women in Mr Dempsey's life to your knowledge?'

'I can't say for sure. If there were Leo never told me. What's all this …' Law's eyes widened as he realised what the policeman was getting at. 'Forget it,' he said, his voice hard.

'Forget what?'

'Any thought that Leo might have killed Georgina and then jumped in the river.'

'We were not suggesting that. We have to explore every avenue.'

'I understand.'

'Could you tell me who was still at the party when you left?' Coates said.

Natalie was dabbing at her eyes now, her handkerchief damp and sodden.

'Everyone,' Law said. 'We left early.'

'OK.' Coates paused then said. 'During the course of the evening did you notice if Mrs Dempsey was particularly friendly with any particular man? Perhaps dancing with him for a long time or …'

'She was friendly with everyone. We're all old friends. Nobody at the party did it. What about burglars?'

'Nothing was stolen and if it had been burglars why would they kill Mrs Dempsey in the house, carry Mr Dempsey to the river and drown him.'

'I don't know, but nobody at the party would have hurt Leo and Georgina.'

The rest of the questions were routine. Had Leo Dempsey had any debts to their knowledge? Had he gambled? Did he have any serious enemies? Where had Law and Natalie met the Dempseys?

'Well, thank you for your help,' the sergeant said when he ran out of questions. 'I'm sorry about all this. We'll find our own way out.'

Law watched the two policemen retreating along the hall as if unable to comprehend the last twenty minutes. Then he stood up abruptly, crossed the room, pulled Natalie to her feet and held her close. He could feel her body trembling under his fingers.

'Who could have done it?' she said. 'What for? Who would want to hurt Leo and Georgina?'

He shook his head slowly. He didn't have any of the answers.

Peter Forrest answered the knock on his front door and

found John Tait, the vet, standing in a fog of pipe smoke.

'What's this Agnes has been telling me on the phone?' the vet said.

'It's true, Henry went for me. The doctor has just left. He put ten stitches in my arm.'

'Where's Henry now?'

Forrest led the way across the gravel drive to the car. At first he could see no sign of Henry, then he saw the dog lying in the valley between the back and front seats.

'There he is, John. I'm warning you … be careful.'

The vet fetched his bag from his van and opened the Jaguar's door carefully, as quietly as possible. The dog lay quite still. Tait placed his bag on the back seat, flipped it open then bent forward, studying Henry, running his fingers across the dog's head and neck. Forrest could see no sign of life. Tait took a flashlight from his bag, lifted Henry's eyelids one at a time and studied the eyes closely.

'He's in some kind of a coma,' he said, putting the flashlight back into the bag. 'I'll take him with me tonight and we'll see how he is tomorrow.'

Forrest looked past the vet, at his dog. It didn't make sense. He had never heard of a placid old dog like Henry going berserk, attacking its master then lapsing into a coma. There had to be a reason.

Law left Natalie's flat at one a.m. after talking her into taking one of the sleeping tablets the doctor had given her when she had been going through an emotional bad patch about a year before. Driving home, the thought of what had happened to Leo and Georgina worried away at him.

He swung the car around a corner and caught a glimpse of a single star in the sky, all alone in the blackness of space, and it started him thinking about life and mortality and eternity and all the other lofty things about human experience that occasionally plagued him but which he always rejected with exasperation because they posed questions which were unanswerable.

Leo was dead. Gone forever. Never coming back this way again. So was Ben. So was Georgina.

A heavy depression closed around him like a metal overcoat. He considered all the events of the past week of his life and wondered how it was possible for one man's life to be plunged into such chaos, such a state of anarchy, in so short a time.

Nothing was going right.

It was as if a part of him had stepped into some kind of other-world lift shaft and all the events of the past week were like floors he was falling past. They came with remorseless regularity, one after the other, going too fast for him to change anything.

Life's like that, he told himself, trying to be philosophical. Mostly it's bland, but sometimes you get a good run ... or a bad run.

Yet there seemed to be no easy way to explain all that had happened to him. He ticked the events off on a mental check-list.

First there was that sickening moment in Srinwanat when the car had lurched away from him, shot down the hill and smashed into the procession, killing the Sedali and God-only-knew how many others. Then there was the nausea and the bad dreams and the feeling of being dirty and the whispers (surely they *were* just part of his illness?). On top of that, three friends had died.

Was all that just a bad run?

And what about the time he had made love to Natalie and hurt her and couldn't even remember it? And what about that moment when he had felt a burning intensity of malice towards her?

A bad run?

Or something else altogether?

He let himself into his flat, got into bed with a large whisky and sat there sipping it for a long time, thinking.

Despite the sleeping tablet, Natalie remained wide awake.

She lay in bed with the light off trying to will herself to sleep but a mixture of tension and confusion kept her mind alert. After about fifteen minutes she got out of bed and started to make cocoa.

And that was when she had the hot flush.

The heat was intense, almost as if she had stepped naked from shade into blazing one-hundred-degree sunshine.

Just like that awful incident in Jack's flat, she thought, and remembered the burning sensation she had experienced and how red her arm had become.

The flush came and went in five seconds and was followed immediately by a sudden heavy drowsiness which seemed to dull all her senses. She told herself it was the tablet doing its job at last and went back to bed.

Sleep washed over her instantly – but she didn't sleep for long. Later she estimated it was no more than twenty minutes.

Twenty minutes in the torments of hell.

She awoke with every detail of the nightmare tattooed on her brain and jumped out of bed, feeling as if she was on fire and the perspiration which matted her body was blazing petrol.

Clawing off her nightgown, she staggered to the bathroom. Now it was as if a thousand tiny flames were searing her flesh. Her brain seemed to shrink into a tiny pinpoint, pulling back from the heat.

As she reached for the shower's cold-water tap, she saw that her arms were the colour of flames. She wrenched the tap around until it would go no further and leapt into the cold jets of water.

That nightmare. That nightmare. How could she have had such a nightmare?

She held her face up to the jets of water, let it saturate her hair, then let it play on her legs, her arms, her feet. After what seemed like a long time, the heat began to diminish.

She let the nightmare run over and over again in her mind, examining every detail.

Why? Why had she had such a terrible nightmare? What did all this mean – the heat and the sleepiness and the terrible images of her sleep?

After about ten minutes she found that the colour of her skin had returned to normal but she didn't get out of the shower. She sat down, her head thrown back, letting the water splash over her face and breasts.

When she realised she was becoming numb and the skin on her fingertips was starting to shrivel, she reached out slowly and turned the tap off.

After she had dried herself, she wrapped the towel around her and walked through to the kitchen to pour herself a glass of cold milk.

Did a nightmare like that mean something? she asked herself. Surely it was a sign of something? Surely *her* subconscious couldn't have conjured up such a thing?

Sipping her milk, she went to the window and looked down into the dark street.

Why? Why? Why?

The dream played through her mind for the umpteenth time.

Why?

Why should she have a dream in which she was staked out on a mound in a yellow desert, her hands and feet held fast by ropes, the sun blistering her skin?

17

Law slept badly, his mind descending into a dark, ugly place of melancholy dreams. As he began to awaken the next morning, the dreams exploded into a thousand fragments leaving no memories, no images, just a loathsome sediment.

Waking was like ascending from a deep wellshaft. After a long time, he became aware of the bed underneath him and of the room around him and of his own body.

And the whispers.

The room was filled with them, terrible, ugly, rasping whispers, as if a hundred hoarse men and women were gathered around his bed, studying him, discussing him.

He blinked his eyes open (they felt like trapdoors) and stared around him.

Instantly the whispering stopped. As if some switch had been flicked to the 'off' position.

As he sat up, listening to the silence in the room, one single thought dominated his mind.

He believed he had recognised one of the whispering voices.

He was sure it had been Ben Wallace.

He shook his head, jerking it violently from side to side. *Just a dream, just a bad dream.* Then he noticed that the nausea had returned – it felt as if greased wires were sliding about in his intestines. There was a band of terrible pain across his stomach and his skin stank abominably.

Apprehension bubbled through him and something that was first cousin to hysteria took root deep inside him and began to wrap chilly tentacles around his heart.

Why was he staying so calm? His friends were dying around him, he was ill, hearing things, something was oh-so-disastrously wrong.

Dammit, don't give in to it, he told himself. *Don't let it grind you down. What you've got is some minor bug so insignificant that it didn't even show up in the blood tests. Don't let it spoil your life. The trouble with being ill is that people give in to it. Ignore it.*

The contradictions were typical of the erratic pattern of his thoughts. His mind was continually zooming from one extreme to the other. It occurred to him that it was as if he had been split in two, as if his mind was a cell in which there were two prisoners. One half, the Jack Law half (*the Jack Law you all know and love, folks*) told him to panic, seek help, but the other half sought to calm him, tell him everything would be all right.

Maybe that was part of human nature, he thought. Maybe even a condemned man shuffling to the gallows never lost hope of a last-minute reprieve.

Everything is OK. There is nothing to worry about …

The soothing side of his brain was dominating again, dulling his fears.

Wasn't that dangerous? Surely he ought to be afraid?

He climbed out of bed like a patient in a geriatric ward and had a shower, scrubbing himself until he was tender and raw, then covered his body from head to foot in splash-on lotion.

He dressed, snatched up his briefcase and headed for the Underground. It was as he walked through a fine drizzle, head hunched low between upturned coat collar, that he remembered the dreams of the night before. His sleep had been teeming with dreams and at the time they had been incredibly exhilarating. But now as he recollected them he felt his hands fold into tight fists. How could his mind have luxuriated in the visions he had seen?

He recalled the dreams like a man glimpsing edited segments from a film.

He had seen a head lying in a yellow desert, a great, black bird pecking at the scalp, and remembered that this had amused him. He had gloated at the sight of Leo and Georgina and Ben Wallace trapped at the bottom of a deep pit, their upturned faces silhouetted against the blackness. The red fog of his earlier dreams had been there too and in the dream he had strolled through it and across the yellow desert to the woman staked out on the low mound, a sensation of malicious delight running through him. He had seen the quivering feet, the ankles chafed raw where she had tried to jerk herself free of the rope, the red blistered legs, the burned skin of the torso ...

And then the face. Thrust back, gasping for air, teeth bared, eyes closed, a tortured mask of blisters and peeling skin.

And it was Natalie's face.

He had laughed and laughed and sauntered away across the desert.

Why? What did it all mean?

He reached the Underground and became part of the hurrying crowd descending into the grey, concrete bowels of the city.

It was as he strode onto the platform that the dizzy spell hit him. The image of the faces in front of him blurred, came sharply back into focus, then began to swim before his eyes. Noses, eyes, elongated faces, a red jacket, the shining lines of the track, a blue skirt – all were smeared together against the walls and the concrete floor and the lager and motor-car posters like some kind of abstract art interpretation of a station.

A tidal wave of nausea seemed to wash up from his stomach and burst into his brain. Sweat oozed from his pores and ran down his face and back and legs, instantly chilly against his hot skin. His legs turned to jelly, his knees buckled and he grabbed for a wall to prevent himself from falling, aware that people had turned to look at him.

'Bloody hell,' he groaned and dry-retched once, twice, three times. It felt as if long claws were being dragged along the skin inside his throat.

Then the dizzy spell receded, as suddenly as it had come. He managed to push himself upright and prop himself against the wall, his vision clearing.

A train was drawing into the station, its doors clanking open. He wondered if he dared make an effort to push himself away from the wall and try to get aboard but decided against it.

Just relax and compose yourself, he told himself, taking out his handkerchief and dabbing at the perspiration under his chin.

That was when he saw the woman watching him from the train.

And the face was familiar.

It couldn't be ...

'Georgina,' he said softly, then he repeated it, almost shouting now, 'Georgina.'

18

'Georgina.'

Law shuffled forward, crouching over and peering into the train.

'Georgina,' he yelled.

Then he realised Georgina wasn't looking at him, she was looking through him, as if he wasn't there.

'Georgina, it's me, Jack Law.'

Still there was no sign of recognition. The gaze remained fixed, the face impassive.

'Georgina.'

The train doors clanked shut as Law reached the window. He put out a hand, touching the glass only inches from Georgina's face.

'It's me ... Jack Law,' he shouted.

Suddenly Georgina seemed to see him for the first time, her eyes round, watchful, sad.

The train seemed to tense, ready to move off, like a carnivore which had spotted game.

Law jabbed a finger at the door.

'The door ... open the door. I'll get on.'

Georgina's face twisted and Law thought she was going to smile. But it was no smile. It was a grimace of intense pain and the eyes were instantly filled with anguish and horror. Georgina's lips parted at one side of her mouth and blood poured down over her chin and spattered her blouse.

Law recoiled from the sight, stepping back quickly, a tic working in his left cheek. A chilled hand caressed his shoulderblades.

The train jerked, hesitated, clanked, then began to glide away.

That was when Georgina's left cheekbone collapsed, a sliver of white bone thrusting through the skin above the jaw. Then her nose broke, crushed as if by an invisible hand, blood spurting across the window of the train.

Law dragged his eyes away and stared at a group of people a few feet away.

'Look,' he yelled, pointing at Georgina. 'Look.'

But they weren't watching the train, their eyes were fixed on him.

Law swung back towards the train just as Georgina's jaw twisted and snapped and her skull caved in beneath the left eye. Law stumbled and almost fell but his gaze remained fixed on Georgina's face.

'Georgina,' he rasped.

The face was a mangled ruin of ripped flesh, spurting blood and jagged white bones.

As the train gathered speed and disappeared into the black tunnel, Georgina's single remaining eye watched Law. It seemed to be pleading with him.

'Oh my God,' Law said and his voice broke.

He spun away from the tracks and all round him the faces and posters, the walls and the concrete floor swam and danced in some kind of perverted mockery of reality.

He staggered through the exit, elbowing his way past people, cracked his knee on a wall and began to run.

What did it all mean? It had to be a nightmare, didn't it? He would wake up soon, wouldn't he?

A moment later he burst into the street, his breath catching in his throat, his chest wheezing, a sticky perspiration matting his body like warm oil.

He turned left and ran on, the cars and shop windows and people a blur of unreality, a single multicoloured mass that seemed to have no relevance to his life. He swung into a dim lane, dashed along it, burst into the sunlight at the far end and darted between slow-moving cars.

Not a nightmare. It wasn't a nightmare. It was real. and it was WRONG. It was all WRONG.

WRONG. WRONG. WRONG.

He had to do something about it.

By the time he had run all the way back to his flat, he was gasping for breath, his heart thudding savagely and erratically.

He threw his briefcase into the corner of the room, snatched up the telephone and dialled Natalie's number with a violently trembling hand.

It rang three times then he heard her voice.

'Hello ...'

'Natalie, it's Jack.'

'How are ...'

'Natalie, listen to me,' he said, cutting her off. 'I've been a fool about all that's happening around me and to me, burying my head in the sand, pretending, just pretending all the time that it's about to go away and ...'

'What are you getting at?'

'Natalie, something is making me ill, something is killing my friends, something is making me see things – visions. There's a terrible stench about my body sometimes, I hear whispers, I have strange dreams, I virtually raped you once and couldn't remember doing it. And now ...'

'Now what?'

'I can't explain it, Natalie. I don't know exactly what's going on, but I'm positive now that *something* is going on and that it all started with the accident in Srinwanat when the Sedali was killed.' His speech began to falter. 'Natalie ... something I can't explain is ... trying to hurt me ... killing my friends.'

'Jack, you can't be serious, you ... What are you talking about? Some kind of a curse on you?'

'Maybe,' he said flatly. 'All I know is I should be fighting this thing. Will you help me?'

'Are you sure ...'

'Will you help me?'

'Yes, of course.'

'All right, here's what I want you to do. First and most important: you could be in danger being around me. I don't want you to come near me. I want you to move out of your flat for a couple of days, stay with friends or book into an hotel.'

'Why?'

'I want you to be someplace I don't know about.'

'But why?'

'I can't explain it, call it a hunch. I saw Ben – he was killed. I saw Leo and Georgina and the same thing happened ... I just think you'll be safer if you do what I ask.' He paused then said: 'Natalie, one of the dreams I've been having regularly is of a woman staked out in the sun. Until last night I had never seen the face of the woman. Last night, I did. It was you, Natalie, and in the dream I was standing over you and laughing.'

'I've had that dream too,' she said quietly.

'What?' He shouted the word into the telephone.

'Other things have happened too, Jack.'

'What other things?'

'I couldn't explain them if I tried.'

He sighed and flopped into a chair.

'In that case, you'll definitely be safer away from me. You can see that can't you?'

'All right ... maybe you're right. But you said you wanted me to help?'

'Yes. I want you to find out all you can about the Sedali and Dacahri. Go to libraries, bookshops, ring universities, try anything. If you find anything that might be useful call me at my flat. Don't come in person. I don't want to see you until all this is sorted out.'

'OK,' she said, then added: 'But you're frightening me.'

He bowed his head and said: 'I'm frightened too.'

'I love you, Jack,' she said and the words caught in her throat.

'I love you too, Natalie ... Goodbye.'

He hung the phone up firmly.

A curse, Natalie thought, as she packed her suitcase. *Was Jack really considering that?*

You're the one who used the word, my dear, a voice in her brain reprimanded her, sounding very much like her mother. He hadn't said anything about a curse. He had just said that all the events since Srinwanat added up to something and he intended to find out what that something was. And he was right, wasn't he? Surely it was too much of a coincidence that he was ill, hearing things, seeing things, that his friends were being killed off one by one, that he was having strange dreams and at least one of them was almost identical to one of hers.

She paused, a pair of jeans in her hand. It all seemed too much to be a coincidence, yet coincidences happened all the time. Why should there be a family living happily in the same suburban house for twenty years, then in the space of a few months the wife dies of a heart attack, the husband falls off a train and the son gets a fatal dose of pneumonia – yet it did happen. All the time.

Law was right to probe the situation, she decided, resuming her packing, but she was sure now that in the end he would find a straightforward explanation. The answer would not lie in the world of curses or psychic phenomena or … (*what was it they called it?*) … the paranormal.

If Law was ill with some eastern disease, hearing things and seeing things was hardly unique and nor were bad dreams. Their shared dream could be explained by some kind of telepathy. *Sympathetic telepathy,* she thought, coining a phrase. *I love Jack and I'm hurt when he's ill. Therefore I pick up some of his brainwaves, tune into his emotions. Stranger things happen. As for the rest of it? Coincidence. So I've had a couple of bad turns, dizzy spells. So what.*

She clipped her suitcase shut and hefted it off the bed, grunting at its weight. Ten minutes later, she was heading for the Midd Hotel in South Kensington where she had booked a room.

*

Law felt the nausea and the pain in his stomach easing and new energy and vigour pouring into his body.

It's because I'm fighting back, he told himself. (*But fighting back against what?*)

He felt as if metal filings were being knitted into his system, toughening him up. But how long would it last?

He rang the international operator and asked for the number of the Kokangarth barracks in India. It took her about a minute to find the number but it felt like an hour. He jotted it down, prodded at the telephone until the dial-tone returned then rang India.

'I'd like to speak to Major Fariya,' he said when a voice answered.

There was a crackling and hissing on the line and Law could hardly understand what the man on the other end was saying.

'Major Fariya,' he repeated. 'I wish to speak to Major Fariya. I'm calling from London, Jack Law's the name.'

There was a click, thirty seconds passed then a voice said: 'Major Fariya speaking.' The words faded away at the end and Law was afraid for a moment that he had lost the line.

'It's Jack Law here,' he said. 'Can you hear me?'

'Yes, I can hear you. I've just arranged for the things you left at Baisakh's hotel to be posted on to you and ...'

'That's fine, major, but ... (*bzzzzzz, hissssss*) ... that's not what I'm calling about.'

'Oh ... I ...'

The buzzing on the line became worse and Law didn't catch what the major said.

'Major,' he shouted. 'I don't know how to ask you this ... but some strange things have been happening since I returned home. Is there any way that some of the Sedali pilgrims could have followed me here ... (*bzzzzz*) ... could be doing things to me?'

There was a pause and a click on the line and when the major spoke again the line was clear, his voice sharp and distinct.

'I can't see how,' he said. 'I would say there was no chance. The Sedali's followers are very primitive people, very poor people. They don't use aeroplanes, they wouldn't have the money for aeroplanes, they wouldn't have the money for a train to Bombay. Anyway, how would they know who you were?'

'I ...'

'You didn't sign any register at Baisakh's hotel?'

'No, but ...'

'And the information in your file here has been seen only by senior officers of the Indian army and senior policemen. There's no way it could have got out. What kind of things are happening?'

Law thought for a moment then said' 'There's no way I could explain it over the telephone.'

'Mr Law, you can rest assured that whatever is happening it's nothing to do with any of the Sedali's followers. For them, going to Delhi would be a trip of a lifetime, something they can hardly conceive of, almost like you going ... to the moon. The thought of any of them following you overseas is absurd. I guarantee it.'

Law nodded. 'OK. Thank you, major. You've been very helpful. Goodbye.'

He hung up, feeling the last slender thread of a rational explanation slipping away.

Porkat: The Search

When the sun reached its highest point the crowd of about fifty girls who had been gathered together by the priests because their signs indicated they might be the new Sedali were shepherded from the blistering heat of the courtyard into the cool interior of the temple. When they were all inside and the adults had withdrawn Subhash came from the altar room, the bloody symbols on his naked body caked hard now. Those who recoiled from the sight of him were sent away immediately. The girls who were left were gathered around him and he spoke to them one at a time, questioning them closely, listening to their answers, studying their faces, looking deep into their eyes.

His lips began to move, slowly whispering the words of the incantation: 'Oh Lord Dacahri, oh Great King Dacahri, oh Master of Eternity ... show yourself to me ... your Seeker ... Subhash ...'

19

John Tait, the vet, brought home the Forrests' Golden Labrador early in the afternoon. He couldn't offer Agnes much in the way of an explanation for Henry's behaviour. 'Who can tell for sure,' he said. 'He's an old dog, maybe he had some kind of fit, maybe it was something he ate. He seemed to be in some kind of coma when I picked him up. He slept for ten hours. After that he was as good as new.'

About an hour later, Agnes heard Henry pawing at the front door.

She opened it and spoke to him in that tone of voice usually reserved for very small children. 'Do you want to go into the garden? All right, out you go.'

She watched him walking heavily across the driveway then closed the door and went upstairs.

When he heard the door shut, Henry broke into a stiff run, padding across the lawn and into the trees and shrubs at the bottom of the garden. Running in wet leaves now, he increased his pace, following the line of the high stone wall. There was a fluidity in his movements that had not been there for years and he went faster and faster.

He reached a small rise overlooking the front gate and settled down between two bushes.

A few minutes later, he cocked his ears and raised his head when he heard Agnes calling him. But he did not get up. Half an hour after that he heard her walking about the garden, shouting: 'Henry ... where are you, boy ... come on, Henry ...'

But again he did not answer her call. He lay quite still on the damp leaves. Waiting for Peter Forrest.

Natalie went to the British Library, the India Office Library, the University of London Library and a dozen other libraries, at each one being referred to two or three others. She lost count of the number of books on India or religion or the paranormal she leafed through, almost all without success – only one or two of every dozen books she lifted down from the endless shelves yielded up anything about Dacahri and more often than not he received only a passing mention in some story about Shiva or Kali or simply appeared in a long list of obscure Indian gods.

Occasionally she struck lucky and found entries like:

'Dacahri, God of a Thousand Faces. The belief is that this god is incarnated on earth forever in the person of the child goddess, the Sedali, who rules as religious leader of Dacahri's followers for a thousand days, each day representing one of the true incarnations of Dacahri on earth. The girl returns to normal life after her reign as the Sedali and Dacahri enters another girl who becomes the new Sedali. The Sedali's temple is in the town of Srinwanat.'

The religion's holiest place was the ancient ruined city of Didrana, one book told her, and another that the holiest day was August 14 on which day pilgrims gathered from hundreds of miles around Srinwanat to celebrate the Festival of the Sedali. A small dog-eared volume printed in 1916 described Dacahri as an extremely malevolent god who was considered by some to be third in the hierarchy of the Old Gods, traditional enemies of mankind. In each of his true incarnations, it said, he moved steadily towards a state of perfect evil. 'Having achieved that, he chose to live for eternity in the body of a young girl, his every whim satisfied by his priests.' In various incarnations, he had appeared as man, woman, half-man half-animal, half-man half-bird, and the Divine Snake of Didrana among others. Five of the kings of Didrana in ancient times bore the name Dacahri,

Natalie read, and each was believed to be the god incarnate.

Three hours after Natalie began her search she found herself standing in the doorway of a library, staring down into a park, gripped by a thought that had been worrying away at the back of her mind for an hour.

What she was doing was silly. Absurd. It was a lot of hooey.

And it wasn't helping Jack.

She had to find a way to do something for Jack. All the scribbling in her pad, all the notes about superstitious nonsense were not going to help make him better. He needed medical help.

Absently she watched a boy about eight running through the park with a football at his feet, beating imaginary opponents and sidefooting a goal between two tall oak trees. He jumped about and punched the air, imitating the delight of real footballers, then fetched the ball back and began to run with it again. Beyond him, a woman sat on a tartan rug, nibbling at a sandwich, watching the boy with a small smile. *They were the real world.* Natalie looked all around her. *This was the real world.* Cars and buildings and people going places and trees and grass and asphalt. *Not Dacahri and the Old Gods.*

Jack was right to want to eliminate all possibilities and he was probably tackling the most likely prospects himself and leaving her to gamble on the long shots but …

She had to do something for him. *She* had to help.

Maybe he needs a psychiatrist?

The thought trickled into her mind like a thick, gooey substance. She didn't want to conider the possbility but it had to be faced. *Something is trying to hurt me,* he had said. *Something is killing my friends. You're not safe if you're near me.* Were they the words of a rational man?

She looped her thumb into the strap of her shoulder bag and tugged nervously at it for a moment then pursed her lips, the decision made, and walked purposefully across the road to a phone box. She consulted the phone book and rang Dr Williams.

The doctor was with a patient, the receptionist said, and

Natalie told her she'd wait. She had pushed five ten-pence pieces into the slot by the time a voice said: 'Dr Williams speaking.'

'Hello,' she said, not knowing where to start. 'My name is Natalie Field, I believe that a friend of mine, Jack Law, is a patient of yours.'

'That's correct,' the doctor said, his voice formal, sounding a little dubious.

'I don't know how to say this, doctor, but ... Jack ... isn't ... himself at the moment.'

'Yes, I saw him a week ago and we did some tests. The results were negative. Has he been vomiting again?'

'I ... I don't know. It's just that ... I spoke to him on the telephone and he ... just didn't sound like himself, doctor. I can't really put it into words.'

'I probably shouldn't be discussing this with you at all, I ...'

'I'm only thinking of Jack.'

'Yes ... when Jack was in here last week I had a word with him about overwork. I ...'

'The point is, doctor, I don't think he's going to get in touch with you, and I'd like him to see a doctor. I wondered if you could possibly just call in on him.'

'Well, of course, he doesn't have to see me if he doesn't want to,' the doctor said.

'I don't think Jack knows what he wants at the moment. *Please* see him. He needs help.'

The doctor sniffed: 'All right. I'll call in at his flat after surgery this afternoon. I think I've known him long enough to just drop in and have a chat.'

'Thank you, doctor.'

'Goodbye.'

'Bye.'

Natalie visited another library then a series of bookshops without any success at all. It was as she left Dryers' bookshop – ready to give up and call it a day – and headed back towards Oxford Street that she saw the second-hand bookshop. There was no name outside, just a sign which said: 'Second-hand paperbacks, excellent condition, one-tenth shop prices. Old books bought and sold. Come in and look.'

An old man in a well-worn grey cardigan with uncombed hair, nicotine-stained fingers and a huge red nose covered in lines and bumps was seated behind the counter. He lowered his head and peeped at her over his thick glasses as she went in, then returned to his book.

She restrained a smile when she saw the title. 'Elaine, the story of a Victorian Courtesan' read the purple letters above a picture of a woman holding a whip and wearing only sagging stockings and a mocking grin.

Dirty old man, she thought.

The shop was musty, stale and airless and there was an ageing-paper smell about it.

She strolled along the lanes between high shelves labelled with small pieces of pink cardboard – Thrillers, Horror, Medical, Sex Education, History. *Religion.* She worked her way from left to right. There were books on everything from the history of Mecca to Saul of Tarsus, the life of Buddha to famous missionaries in Africa. But nothing that looked likely to contain any revelations about Dacahri. There was a space in the middle of the shelf and five paperbacks at the far end. She walked over and let her eyes flick across the titles. The books had names like 'Exorcism in Britain, 1985' and 'Real Witchcraft' and 'The Haunted.'

She took them down one at a time, wearily, and flicked through each index.

Three of the five books mentioned Dacahri or the Sedali.

A gold mine.

She was about to look up the appropriate pages when the old man who ran the shop appeared at her side. She was surprised at his height – well under five feet, she guessed. She thought he looked like a gnome.

'I'm sorry, love,' he said, looking up at her, 'but we're closing now. Is there something I can help you with?'

'I'l take these,' she said, showing him the three books.

'One pound seventy-five,' he said as she put the books in her shoulder bag.

She handed over the money and left, hurrying to get to her car before the meter ran out.

Dr Williams left his surgery at five o'clock and drove through the heavy traffic humming along with 'Men of Harlech' as it thundered from the twin speakers in his rebuilt, personalised 1970 Mini. The traffic didn't annoy him, nothing annoyed him – things only irritated you if you let them, that was his belief. He was a man at peace with himself and the world. He liked his job because helping people satisfied him, enjoyed the money he earned, considered his wife to be the nicest woman he had ever met, adored his children, and believed the young widow in Wimbledon who had been his mistress for a year was the sexiest thing ever to draw a pair of black stockings over plump thighs.

He found a parking place in front of Lissils Mansions, took his black bag from the back seat and strolled into the building. Ten minutes with Law then it would be home to put his feet up for the weekend. He nodded to the porter, prodded a finger at the third-floor lift button and leaned against the rear wall of the lift as it sighed and began to ascend with a mechanical hum.

There was a rectangular glass section in the lift door, about eight inches wide and three feet deep, and he bent forward and peered through it as he passed the first floor. He caught a glimpse of a corridor – patterned maroon wallpaper, maroon carpet, Constable prints, a table with fresh flowers in a vase.

Then he was climbing through the darkness between floors again. No maroon on the second floor, he noted. It was done in an unusual blue.

He took a step towards the door, watching the floor lights above his head, as the blue gave way to blackness.

Third floor, a nasal, department-store-lift-girl's voice said in his head. *Sick journalists, problems, nausea, vomiting, and behaviour that worries girlfriend. Credit cards welcome.*

He laughed quietly and the grin was still fixed on his face when the lift stopped. Between floors. He jabbed his thumb into the button marked '3.'

Nothing happened. His frozen grin began to melt. He poked at the second-floor button then the first and waited. Silence. No movement. No mechanical hum. He prodded the red emergency button and expected to hear an alarm go off – but there was no sound.

Someone would come any second now, he told himself, and throw a switch that would get the lift moving again. This kind of thing probably happened all over London a hundred times a day. It was inconvenient but you just had to be patient … Yet he couldn't escape a primitive, trapped-in-a-confined-space feeling.

'Hey,' he yelled after a minute. 'Is anybody there?'

What a stupid thing to shout. Of course somebody was there. They'd be working in fuse boxes right now and before you know it …

Suddenly the lights in the lift dimmed and the floor shifted under his feet, trembled briefly. Then the lift began to descend. There was no mechanical hum now, no sound at all. Slowly and silently the lift was falling back the way it had come. Some kind of emergency mechanism, he told himself as it passed the second floor.

He poked at the first-floor button, just to see if he could get it to stop there. But it didn't.

Whoever was operating the emergency mechanism would be going to let him off at the ground floor, he decided, but pressed that button just in case. As he waited he saw that the floor lights above his head still registered '2.'

It was when the lift moved smoothly past the ground floor that something caught in his throat and panic began to knit tension into his shoulders, neck and face.

'Hey,' he bawled as the ground floor disappeared. 'Hey, I'm trapped in here. Get me out.'

Don't make a fool of yourself, a voice in his head said. *On the emergency mechanism the lift probably has to go all the way to the bottom, to the basement.*

Silly newspaper headlines flashed into his mind – *Doctor in lift panic: He screamed like a schoolgirl after five minutes stuck in lift.*

He stared at the glass section in the lift door, waiting for the basement to appear. Then it did and he caught a glimpse of trunks and boxes, rubbish bins and piles of old newspapers. He reached out a hand, anticipating the lift door clanking open.

But the smooth, silent descent continued and he noticed the lift lights were growing dimmer.

'Help,' he yelled as panic surged through him in hot waves. 'Help meeee.'

What the hell was going on? Why would the lift shaft be deeper than the basement? Was there another level?

He counted to twenty seconds but no other floor appeared. He counted forty seconds more but still there was no lower level and the lights in the lift were growing dimmer and dimmer.

I'm not going to be trapped in the dark, he told himself, *not in the pitch black.*

He put his bag on the floor, unfastened the top, took out his doctor's torch and switched it on.

'Heyyyyyy,' he yelled at the top of his voice.

Remorselessly the descent continued.

It was wrong, wrong, wrong. It wasn't real. It was an illusion.

He had travelled three minutes beyond the basement now and he *couldn't* really have been going down all that time. If he had he would be hundreds of yards under the streets of London. If he had …

Suddenly the lift stopped, with a tiny sigh. The doors clanked open and he found himself staring out into darkness beyond anything he had ever seen before, unvarying pitch blackness that seemed to have no end.

He shone his torch out in front of him and the slender

shaft of light penetrated a hundred feet but picked up no feature. Nothing.

He pointed it in front of his feet and saw that there seemed to be some kind of floor outside the lift.

'Hello,' he said, his voice breaking. He cleared his throat. 'Hello.'

He put one foot tentatively out of the lift, testing the floor. It felt like cement.

This had to be some kind of lower floor therefore there had to be a way out.

He took one step into the darkness, shining the torch a few feet ahead of him.

'Hello-oh.'

The word seemed to be swallowed up in an eternity of emptiness. How big could this place be?

'Is anyone there?'

He knew no-one was here but the sound of his voice was comforting.

He took another step into the blackness, then another and another. Pausing, he shone the torch up ahead of him. There had to be a wall there somewhere and once he found it, he could follow it until he discovered where the door was. But the torch beam picked up no wall, no feature of any kind.

He lowered the shaft of light to his feet and began to shuffle forward again.

That was when something that felt like a huge hand hammered into the centre of his back, sending him sprawling, the torch flying out of his grasp and smashing on the floor.

He rolled onto his back yelling, babbling incoherently, pleading, his mind shrivelling in terror.

Something fell on top of him and he felt hands close around his throat and smelled fetid breath.

'No, no, no, no, no …'

He scrambled to get free, pushing his palm up against the hands which held him.

But they were not hands. They were claws. And razor sharp talons were ripping at his face and neck now.

He struggled, kicking and punching as the talons bit into his flesh and raked across him again and again. But the weight of the thing kept him down.

Then he was aware that the lift doors were closing, the last of the light disappearing.

20

Law woke up and found himself lying face down on his bed. No matter how hard he tried, he couldn't remember going into the bedroom or falling asleep. He glanced at his watch. It was almost six o'clock. He had slept all day. He decided he needed some thinking time and went for a walk, but he didn't come up with any answers.

The nausea came back the moment he re-entered his flat, in a sudden great wave. He staggered and felt warm sweat dribbling from his pores. He held onto the door handle as the room began to swim. Then his vision cleared and the nausea receded, returning to another horrible wave ten seconds later.

Why? Why had it come back so suddenly?

He stumbled into the kitchen and splashed water into his face and again the nausea receded. When it came the third time, he retched over the sink and tasted bile in his mouth. He lurched into the bathroom and gulped a mouthful of the medicine the doctor had given him.

Groping his way along the wall, he managed to get back into the lounge and sit down.

And that was when he lost seventeen hours.

Natalie called Law from her hotel room at seven o'clock then again at eight and eight-thirty, but there was no answer. She had to talk to him – not to tell him all she had found out about the Sedali and Dacahri but just to hear his voice and tell him everything would be all right. She wanted to ask what Dr Williams had said, what his opinion was. Maybe the problem had been solved already, she thought.

I told him he was working too hard. Hadn't the doctor said something like that?

She sat watching television, taking nothing in, just letting the words and images wash over her, elbows propped on her knees, her chin in her palms, from eight-thirty until ten, then called Law again. She let the phone ring for a long time then hung up and stood with her hands on her hips, thinking.

What should she do? Confronting him and talking it out was the best course of action, she decided. She had to make him see sense. But …

She glanced at her watch. If he wasn't answering his phone that could mean only one of two things – either he was out or he had gone to bed with a sleeping tablet (perhaps Dr Williams had given him something extra-strong?). Either way there was no point in going to his flat that night.

She made up her mind to get a good night's sleep and go there in the morning then went downstairs and had a large gin and tonic in the hotel bar (*why not? I need it and I've earned it*). Back in her room, she showered and slipped between the cool sheets of the strange bed.

Turning off the bedside lamp, she closed her eyes and tried to fall asleep, but she shifted and rolled about restlessly. Ten minutes later, she knew it was useless and flicked the light back on, blinking. She felt like reading and her gaze shifted across the bedside Bible. No. She shook her head. She wasn't in the mood for the Bible.

Then she remembered the books she had bought in the second hand bookshop. She hadn't given them a thought since she had put them into her shoulder bag. She had been thinking about Jack, relying on Dr Williams and good sense to get him well and make him snap out of his strange mood. But now, considering the fact she couldn't sleep anyway, she decided she might as well see if she could add to her notes on Dacahri and the Sedali.

She fetched the books and her pad and pen and got back into bed, propping the pillows into an upright position to support her back.

She took the first book and thumbed her way to the index. It fell open at 'S' and the word 'Spells' caught her eye as she raked the pages back towards 'D.' When she reached 'D' her eyes brushed across 'demonology' and 'devil worship' before she found 'Dacahri.'

What rubbish, she thought, irritated. *What was she doing reading this nonsense?*

'Dacahri, page 106,' the entry read and she leafed through the pages to page 106.

'Dacahri, God of a Thousand Faces,' the book told her, 'Indian god who is said to be incarnate in the body of a young goddess, the Sedali.'

Big deal. Oh yes, that was a great help.

She tossed the book aside with an exaggerated gesture of annoyance and took up the second. There was even less in this one. Dacahri was only mentioned in a story about another god she had never heard of, who was referred to as being 'as malevolent as Dacahri, another of the Old Gods.'

Who wrote books like these?

She grabbed the last book, thumbed it open with a bored, impatient flick of her hand, and let her eyes run down over the brief biography of the author inside the back cover.

Professor John Bahashasda was a retired professor of history, she learned. Born in Coventry ... (*oh, how exciting, one of the Coventry Bahashasdas,* a voice in Natalie's head said caustically, and a smile twitched at her lips) ... he was an expert in eastern mythology. He had lectured on the occult and the paranormal all over the world. Throughout his life he had carried out more than 500 exorcisms, the vast majority since he had moved to London after retiring from an American university five years before.

His most difficult exorcism had been the removal of an entity from the house of an Indian living in Bradford.

Bradford, my God, Bradford. Natalie restrained a giggle.

Hardly the most exotic place to find an entity. They must be everywhere.

It seemed the house was inhabited by an evil force determined to make the man's life a misery. The professor had discovered that the man had once, many years before, removed a small and seemingly unimportant object from a temple in Madras – a carved metal cup of little value. The professor had carried out a series of exorcism rituals, the object had been sent back to India and ... (*lo and behold,* Natalie thought) ... the house had been cleansed.

What nonsense.

She found the reference to Dacahri in the index and turned to page 156. It was near the beginning of a chapter entitled 'Death by Suggestion' and she started to read the introductory paragraph which told her about how Australian aborigines used a *munguni* – made up on a bone, a string and a receptacle – to kill or torment their enemies. 'Even if they are miles away,' Professor Bahashasda asked her to believe, 'the victim will be smitten with the deadly force.'

She tutted and ran her biro down the page until she found the section on Dacahri. Her eyes sprinted through the first paragraph which told her about an Indian with a long and unpronounceable name who had been farming land ten miles west of the city of Kokangarth in 1972. He was prosperous, happily married, thirty-seven years old and had three children.

She skimmed the second paragraph which outlined the basic facts about Dacahri and the Sedali with which she had become so familiar and plunged into the third.

The farmer, who came from a family which had always worshipped Dacahri and the Sedali, attended the Festival of the Sedali in August, 1972. However ... (*ah, here comes the crunch,* Natalie thought) ... he had become worldly, disinterested in Dacahri and openly sceptical and cynical about the Sedali and her powers.

'During the procession,' the passage continued, 'as the

Sedali passed by, the farmer was stricken by a sudden
blinding headache. Barely able to stand because of the
intense pain, he was attended to by members of his family
but nothing they did helped to alleviate the headache. He
returned to his farm where the headache persisted for three
days then vanished abruptly.

'His next crop failed, his animals began to die one by one
and his family became sick with a strange disorder which
made them too tired and lethargic to work. Another crop
failed, then a third. Members of his family approached the
priests of the Sedali to ask for help but were turned away.

'Ten months after the festival, he became seriously ill,
horrible sores appearing all over his body. After a fortnight,
he was admitted to a hospital in Kokangarth where he
lapsed into a coma. Various tests were carried out at the
instruction of an American doctor, Walter Kraitsch, who
was then based at the hospital, but nothing physically
wrong with the farmer could be found. A week later he
died.

'Dr Kraitsch told me that he had never seen ...'

Natalie raised her eyes from the book.

'The old evil eye,' she said aloud, shaking her head
slowly. *How could people believe in such drivel?*

'Superstitious shit,' she said venomously and threw the
book across the room.

Peter Forrest felt good. It had been a long hard day but a
satisfying one. The gentle crisp patter of tyres on gravel rose
through the window of his Jaguar as he swung the car up
his driveway. He gave Agnes a brief jerk of a nod and a big
smile when he saw her waving from the window.

As he opened the car door, snatched up his briefcase and
stepped out into the darkness, he heard a sound away to his
right – a crackling, leafy sound as if something was rushing
through the bushes.

He had started to swing his head round when Henry
leapt at him. The pain as the dog's teeth bit into his throat

was unbelievable – fire scorched through every part of his body.

Instinctively he raised his hands to defend himself but his arms were suddenly weak and heavy and he fell backwards, hitting the car and sliding to the ground.

He saw a half-moon in a black sky and felt his flesh rip and a huge chunk of his throat being torn away.

God Almighty. What was happening?

A dark geyser of blood shot up in front of his eyes and splashed over his face. *His blood.*

He tried to yell but no sound came.

In the light from the porch, he saw the dog's bloodshot eyes, its slavering mouth, its white teeth covered in blood.

Henry.

He tried to push the dog away but his hands were like plasticine, all his strength ebbing away.

The dog's teeth clamped over his face and he felt himself being shaken like a cloth doll.

There was no pain now, only a numbness that gripped his entire body, scoured away the agony.

He heard Agnes screaming and caught a glimpse of her running towards him.

Stay away, he wanted to say. *Stay away.*

But the world was rising away from him now – he was tumbling into a deep, silent, painless hole.

It entered Natalie's flat in a millisecond and hovered, low down, just inside the front door. Anyone seeing it in the dimness would have thought it was a two-feet by two-feet defect in the pattern of the wallpaper or a stain on the wall. It was finer than mist, almost entirely transparent and had no definite outline. In its depths, beyond the pale grey folds, two merciless eyes of the palest blue, slanted like a cat's eyes, darted from side to side. After a moment, it began to move, drifting through the lounge, kitchen, bathroom and bedroom, slowly searching the entire flat. The eyes quivered with a strange brutality when it became obvious there was no-one there. It lingered for almost an hour at the front window, looking out, waiting for Natalie. When she did not appear, the grey folds began to tremble violently, then disappeared, melting slowly into the wall.

21

In the dream Law was astride a woman, making love to her, thrusting deep inside her, trembling shafts of pleasure shooting through his body.

Suddenly a minute tickling sensation began to creep up one of his nasal passages, like a cold hand caressing sensitive nerve ends. It became unbearable and he felt his body tighten an instant before he sneezed violently, his head lashing forward.

Sneezed. Did people sneeze in dreams?

His mind began to clear, the dim shapes and outlines of the dream disappearing.

'Well?' a voice said in his ear, a rasping, ugly, woman's voice. 'Are you going to finish or not?'

He opened his eyes and stared down at the woman beneath him. She was about forty-five, he guessed, but an old forty-five, her face puffed up, ravaged by alcohol. Mascara and powder failed to hide the deep lines and wrinkles on her face and the dark trenches under her eyes. Her black hair had grey roots and her red lipstick was smeared across her teeth. He stared at the face, the bare shoulders, the immense breasts, hypnotised, horrified.

It was still part of the dream of course.

He climbed off her, pulled the blankets back and started to get out of the bed.

He noticed unpleasant smells now – face powder, cheap perfume mingled with sweat, stale beer, reeking cigarette butts in an overflowing ashtray, a mustiness that seemed to ooze from the carpet and from the walls of the room.

The room.

He looked around him. An old dressing table with one of the drawers open, a stocking hanging out, white curtains turning grey with grime, a stained easy chair, faded pink floral wallpaper, a dog-eared poster of a woman reclining obscenely on a settee.

'Is that it then?' the woman in the bed said hoarsely and he snapped his head round and looked at her again. He didn't have to answer of course – it was all part of the dream. *It was.* He remembered the earlier part of the dream quite clearly. There were no faces in it, no individuals, just his body tangled with a shadowy female form.

But the things he had done in the dream. The perversities he had indulged in. They flooded back into his mind now. How could he dream of such things? How could he imagine himself indulging in such horrors?

It doesn't matter, he told himself. *Nightmares aren't important.* This was the last part of the fantasy as he moved towards wakefulness. It would be over any second now. He would find himself in his own bed, sweating and irritable.

Wake up, said an urgent voice in his brain. He dug his fingers into his palms.

'If you're finished, you still owe me twenty quid,' the woman was saying. She was getting out of bed, breasts bobbing, stomach and thigh-flesh jiggling. He saw that her toenails were painted pink.

It was a dream, wasn't it? This couldn't be real.

'What are you staring at?' the woman said, standing in front of him, looking up into his face. 'You needn't think you're going to get out of giving me the other twenty quid.'

'T-twenty pounds?'

'Don't play games with me,' she said, her voice shrill.

'Y-yes. Twenty pounds … that's OK.'

He was aware suddenly of his own nakedness.

'My … c-clothes?' he said.

She jerked her head at the far side of the bed and he saw

them there, scattered about the floor.

'You said an extra twenty if I made it real good for you,' she said as he stumbled around the bed.

'Y-yes. Oh,' he said, starting to dress, noticing his hands were shaking.

'This has to be a dream,' he mumbled.

'What? What did you say?'

'N-nothing.'

'Well hand it over then. You've had your money's worth.'

She half turned, showing him her back. It was striped from her neck to her knees with red weals.

'When I let a man do this to me, I expect to get paid.'

It seemed too real to be a dream. Yet it had to be. There was no other explanation.

He fumbled in his jacket pocket and took out his wallet. There was more than a hundred and fifty pounds in it. Why did he have so much money with him? There was only one place it could have come from – his emergency fund, the three hundred pounds he kept in an envelope in the vegetable tray in his fridge. Why had he taken it? What had he been doing for the last …

He glanced down at his watch.

… the last seventeen hours.

But why was he asking himself these questions? *THIS WAS NOT REAL.*

He handed her two ten pound notes.

'Thanks,' she said, 'now piss off and don't come back.'

Dreams were like this sometimes; they tricked you, deceived you into thinking they were actually happening. Once he had dreamed of running in a forest, being chased by someone he couldn't see, and he had been able to smell the pine cones and feel the branches lashing at his face.

He finished dressing, stuffing his tie into his pocket, and hurried to the door.

When he opened it, he would wake, he told himself. He would be in his own bed.

He snatched at the handle, but there was no awakening.

Beyond the door there was a narrow staircase. Sunlight trickled around the edges of a door at the bottom. He rushed down the stairs, fiddled with a lock, then was outside, the sun on his face.

How long would it go on?

IT'S REAL, a voice yelled in his head. *REAL*.

He stumbled along a pavement, pushing his way through crowds of shoppers.

REAL. You spent the night with that woman. REAL. REAL. REAL.

He bumped into a parked car, staggered across a narrow lane and found himself staring at his reflection in a mirror in an Oxford Street department store window. He looked terrible, his eyes wild, his hair a chaotic reddish-brown mop, his shirt collar turned up at one side, his shoulders stooped. There was lipstick smeared across his chin and mouth. He took out a handkerchief, spat on it and wiped the mess away, rubbing until his face was red and sore.

He saw the cab as he folded his collar into place and dragged a comb through his hair.

'Hey,' he yelled and sighed with relief when it stopped.

He got in and rested his head back on top of the seat.

'Chelsea,' he said.

As the taxi nudged its way through the traffic he began to recall a dream he had had the night before, a real dream, not something which had happened and he had thought was a dream. In the real dream, he had gone to Natalie's flat to search for her and he had been so angry when she hadn't been there.

He had wanted so much to hurt her.

Natalie began to brace herself for her visit to Law's flat from the moment she got out of bed. He had said to stay away and she was going there so she couldn't expect him to be pleased – but she had to go, had to look after him, had to reassure him (and herself) and help him get rid of his stupid notions.

She paused once as she dressed, looking at the telephone. Should she call him first? Would that be a better course of action? She shook her head, hooking up her bra. *No.* It would be better to meet him face to face. That way he couldn't say no. He could hardly turn her away when she was standing on his doorstep.

Her mind made up, she ate a good breakfast and let time slip by. She reckoned between eleven and eleven-thirty would be the best time to knock on Law's door. That would give him plenty of time to sleep if he had, as she guessed, been given sleeping tablets by Dr Williams.

Her watch was flicking off ten forty-five when she handed her room key to the desk clerk. She didn't like the man. He was well dressed – pin-stripe suit, white shirt, dark-blue tie – but his sober clothes didn't change the fact that his shiny black hair, switch-on switch-off smile and eyes she always thought of as 'oily' conspired to give him the look of a Cypriot pimp. She felt the eyes studying her as she headed for the door, looking *through* her clothes, *sliding* over her.

She felt relieved when she was out of his sight and as she drove through the Saturday morning traffic she tried to strengthen her resolve to help Jack by raising her mood, getting herself into a positive frame of mind.

But it wasn't to be.

It seemed everywhere she turned there was something depressing. Why today when she needed to be bright and cheery?

First she saw an old woman shuffling slowly across a road and a bus driving too close to her, its horn blaring. Then she saw two drunks fighting on a street corner, throwing badly aimed punches at one another. (*Drunk, at this time in the morning. What was the country coming to?*) A couple of minutes later, as she rounded a corner, she saw a junky in an old army greatcoat, clinging to a lamp post, his eyes shut. He seemed to be praying the world would stop spinning.

One of those days, she thought. One of those days when it

seemed a scab had been ripped off the face of the world, exposing its wounds.

She tried to shrug aside the ugliness of the day, to coax herself into a good humour, to think positively. She had to be in the right frame of mind when she saw Jack if she was going to solve anything. She couldn't walk in there with a long face.

You're going there to cheer him up for Christ's sake, she told herself as she cruised past the front of Lissils Mansions. There were no parking places in the street so she drove around to the back and left the car in the residents-only section.

It was as she hurried around to the front of the building that she saw the porter, Bert Miller, pushing a large cardboard box into the back of a van.

'Morning,' she said as he straightened up, giving him a polite smile.

He nodded and returned her greeting. 'Morning,' he said but as he bent forward again, his head disappearing into the back of the van, she had a feeling his face had twisted into a scowl.

Imagination, she thought. Bert Miller was always so cheerful. Or maybe he was having a bad day too.

She heard him coming up behind her as she approached the door. He moved past her without speaking, pushed the door open and held it for her.

'Thank you,' she said.

There was no scowl there now, but his face was impassive, his eyes not meeting hers.

She nodded to the van as he followed her into the building. 'Somebody leaving?' she said.

He hesitated then said: 'Yes, me.'

'You're leaving?' she said. 'For good?' She stopped, facing him.

'Yes, I won't be coming back here,' he said and she thought she detected a trace of venom in his voice.

'Oh ... a better job?' she said.

'I haven't got another job. I'll probably work for my brother. I'm not sure yet. All I know is I'm not staying in this place.'

She realised his eyes were still avoiding hers and he seemed ill at ease. She felt her brow furrow.

'Is something wrong, Bert?'

Again he hesitated, for a longer period this time, then his eyes rose and looked into hers.

'Look ... I've always liked Jack Law. Do you know what he's up to ... in his flat?'

'Up to? What do you mean?'

'You mean you *really* don't know?'

'Know? Know what? I've no idea what you're talking about.'

Alarm bells were ringing in her brain now and she wasn't sure why. What was Miller trying to say? What was he getting at?

'Nothing in this building has been the same since he came back from abroad,' Miller said. 'I don't know what's going on but I do know I want to be far away from the things that are happening here. I don't want to be any part of it.'

'I've no idea what you're talking about,' she said slowly. 'Explain to me what you're talking about. I've been worried about Jack too. He hasn't been well and ...'

Suddenly his eyes narrowed and looked deep into hers and she thought she saw anger and fear there.

'Do you know what I saw this morning?' he said.

'What?'

'You know that friend of Jack Law's who was killed ... Leo Dempsey?'

'Yes.'

'I knew Leo Dempsey. I'd seen him here a couple of times and I saw his picture in the paper when he died.'

Miller swallowed and Natalie said: 'And?'

'I saw Leo Dempsey today, on the third floor of this building, heading for Jack Law's flat.'

22

Jack Law knew he had been out again because he was wearing a different jacket to the one he had worn the night before, but he could not remember where he had been or for how long.

A blackout. He had had another blackout like the one the night before when he had been with that horrible woman, when he had beaten her. That was the only answer, he decided.

He recalled arriving home that morning and phoning Natalie's flat and an incredible fury rushing through him when she hadn't answered.

Then it had been as if a curtain had dropped.

He was seated on the edge of his bed now, staring at his right fist which was bruised and discoloured, caked in blood. It looked as if he had punched somebody but no matter how hard he tried he could remember nothing. Perhaps he had slipped, scraped his knuckles on a wall? Perhaps anything?

He had vomited twice since he had re-entered his flat half an hour before and the nausea was surging through him, more terrible than ever before. It seemed to wash from his groin up to his throat in long vile waves. The stench that clung to his body now was so horrible that it began to make him gag again and he brought out a handkerchief and clutched it over his nose.

He tried to think clearly but his mind was like sludge slowly churning in a cement mixer.

A shower.

At least if he showered the smell would go.

He tried to get up but he was too weak and he fell sideways onto the bed and rolled onto the floor.

'But you can't have seen Leo Dempsey,' Natalie said, staring at Bert Miller.

The alarm bells in her brain were ringing more shrilly now. Tiny doubts began to gnaw away at her certainties.

What if ...

'You can't have seen Leo Dempsey,' she said again as Miller watched her, his gaze steady.

'I saw Leo Dempsey,' Miller said evenly. 'I know it was him. I got out of there as quickly as I could. I ran faster coming down those stairs than I have at any time in the past twenty years.'

'But it can't be ... it's impossible ... I ... What are these other things you say are happening in the building?'

Miller looked from the closed lift doors to the stairway and back at Natalie again.

He's scared, she thought. *He's actually scared of something. WHAT?*

'Come into the office,' he said quietly and Natalie followed him into his small office and sat down in the easy chair he gestured to, leaning forward, eager to hear what he had to say. Miller lowered himself into a kitchen chair near the window like a very tired man, sighed and said: 'I don't know where to start ... what to say ...'

'Just tell me what's been happening.'

'It started with little things,' Miller said slowly. 'Spoons that clattered and jumped about when Jack Law walked past. Objects being dragged towards him. That table out there in the entrance hall ... it weighs a ton I can tell you. Once when he got into the lift I saw it shift a full six inches. There were pictures which trembled on the walls ...'

I'm not hearing this, Natalie thought. *I CAN'T be hearing this.*

'Then there was Mrs Lessor,' Miller continued. 'She's got the flat beneath Jack Law's. Her television set kept coming on even when she was positive she had switched it off properly. The TV repair man couldn't find anything wrong with the switch mechanism. I think there were other things that Mrs Lessor didn't tell me about.'

She felt as if her place in the world had shifted dramatically – as if she had gone to bed in her flat and woken up in Outer Mongolia or like a woman plucked from the splendour of an upper-upper-middle-class house who found herself in a truck heading for Auschwitz.

'And there was Don Singer,' Miller said. 'He has the flat next door to Jack Law's. I don't know what happened to Mr Singer. All I know is he left in a hurry yesterday and he was so scared he could hardly speak ... Then there's the lift. It keeps jamming. The maintenance man can't find anything wrong with it. Yesterday evening it was jammed for an hour between the second and third floors.'

'But what does all this have to do with Jack?'

'Believe me, it all started when he came back from India.'

'But how *could* it have anything to do with him?'

Miller sighed. 'Don't ask me. I'm only a porter. I don't have the answers.'

He stood up, walked heavily to the window and looked out.

'Did you know I spent most of the my life in the army?' he said, turning to face her again.

'Yes.'

'I travelled everywhere. You see a lot of things when you travel. I saw ... some things that ... I don't like to talk about. At my age I'm afraid people might think I'm senile and ...'

'What kind of things?'

'Things you don't see in this country or ...' He thought a moment then added: 'Maybe they happen here too ... but I've never seen them.'

'What ...'

'When I was in Egypt, I was with some soldiers one evening in the barracks and we started playing with a ouija board one of the lads had bought. We all thought it was a bit of a joke the way the board gave answers to questions we asked. From that evening on things started being shifted around in the barracks. We'd find shaving gear moved from one place to another, all the pillows piled on one bed or two beds pushed together – that kind of thing. We joked about it being some kind of spirit we'd conjured up but really we thought it was one of the lads playing a practical joke.'

He paused and his upper lip twitched. When he spoke again, his voice was low and even, like that of a man reciting the words of a hard-to-remember poem. 'One night I was alone in the barracks. Suddenly I knew something was there with me. I knew exactly where it was. It was on the end bed and it was watching me. I couldn't actually see anything but I was sure it was there and there was his terrible feeling of nastiness, badness ... like I was in danger. then I knew it wasn't on the end bed any more. I knew it was coming towards me. It's funny but you know I really felt like my hair was standing on end – you read about that in books but I really felt that. I got out of there so fast my feet hardly touched the ground.'

A voice inside Natalie's head was jabbering, urging her to tell Miller to stop it, to shut up. She didn't want to listen to any more but she knew she had to.

Miller cleared his throat. 'Another time, in Malaya – Malaysia now – I saw something in a temple. There were about six of us walking back from the town, drunk as anything. We came across this temple and went inside. We lit some candles that were there, sang songs, played cards. We did things we wouldn't have done in a Christian Church but it was just an old building as far as we were concerned. We ... relieved ourselves in one corner and one of the lads was sick on the steps at the front. We didn't mean any harm, we were just drunken soldiers ... but it was no way to behave.'

He returned to his chair and sat down, hunched and tense, his palms resting on his knees.

'Anyway we had been there about an hour when we saw this shape at the back of the temple, beyond the altar, in the shadows beyond the candlelight. At first we thought it was moonlight but it wasn't. It was ... well it was just a shape. But there was the face of a man in the shape and it began to move towards us, sort of gliding. We ran for our lives and I'll tell you something ... when we got back to camp there wasn't a drunk man among us. We were as sober as judges. I saw other things too and heard lots of stories about things that happened to other soldiers in the east.' He bit his lip. 'You can see things in Malaya you never see in Hammersmith,' he said and tried to twist his face into a smile, but his eyes were too scared for it to work.

Jesus ... Ghosts. Hobgoblins. Was that what this man was talking about? This was London. This was the late-eighties. Men had gone to the moon. Space probes had photographed the Rings of Saturn. How ...

'Getting back to what's been happening here ...' Miller said and she noticed his voice had grown hoarse. 'Early this morning I was sitting right where I am now when the lift doors opened. I saw what looked like a pool of blood on the lift floor. I went over but when I got there it had gone, disappeared. Then something on the back wall of the lift caught my eye. It was like a small ... pattern, a circular pattern of light ... like light light reflecting off some kind of medallion, something like that. I told myself it had to be reflection of some kind. I told myself that if I raised my hand, blocking out the light, that a shadow would fall on this thing on the wall. Well ... when I put my hand across it there was no shadow. I moved my hand all around but whatever it was ... it was coming out of the wall. Then it seemed to get ... I don't know. Angry. It seemed to get angry. It began to grow bigger and ... pump, you know, like a heart.'

'Pulsate?'

'Yes, pulsate, that's it. I got out of the lift fast and pressed the basement button. Funny thing though the lift didn't go down. It went up – to the third floor. It was about half an hour after that that I saw Leo Dempsey.'

Natalie felt as if the rational part of her brain had just fragmented and something in her mind was struggling to get all the pieces back together again.

Miller was still talking but she was only half listening now.

'I don't know what's happening in this building,' the porter was saying. 'All I know is I'm getting out. Maybe Jack Law has tampered with something he shouldn't have, something ... I don't know the word for it, something he should have left well alone ...'

Something. Something. Something's trying to hurt me. That's what Jack had said. *Something is killing my friends. Something.*

She hadn't believed because she hadn't wanted to believe. It hadn't been in her to believe. But now?

'If I were you,' Miller was saying, 'I'd stay away from him.'

'What?' she heard herself say. 'Yes. Yes.'

Suddenly the skin on her face felt like damp, warm clay. She stood up and walked out of Miller's office, moving stiffly like a zombie. Then she was in her car, cruising down street after street, driving mechanically, heading nowhere, her mind in turmoil.

(*Jack needed me and I wasn't there. I did NOTHING. I didn't believe him. What did I really find out about the Sedali and Dacahri? Nothing. But I tried, didn't I? I did try. And how could I find out more? What else could I have done, even if I had believed he was right. I could have ... I could have ...*)

Then she remembered the story she had read about the Indian farmer who had died after showing disrespect to the Sedali. Maybe the man who had uncovered that story could help her? The author had been a professor, she recalled, and based in London. John Baha-something. If she could get in touch with him, maybe he knew more about the Sedali and Dacahri than appeared in the book. Maybe ...

He had carried out more than 500 exorcisms. She remembered the biographical note had said that and her mind stood still at the word exorcism. Was that what Jack needed to throw off this spell or curse, this whatever it was, this unclean chunk of paranormal activity? It was obvious now that something inexplicable was happening. There was no point in pretending otherwise.

Unclean.

The word hung in her mind.

Was that what Jack was? A leper of the paranormal?

Unclean?

Maybe he'd have to wear a little bell around his neck to warn people of his approach.

Unclean.

A sign around his neck maybe?

She began to giggle hysterically, her shoulders shaking, tears filling her eyes. She realised she was losing control, laughing and crying at the same time.

Stop it, a voice in her head shrieked. *STOP IT. Get a grip on yourself. You have to help Jack, not go potty. You may be his only chance. You'll be ready for an asylum if you carry on like this. GET A GRIP.*

She began to sob then controlled it and blinked the tears away. This was not the time for emotion – this was the time for action. Swinging the car around in a sharp U-turn, she headed back towards her hotel.

Five minutes later, she saw the newspaper bill which read: 'Globe editor dies after dog attack.'

23

Four.

That was Natalie's estimate.

Four of Law's friends had died now – Ben, Leo, Georgina and Peter Forrest.

She could accept now that Law's illness and phenomena such as shifting tables and jammed lifts were being caused by some kind of force of suggestion or some other inexplicable paranormal activity ... but four deaths?

She spun away from the window of her hotel room, brought up the paper in her hand and stared at the picture of Peter Forrest on the front page.

His dog had killed him. How could that possibly be connected and yet ...

You know as much about the kind of thing that's going on here as you do about Japanese flower arranging, she told herself caustically.

DO SOMETHING.

She threw the paper onto the bed, hurried across the room and found the book by Professor John Bahashasda on an occasional table.

"Bahashasda," she said aloud, snatching up the telephone.

She dialled the operator and when a voice answered, said: 'I'm trying to get the number of a Professor John Bahashasda. I know he lives in London but I don't have an address. There can't be too many professors called Bahashasda.'

'One moment please,' the voice said. There was a pause then the operator spoke again. 'Yes, I have that number.' Natalie scribbled it into her pad and hung up. She snatched the receiver up again immediately but hesitated, her finger poised over the first digit of Bahashasda's number.

What was she going to say to him? Where could she start?

Do it, a voice in her head said and her index finger flicked out Bahashasda's number.

'Hello,' a pleasant, well spoken, woman's voice said almost immediately.

'H-hello. My name is N-Natalie Field. May I speak to Professor Bahashasda?'

'I'm afraid the professor is not at home.'

'When do you expect him?'

'Not till five o'clock.'

'It's important I speak to him,' Natalie said and realised her voice was breaking.

If she couldn't get in touch with Bahashasda, where could she turn? Who could help her? She had no other ideas.

'I'm sorry,' said the woman on the other end of the line. 'Is there something I can help you with? I'm the professor's wife.'

Natalie found herself sobbing. She covered the mouthpiece of the telephone and managed to control herself.

'Is it something urgent?' Mrs Bahashasda said.

'It's ... it's my boyfriend,' Natalie heard herself say. 'Something is happening to him. I'm scared, I'm scared. I don't understand any of it.'

Suddenly her mind seized on a thought.

'I've been trying to find out everything I can about an Indian god called Dacahri. There was something about it in a book your husband wrote. Would he have any more information on this Dacahri? Does he ...'

'He's working on a new book at the moment,' Mrs

Bahashasda said. 'It's possible there might be something about Dacahri in his research notes. He's not a god I've ever heard of. I'd be delighted to check.'

'Could you … please.'

'Of course.'

Mrs Bahashasda seemed to be gone a long time. Natalie sat staring at the blank hotel-room wall in front of her. She no longer felt *real*; she felt as if she was playing some part in a sick play. Would a director shout 'Cut' at any second? Would it all be a dream?

She heard a dull clunk as Mrs Bahashada picked up the receiver again.

'There isn't much here,' Mrs Bahashasda said. 'Dacahri, the notes say, God of a Thousand Faces. Incarnate on earth in the body of the Sedali, a young girl …'

'Yes, I know all that,' Natalie said. 'Is there anything else?'

'Yes. There's a piece here about a farmer. In August, 1972, it says, he …'

'I read that story in one of your husband's books. Anything else?'

'Yes. There's one last piece here. It's hard to read, my husband's handwriting is atrocious … There were five kings called Dacahri in the ancient city of Didrana and they were believed to be the god incarnate …'

Natalie knew that. She knew that. It was in her notebook.

'Yes?' she said.

'The last of the kings was the most evil. The notes here are about … well, horrible things the king did. He impaled people … had men thrown into pits of snakes … and there's a long section here about …'

There was a brief pause then Mrs Bahashasda continued. 'It seems a piece of gossip reached the king. People were saying one of his two hundred concubines had had an affair with one of his priests. The priest was cut to pieces but would not divulge the name of his lover. Dacahri had all of the two hundred concubines taken into the desert and staked out in the sun to die, while he watched their agonies.'

It was what she had seen in her dream. Their dream.

For an instant it was as if the world stood still. Natalie realised the receiver was slipping from her damp palm. She snatched at it.

'Mrs Bahashasda,' she said, 'I have to talk to your husband.'

'I'm sorry, there's no way I can contact him. He's driving home from Manchester. Can you tell me what's happening?'

'I … I can't explain it really,' she said and realised she had shrieked the words like some kind of lunatic.

'Just try to tell me. I might be able to suggest something.'

For five minutes Natalie blurted out disjoined chunks of the story, swallowing her sobs.

'I don't know what it means,' she said when she had finished. 'All I know is Jack needs some kind of help. What do you think? Could there be some kind of evil force … hurting him, doing these things?'

'I can't answer that. It … it …'

'I've got to get help for Jack now.'

'My husband might be able to help but …'

'I must get help now.'

'I can give you the name and address of a man, a priest my husband sometimes works with on … things like this. Maybe he can answer some of your questions. Maybe he can help.'

'All right,' Natalie said.

She picked up a pen and wrote down the name and address, watching her hand shaking violently.

'He runs a kind of soup kitchen and hostel there for down-and-outs,' Mrs Bahashasda said. 'I'm sure you'll find him there. If you still want to talk to my husband, call at five.'

'Th-thank you … for all your help.'

She hung up and stared at the name scrawled in her pad.

Father Francis Quigley.

Emotionally and physically, Jack Law was in chaos. He was on a rapidly spinning carousel which snapped him from horrible, stomach-cramping pain to unbelievable ecstasy, from total blackness to a state of seeking to devour everything around him — from images on the television screen to alcohol, food to the odours of such things as soap, aftershave, wood, cheese and fruit (and they all seemed so new and fascinating to him now).

Once, he stripped naked and found himself standing in the bathroom, studying himself in the full-length mirror, feeling his hair, touching his flesh. He smashed a glass, took up a tiny sliver between thumb and index finger, and ran it slowly down his forearm watching the blood which oozed out of the cut, finding the sight intensely exciting.

As he began to cut into his knuckles, the pain hit him in a sudden stab and he had a moment of clear, rational thought.

Something is trying to hurt me, something is killing my friends. That's what he had said to Natalie and he had been right.

But it was more than that ...

(He grabbed for the answers like a man who knew it was now or never, his face twisted with the effort of thinking.)

It was more ...

That something was now using his body, his mind, his senses for pleasure; using him to obtain perverted satisfaction.

Then the moment of rational thought was gone and he found himself mechanically wiping away the blood and bandaging the cut.

Back in the lounge he caught sight of the picture of a woman on a magazine cover and he felt a sudden irrepressible lust, a need to have a woman ...

To hurt her.

Like he had hurt that woman the night before.

He began to dress, laughing quietly to himself, an astonishing surge of strength running through him.

24

Number twenty-four Buckberry Street had end-of-the-line
written all over it. Crushed between warehouses and
derelict buildings it was a gaunt, bleak, three-storey
Victorian monstrosity, its red bricks blackened with grime.
A flaking sign above a heavy steel door read simply 'Men's
Hostel.'

Natalie pushed the door open and stepped into a dim
corridor which smelled of carbolic with a score of
undersmells – she had identified vomit and musty decay,
urine and linoleum polish when she saw the grey-haired
woman leaning on a mop at the bottom of a dark stairway
not ten feet away from her.

'Yes?' said the woman.

'I'm looking for Father Quigley.'

'Dunno where he is. He might be …'

'It's very important,' Natalie said quickly.

'All right,' the woman said, putting down her mop and
wiping her hands on her apron. 'You can wait in his office
while I see if I can find him.'

Natalie followed the woman to the end of the corridor
and went through a door the woman opened for her.

'He's probably in the dormitories upstairs,' the woman
said and disappeared.

The office was sparsely furnished – a scratched metal
desk with an empty wire basket in one corner, two brown
kitchen chairs, one behind the desk and one in front of it,
the pale green walls adorned only by a single crucifix
two feet long.

Natalie went to the window and watched a succession of lorries manoeuvring their way along Buckberry Street and in and out of the warehouses. She had the sudden strange feeling that she wasn't sure who she was, what she was doing there. The place seemed so far removed from her *real* life. What had life been like in that distant country where she had lived until Jack had returned from India, that everyday place with its everyday worries, its little successes and little failures? Where was it now?

She was alone for about five minutes then the door opened and she turned quickly from the window.

The man facing her was about six feet tall and dressed in a blue check shirt and faded blue jeans. He had the striking good looks of a film star and reminded her immediately of Robert Redford as he had been in a film she had once seen called 'Downhill Racer.' He was wearing a crooked smile that showed two lines of perfect white teeth and there was an overwhelming impression of cleanliness about him, about his skin, his hair, his clothes.

'Hello,' he said, and his blue eyes invited her to speak.

'Hello. I'm waiting for Father Quigley. I ...'

He chuckled and walked behind the desk.

'I'm Father Quigley,' he said, then paused and added: 'We don't always wear our back-to-front collars, you know.'

'Oh.'

'Please sit down.'

When she was seated he lowered himself into the chair opposite her and said 'How can I help?'

'I ... I don't know where to start. I spoke to a Mrs Bahashasda by phone and she said you might be able to help me. I know I should have called first but ... I ... I'm desperate.'

She thought she saw a tiny frown knit its way into his brow at the mention of the name Bahashasda but it was gone in an instant.

'I understand you have worked with Professor Bahashasda on some ...'

She let the sentence trail away, uncertain of the words to use.

The priest nodded patiently.

'That's right. We've tackled a few problems together.'

'What ... what kind of things?'

'We've carried out exorcisms, usually simple cases, psychic energy of a nasty kind trapped in old houses, that kind of thing. Why don't you start at the beginning and tell me what your problem is.'

She studied his face for a moment. At first glance she had put him at about thirty but now, looking more closely, she saw the grey lacing his hair and the patterns of lines around his eyes. She guessed her first estimate had been about ten years out.

'Go ahead, tell me,' he prompted, 'believe me, nothing you say is going to shock me.'

He gave her an easy smile and she began to talk, telling the whole story in fifteen minutes, garnishing the facts with her own thoughts and doubts and feelings of confusion. She felt better when she had finished, as if she had unburdened herself ...

As if she had been to confession.

(Was that what confession was like for a Catholic, she wondered. A sense of having packed all your troubles and failings into a bag and handed them over to the priest like old clothes you never wanted to see again, a sharing of problems, a chance to rid yourself of guilt.)

Father Quigley thought in silence for a moment, his face serious but untroubled, then he said: 'Would it shock you or hurt you if I told you that the odds are that what your boyfriend really needs is a psychiatrist.'

She shook her head. 'I don't understand. How ... I thought that myself but ...'

'Many things can affect the human mind,' he said quietly, kindly. 'Alcohol for instance, stresses and strains, thoughts that worry away at you, fear, love, even the moon. Yes ...' He gave a half laugh. 'Many doctors in mental homes will tell you that patients can be influenced by the full moon. It's to do with magnetic forces, it's where the word lunacy comes from.'

'But how does all this explain what's happening to Jack?'

The priest clasped his hands, crossed his legs and bit his lower lip.

'Let me give you a scenario. A man under stress, overworked, is involved in an accident in a faraway country, an accident for which he feels partly to blame. He returns home and by pure coincidence a number of his friends die. The strain on him and his feelings of guilt combine to ...'

'But ...'

'The human mind is awesomely powerful. You've heard of psychokinesis, you've probably read about poltergeist activity, hysteria and other paranormal phenomena. In the presence of teenage girls for instance furniture has been known to move, light bulbs do explode, tables can tremble and rise. All these things do happen and they do defy scientific explanation. However, it is all the power of the mind. It is not spirits or entities from beyond. An emotionally disturbed person can unleash some very strange phenomena.'

'How could that explain what the porter saw? He said he saw Leo Dempsey.'

'If my theory is correct, it could be that the porter observed some unusual phenomena and was therefore himself under strain. What he probably saw was a man who looked like Leo Dempsey.'

'And the deaths were just coincidence,' Natalie said doubtfully. She didn't know what to believe now.

'Probably. I would think they were not related to Mr Law in the sense you were suggesting but rather the opposite. The deaths helped to create his state of mind.'

'But Jack's illness, it ...'

'Stress, overwork, guilt.'

'I just can't ...'

'Let me put it this way. You appear to be distraught

because you believe your boyfriend is in danger from some kind of psychic force. What I'm saying is, you're probably wrong. The best thing for us to do is to go quietly and calmly to Mr Law's flat and talk to him.'

'Now?'

'Yes, if you like.'

He pushed his chair back and stood up.

'I'll just get my jacket,' he said, striding across the room.

He hesitated, resting his right hand on the door handle, turned and said: 'Mentally disturbed people can have many symptoms. I have many friends who are psychiatrists. Most of the people they deal with have everyday emotional problems. Leaving those aside, there are thousands of people who have extraordinary and unusual problems. In nine hundred and ninety-nine cases out of every thousand, they can find a solution or at least a psychiatric explanation.'

As he tugged the door open, she said: 'And the other one?'

The priest frowned briefly and shrugged. 'The other one is something else altogether,' he said quietly. 'Something out of their field. That's when they give me a call ... or someone like me.'

He went out and returned a few moments later wearing a zip-up leather jacket and carrying a black briefcase.

'Your car or mine?' he said and gave her the same boyish smile he had been wearing when she had first seen him. She knew it was meant to be reassuring but all she felt now was a deepening confusion.

'It'll be easier if we take my car,' she heard herself say.

Suddenly Law was aware he was walking along a street but he was uncertain where he was going or where he had been.

He knew his lucid moments were becoming fewer and fewer. *It must be some kind of fever brought on by the illness, affecting my brain, he told himself, grabbing for rational thought. But ...*

NO.NO.NO.

It wasn't that.

He fought to clear his mind, to examine his predicament, to make sense of it.

But that was when the visions began, strange images that floated up from his subconscious – not like dreams, more like memories, he was to think in his next moment of clarity. Yet they were not his memories, not memories of events in his life.

The first image (which recurred constantly, punctuating all the other images) was of a void, black and empty and seemingly endless. He was aware he was travelling at an incredible speed, aware of the exhilaration of that speed, but irritated by a feeling that this journey through the void would take a long, long time.

Then he saw a host of men and women being prodded by spears towards the edge of a pit and watched, elated, as they fell one by one into the wriggling mass of snakes which covered the bottom.

Something glinted in his mind, like sunshine on naked, polished metal and an instant later he was looking down into a vast valley where two armies were locked in combat, their swords and spears and shields flashing, distant cries of anger and pain, the thud of horses' hooves and the clash of weapons whispering past him in the clear air. A horse snorted, something beneath his feet shifted and he knew he was in a war chariot.

Then he was in a silent room, watching three young women crouched over the reclining figure of an old man. After a moment the man rose and came towards him and he saw that the man's body was covered in symbols drawn in blood.

The image quivered and disappeared and he found himself staring into a mirror. Slowly he lowered his eyes and saw that he had the body of a young girl, a girl of no more than eight. He studied it intently, running his fingers over the child-flesh.

Something bumped into his shoulder and he blinked and saw it was the corner of a building.

This was London. Cars were driving past him. Women with shopping baskets and prams were hurrying along the pavement. He could hear car engines and people talking and a horn sounding in the distance. A cool wind blew in his face and he was aware that his hair was damp.

It must have been raining, he thought, yet he could recall no downpour.

Why hadn't he taken shelter?

Why ... what ...

He snatched for rational thought again, but another image was filling his brain ...

The image of a vast, empty, yellow desert.

He knew he was returning to the fairground-ghost-train of memories.

Memories which were not his own.

25

'What if it's not a psychiatric problem?' Natalie said to Father Quigley as she drove towards Law's flat. 'What if Jack is the one in a thousand?'

'I ...'

'It occurred to me that you are probably concerned that I'm upset but ... *please* tell me.'

She swung the car around a corner, accelerated through traffic lights as they dropped from green to amber, then threw a quick glance at the priest.

'I have told you the absolute truth,' he said.

'Yes, I know that,' Natalie said. 'But ... what if your theory's wrong?'

Father Quigley sighed. 'There are all kinds of unclean psychic activity on this earth. For instance, anything that is living has some kind of energy force. Take a rat. When a rat dies its energy force does not dissipate immediately. It could become tangled up with a man's energy force ... or spirit or soul or whatever you wish to call it ... say while he's under the influence of alcohol or drugs. That can cause a lot of problems. Then there are truly powerful evil forces. No human being can really understand them but there are many ways that people can become ensnared in this kind of evil, become possessed if you like by some kind of psychic filth.'

'Demonic possession,' she said quickly.

'No,' he said firmly. 'True demonic possession is very rare. In all the years I've been working with the paranormal, carrying out exorcisms, I've been involved in only one case of true demonic possession. This kind of possession does not involve a body being violated by some kind of inexplicable psychic filth or even by some earthbound spirit ... No, demonic possession involves something else altogether, not something confused or lost or simply unclean but something coherent, something that knows what it's seeking, what it's trying to do, something that has a consciousness, a knowledge of its purpose.'

She drew up beside a parking spot opposite Lissils Mansions and began to reverse in.

'What do you know about this Dacahri?' she said.

'Nothing,' he said as she pulled on the handbrake and killed the engine with a flick of her wrist. 'The name rings a bell, that's all.'

'That's where Jack lives,' she said, nodding to the building across the road.

It was as she reached for the door handle that Quigley's hand snaked across in front of her and grabbed her wrist, hard enough to hurt her.

'Don't open the door,' he rasped.

'What ...'

'Just listen carefully.'

'Why? What is it? What's wrong?'

She looked up into his face and saw that he had grown pale and his upper lip was twitching.

'Look at that man across the street ... there ... is that Jack Law?' the priest said.

She swung her head round, following the direction of his gaze, and ran her eyes along the pavement at the front of Lissils Mansions. At first she did not recognise the stooped figure hobbling along the pavement, his hair dishevelled, his oddly bloated face slumped forward, eyes fixed on the ground in front of him. She was about to say *'Jack Law, no that's nothing like Jack Law'* but then something caught in her throat. This man *was* nothing like *her* Jack, nothing like the tall, erect, athletic newspaperman she had fallen in love with.

But the truth came to her with a burning certainty.

It was Jack Law.

'Yes,' she breathed as the figure drew level with them and turned into Lissils Mansions. 'That's Jack.'

Natalie was aware that the priest's grip on her wrist had loosened but his fingers still rested on her flesh and she could feel them trembling.

'Drive,' Quigley said hoarsely and she turned and saw that his face had been transformed ino a stony, impassive mask that attempted to disguise the horror that he felt, the horror that was obvious in his eyes – they were wide and staring, tormented. It was as if he had just caught a nightmare glimpse of the horrors of hell itself, Natalie thought.

'What do you mean?' she said. 'Aren't we …'

'Drive,' he repeated and she noticed a note of pleading in his voice. 'Get us out of here.'

'I …'

'Get me to a phone box.'

He slumped back in his seat as she started the engine and swung the car out into a line of traffic.

Jack. How could that have been Jack?

Mechanically, she drove the car to the next corner and turned left, heading for a phone box she knew two blocks away.

Jack. How …

But it had been Jack.

And what had the priest seen that could have such an effect on him?

A terror beyond anything she had ever known coated her body and face in a strange, oily numbness and made her hands and the back of her neck tingle with a sharp pins-and-needles sensation. A senseless voice jabbered wildly in her brain.

'There's a phone box,' Quigley said, failing to control a tremor in his voice, and she drew into the kerb.

The priest was out of the car before she had brought it to a stop. By the time she had turned off the engine and reached for her door handle he had crossed the pavement, entered the phone box, dialled a number and inserted a coin.

'Mrs Bahashasda?' Natalie heard him say as she approached the phone booth. She pulled open the door and went inside, standing beside him.

'It's Francis Quigley here,' the priest was saying now. 'I have to see your husband most urgently. Yes, yes I know you don't expect him back until five. Yes ... she's with me now. I'll be coming round there to wait for the professor. In the meantime, if he calls, could you tell him that I must see him urgently and ask him to call back in twenty minutes. I should be there by then.'

She watched his eyes as he spoke and the horror there transferred itself to her like an electric charge, intensifying her own fear.

'Yes ... yes, that's right,' Quigley said. 'Goodbye.'

'What is it,' Natalie muttered as the priest hung up.

'I ...'

She grabbed savagely at the front of his leather jacket, almost ripping out the zip.

'What is it?' she yelled. 'What did you see?'

'It can't be explained easily,' he said slowly. 'I need assistance. I'm a man of God who spends most of his time running a hostel ... a hospital really, a hospital for the sick in spirit, society's walking wounded, a place where they know someone cares about them. We try to help them and ...'

He was talking automatically, like a man in a trance, as if he wanted to say anything except what was really on his mind.

'Tell me,' Natalie shrieked. 'What is it? What ...'

'There are no doubts in my mind,' Quigley said, looking down at her. 'This *is* a case of demonic possession.'

PART THREE
26

The long wait at Professor Bahashasda's house in Putney was made even more unbearable for Natalie because Father Quigley refused to be drawn on what he had seen. Mrs Bahashasda had shown them into a comfortable lounge room with French windows which looked out over a large overgrown garden and made them interminable cups of tea – but she did not join them and they sat alone hardly talking, the minutes passing with a painful slowness.

The phone rang once – at three-thirty – and the priest jumped out of his chair as Mrs Bahashasda rushed in to answer it. But it was a family friend, not the professor, and Quigley and Natalie resumed their wait.

Natalie watched the minute hand of the carriage clock on the mantelpiece flick up to four o'clock and listened to the quavering *piiing, piiing, piiing, piiing* of the chimes.

An hour to go.

But, of course, the professor might be early, she told herself.

Or he might be late. His car might break down. He might get a puncture.

What would happen to Jack then?

What was happening to Jack now?

What ...

She shifted in her seat, watching the minute hand begin its descent, apprehension and barely-controlled, nameless

197

terrors flitting backwards and forwards through her mind. She massaged her temples, uselessly trying to rub away her headache — it felt as if someone had tipped a vial of acid through a hole in the top of her head and the burning fluid was slowly eating its way through her brain.

The priest seemed deep in thought. She guessed he was examining and re-examining what he had seen, studying it in his mind's eye, preparing his story for Professor Bahashasda.

At four-thirty she suddenly realised she was shouting at Quigley.

'Just tell me what you saw. What was it?'

'I can't explain it, you wouldn't understand,' he said with a sigh.

'Try me.'

'Not until I speak to Professor Bahashasda. There's no point ...'

'What was it?' she shrieked.

'Not even I can tell you that,' he said evenly. 'And the professor won't be able to either. If we could answer that we'd know the secret of existence, we'd know the purpose and meaning of everything.'

'I don't want words,' she said bitterly. 'I want facts ... I ...'

'All right, all right.' He held up his hand in a gesture of peace. 'Let me put it like this ... It's something I wish was lost in its own time, its own place, its own dimension ... far, far away from the earth, something that became trapped on earth a long, long time ago... and stayed here.'

'But what can we do about it,' she yelled. 'How can we help Jack? What do you mean by demonic possession?'

'I understand you're upset, believe me. I want to help him too, but it will take two experienced men ... and even then ...' He spread his hands in a gesture that said he could offer no guarantees.

Tears filled her eyes and she felt her anger drain away. What right did she have to take her feelings out on this man who was trying to do his best to help Jack?

'I'm sorry,' she said. 'I shouldn't have …'

That was when the door opened and Mrs Bahashasda hurried in.

'He's home,' she said. 'His car is coming up the driveway now.'

Porkat: The failure

Manali found Subhash just inside the temple door, standing with his feet apart, his hands dangling loosely at his sides, his chin on his chest. Subhash heard Manali enter, raised his head and saw the question in the other man's eyes.

For twenty-four hours Subhash had talked to the girls who had been brought to him but Dacahri had not shown himself. He knew this had never happened before. Dacahri always showed himself quickly, unmistakably. Often the people of Porkat knew who the new Sedali was before The Seeker arrived so obvious was the manifestation of Dacahri.

He had assumed Dacahri was setting him some kind of test and had seen all the girls many times, but still he had been unable to find the Sedali.

He spun away from Manali, strode across the temple and stared up the wide stairway at the statue of Dacahri in his half-man half-tiger incarnation as if seeking some sign, some answer.

The statue was of yellowish stone, unpainted and unadorned. The genius of its long dead sculptor shone through each stone muscle and sinew. The bottom half of the statue was of a tiger, crouched, ready to pounce, its legs corded muscle. The upper half was of a handsome young man with a perfectly proportioned torso and four arms held out in front of him, the palms of his hands turned up. The long hair seemed to fly away at the back of the head as if caught in the wind.

Subhash had always found that these statues were more than just symbols of Dacahri, more than just artists' interpretations of Dacahri's one thousand earthly incarnations – it had seemed to him that each contained a tiny piece of the essence of Dacahri, some almost magical quality.

But not this time.

Now he felt as if he was just looking at stone – brilliantly carved stone, but just stone nevertheless. He turned away from the statue and his eyes locked with Manali's again. Manali shook his head slowly from side to side as if he knew what Subhash was about to say and did not wish to hear the words.

'There is no error,' Subhash said and his words seemed heavy and leaden in the hush of the temple. 'There is no Sedali.' He covered his face with his hands and between his palms he said: 'Dacahri is no longer among us.'

27

Professor Bahashasda's appearance surprised Natalie. He was the thinnest man she had ever seen and short, not above five feet tall. Swarthy, papery skin was drawn tight over the jutting bones of face cut in half by a huge moustache as coal black as his wild mop of curly hair. He was dressed in a sober blue suit, white shirt and striped tie but his clothes did nothing to lessen the startling impact of his appearance. Natalie found his wide, watchful eyes a little frightening. As he came into the lounge they were turned on her for an instant and they seemed to look inside her as if seeking out some dark place there.

When the introductions were over, the professor took Quigley to his study upstairs, leaving Natalie alone in the lounge with a curt 'Excuse us, please Mrs … uh … Miss Field …'

'Natalie,' she said as he closed the door behind him.

She managed to contain herself for fifteen minutes. (Let them get on with it, she reasoned. They knew what they were doing, didn't they.)

Finally she decided she couldn't hold on any longer and hurried upstairs. Only one door was closed and she assumed that was the study and threw the door open.

The men were standing in the middle of the room, deep in conversation, the priest towering incongruously over the professor. They were half turned away from her and at first they didn't seem to realise she was in the room.

'You're sure about what you saw?' she heard Bahashasda say.

'Yes,' Quigley answered. 'They were shooting out of him like flames.'

They, Natalie thought. Who or what were *they*?

'A thing like a snake,' the priest said, running the fingers of his right hand through his hair, 'a huge man with a shaven head, a thing ... like a bird and the strongest of all was ...'

'I don't want to be left out of this,' Natalie interrupted and noticed an abrasive, near hysterical edge on her voice. They turned to face her and she added: 'I *can't* be left out of this. I've got to know what's going on, what you're going to do, what you think.'

Quigley threw a glance at the professor and Bahashasda sighed and gestured Natalie to an easy chair.

She sat down and the professor said: 'I believe you've been reading up on Dacahri?'

'Yes,' she said.

'Then you'll know it's one of the Old Gods.'

'Yes, whatever that means.'

Bahashasda strolled across the room and half-sat, half-leaned on the edge of his desk.

'Is it like a ... demon?' Natalie said.

(*Demon. My God' Natalie, what are you saying? What is a demon anyway?*)

'Something like that,' Bahashasda said. 'It's an entity that is not of the earth. It came here a long time ago ... and stayed, perfecting its evil in a thousand incarnations. Its followers worshipped it and gave it a name – Dacahri.'

'Yes, but what has it done to Jack?'

The professor took a deep breath. 'From what I've heard I'd guess it has entered him.'

'Taken possession?' she said, her voice as cold and hard as a block of ice.

'I didn't say that. It may not have taken full possession yet. It takes some time for even a very powerful entity like Dacahri to take full possession of an adult male. It's not quite the same thing as taking possession of a young girl. When did you last speak to Law?'

'On the telephone yesterday.'

'How did he sound?'

'I don't know … worried … irritable … short-tempered …'

'But did he sound like himself?'

. Natalie thought a moment then said: 'Yes, he was just a worried version of Jack.'

'That means possession was not completed at that time.'

'None of this is making much sense to me,' she said. 'Possession, entities. You may as well be talking about nuclear fission. Tell me … in simple words … what is happening to Jack.'

'All right. First you must understand that Dacahri is a discarnate entity … sorry, that means he has no flesh, no body. In order to experience the earth, the sensations of existence here, he must have a … a home if you like, a body in which he can live …'

'Why Jack?'

Bahashasda shrugged. 'Probably unintentional, that's my guess. The transfer probably took place instantaneously at the split second the Sedali died, during the instant of shock when Dacahri found he had no living human body in which to exist. Dacahri simply spat out of the Sedali's body and into Law.'

'Will it kill him? Will he die?'

Father Quigley took two steps towards Natalie and looked down at her. She saw that his eyes were filled with emotion.

(*Compassion,* she thought. *He cares. He wants to help so much.*)

'It will not deliberately kill his body,' he said quietly. 'It will … attempt to complete the possession. This loathsome thing needs Law. It has no other place to go. To enjoy existence here, it will have to use him.'

'Father Quigley is trying to be kind,' Bahashasda said. 'I prefer to give you the truth bluntly. The fact is that Father Quigley is right when he says it won't kill Law but … it will torment him until it has destroyed what is left of his own spirit … his own soul.'

Natalie sobbed once, staring at Bahashasda, then composed herself.

'How does this explain Jack's illness?'

'Nausea, a terrible odour emanating from the skin, stomach pains ... all these things are classic symptoms of possession.'

'What about all the people who have been killed?' she said. 'Is that just coincidence or ...'

Bahashasda shook his head. 'No,' he said emphatically. 'My guess is that Dacahri is very angry, resentful, and has intensely malevolent feelings towards Law. It wants desperately to hurt Law. Its ... various incarnations and its minions are being sent to kill Law's friends, to cause him as much suffering as possible. It occurred to me that it may be killing people in an ever-decreasing circle, drawing closer and closer to Law ... rather like a psychological death of a thousand cuts. It's taking a perverted pleasure from his pain.'

The room and the words she was hearing were taking on a dreamlike quality now. She felt oddly light, as if she might float away at any time.

'What about me? Why am I alive?' she said and her voice seemed strangely distant, like a voice in another room.

'That's precisely what I mean,' the professor said. 'You're alive. It's drawing closer and closer to Law with each death. You were being saved for last ... perhaps to be killed in the most gruesome way of all.'

No-one spoke for a moment and a heavy silence filled the room.

Natalie broke it, saying: 'What about the porter seeing Leo Dempsey outside Jack's flat?'

'At this level,' Bahashasda said, 'demonic possession is incredibly magnetic, in a psychic sense. Any spirits which have not yet passed over may become trapped in ... in what I can only describe as a maelstrom of psychic activity.'

'What do we do?' she said, the words catching in her throat.

(What if there was nothing that could be done? What if Jack was doomed? Doomed to what? WHAT?)

'Do?' Bahashasda said. 'We do what Christians have to do when confronted with evil – we fight it. We fight it with the weapons that we have, the only weapons this thing will understand.'

'We're going to try to exorcise it,' Father Quigley said, hardly above a whisper.

The nightmare did not begin as a nightmare. It started pleasantly enough. Law left his body (it seemed the most natural thing in the world), floated to the ceiling and rolled slowly onto his stomach.

It was strange to see a room from that vantage point and everything seemed new and intensely fascinating. The sensation of weightlessness was relaxing. He found himself studying his sleeping body, still dressed in trousers, shirt and tie, lying just where he had flopped on the bed when he had arrived back at the flat. He was surprised at how tired and ill he looked and how grey his skin had become.

Suddenly the outline of his body seemed to tremble and shimmer as if it was an image in a mirror and the mirror was being shaken. Then he realised that the figure on the bed was altering, changing form.

It was not him at all. It was someone else. It …

He peered down, intrigued. The shimmering eased and he could see a huge, fat, shaven-headed man lying in his place, in a deep sleep. The first stirrings of apprehension began but there was no real fear yet.

Then this new form began to shimmer and as he watched it became a twitching blur and began to diminish. When the shimmering cleared again, the figure of a thin woman in a sari lay on the bed … but there was no face.

Where the face should have been, there was only a black hole.

That was when the dream became a nightmare and fear began to flicker through him.

He felt compelled to drag himself along the ceiling and look down into the hole. Something told him not to do it but he couldn't hold back. He drifted to his left, corrected his direction by scraping his heel on the ceiling, and found himself directly over the hole.

Fear scorched through him as he saw something rushing up out of the hole.

It was a pale, semi-transparent beam, not unlike a shaft of light.

He propelled himself away acoss the room, heading for the corner nearest the door.

As he watched in horror, the beam twitched and trembled violently. Slowly it began to take on the shape of a man's arm, six feet long, with a powerfully-muscled forearm and long fingers.

Fully formed but with quivering, indistinct edges, it began to inch upwards, the fingers feeling their way through the air. It brushed the ceiling, hesitated, then turned in his direction and shot towards him.

He kicked away from it instinctively but wasn't quick enough. Something with awesome strength fastened itself around his ankle and he felt himself being drawn down.

A strange thought began to filter into his mind. At first it had no clear message, it was just a primitive alarm signal, but he concentrated and the thought formed into words.

This is not a dream, it said. *This is real.*

28

'You were surprised when I said I was a Christian,' Bahashasda said matter-of-factly, throwing a glance over his shoulder at Natalie.

They were cruising towards Chelsea in the professor's Jaguar XJ6, picking their way through the early-evening traffic. Darkness had fallen, the steadily-deepening dimness punctuated by the regimented glow of street lamps, the jagged chunks and pillars and rectangles of light from windows and the garish glare of neon signs.

'No,' she said, unconsciously gripping the attache case the professor had handed to her when he got into the car. 'I ...'

'I saw the surprise in your eyes,' he said. 'But I sensed it as well. I'm intuitive ... a little psychic.'

'I'm sorry. I ...'

'Don't apologise,' he said abruptly and she looked in the rear-vision mirror and saw an odd smile playing on his lips. 'You probably assumed because of my, shall we say, eastern appearance that I was a Hindu or Buddhist or Moslem. For the record I'm third generation English. Before that my family were Indians, but we've always been Christians. There are a lot of Indian Christians. They say it was Doubting Thomas who brought the faith to India.'

'I didn't know that,' she said. She felt she ought to add something but didn't know what to say.

After her conversation with Quigley and Bahashasda that afternoon she had had dinner with Mrs Bahashasda while the two men carried out what Quigley called their 'preparations.' During this time, she had seen the professor only once, when he had come into the dining room to ask if she had a key to Law's flat. She had handed over her key ring saying 'That's it, the silver one, Jack gave it to me so that I could keep an eye on his flat when he was away.' After dinner, Mrs Bahashasda had left her alone in the lounge. Once, tired of waiting, she had gone upstairs to see how long the men would be. Through the study door she had heard Quigley's voice, praying.

'Hail Mary, full of grace,
Our Lord is with thee,
Blessed ...'

She had tiptoed back downstairs, embarrassed and a little ashamed of her impatience.

'How do you feel?' Bahashasda said now, turning his head to the priest as he drew the car to a halt at a red light.

'Nervous.'

'Me too. This could be even worse than that case in Eastbourne, you know.'

Quigley nodded without comment then snapped open the briefcase at his feet and dived his right hand inside. He took out a small Bible, a golden cross about five inches long, a crucifix on a heavy chain and a small bottle of clear liquid.

'Holy water,' Bahashasda said to Natalie, seeing her quizzical expression in the rear-vision mirror.

The priest put the Bible, cross and bottle into the zip-up pockets of his jacket and ducked his head into the chain, dropping the crucifix across his chest. It glinted as he leaned back, reflecting the dashboard lights.

Five minutes later, Natalie saw Lissils Mansions and a strange thrill of fear lanced from the pit of her stomach up into her chest.

She tapped Bahashasda's shoulder and pointed out the building.

'There it is,' she said and he drew up at the kerb opposite the front door and flicked the engine off.

'Ready?' the professor said to Quigley.

The priest nodded and Bahashasda took the attache case from Natalie.

'You're to stay in the car,' he told her firmly. 'Whatever happens, don't enter the building. Do you understand?'

She nodded, three brief jerks, and Bahashasda turned back to the priest.

'Let's get it done,' he said, opening the door.

Quigley swung around in his seat, took Natalie's hand and gripped it for a moment, then said 'Don't worry' and stepped out of the car.

She watched them cross the street, the tall priest in a leather jacket and jeans and the tiny professor in a long blue coat that fell almost to his ankles, his large attache case swinging in his right hand.

They could have been a stockbroker and his son, she thought. Or a shady businessman and his minder making a call on a client who had failed to pay the latest instalment on a loan which carried exorbitant interest. They could have been arms dealers or yacht salesmen or health officers out to check on a dubious restaurant.

But they weren't.

They were *exorcists*.

'God,' she murmured. 'What's happening …'

She tried to imagine the reality of tomorrow or the day after, the old routine, normality, but failed.

There was no reality but *now*.

Law sat up abruptly, leaping out of the world of visions and strange imaginings, aware for a moment of who he was, grabbing desperately for answers.

He was Jack Law. It was Wednesday. He was ill. He was on the floor of his bedroom. He had …

The clarity in his mind wavered but he fought for it. He was like a drunk, he thought, having occasional, brief lucid patches when he was vaguely aware of his condition but unable to do anything about it before he went under again.

If before he had had a panoramic view of his own life, now he saw it in occasional blurred glimpses from a dingy basement in his mind, crammed between fantasy and blackout.

And he couldn't make sense of anything.

'I'm Jack Law,' he mumbled. 'I'm …'

He tried to recall events. The accident in India. Seeing Natalie for the first time on his return. Leo and Georgina's party. But everything was garbled, mixed up.

I'm no longer in control … of myself, he thought, and an idea leapt into a distant corner of his mind.

He struggled to reach for it but a vision washed into his brain. He was descending through thick, dark clouds …

He fought to edge the vision to one side. His idea was becoming clearer now.

It was …

… as if …

The clouds parted and far below him he saw the folds of a great yellow desert, low hills and depressions edged by jagged cliffs.

… as if … he was in a prison cell. He had always been there …

There was no fear in his slow descent towards the desert, just a wild exhilaration. It was as if he was hang-gliding or as if he had wings and was descending like a gliding hawk.

… He had always been in that cell … but now … now …

There were two prisoners in the cell.

He was not alone.

The yellow desert swung up at him and he banked and soared into the burning heat of a depression.

It hovered just inside Law's window, a pale grey form, finer than mist.

Anyone looking up from the street might have mistaken it for a dirty smudge on Law's window, perhaps a two feet by two feet stain left by a careless window cleaner.

Two merciless pale blue eyes quivered in its depths, watching Natalie with a kind of excited, malevolent glee.

The grey folds began to tremble and melt slowly into the glass, reforming outside the window.

Then it began to glide gently down towards the street.

Bahashasda transferred his attache case to his left hand, took the key from his pocket and reached towards Law's door.

'It's hot,' he said, hesitating.

Quigley poked a hand at the door, brushing the tip of his index finger over the wooden surface.

'Yes,' he said and sighed heavily.

Bahashasda thrust the key into the lock and pushed the door open.

29

'Jesus and Mary,' Father Quigley muttered hoarsely as he stepped into Law's flat.

The lounge was crowded with vague drifting shapes and dim forms and filled with a cacophony of low whisperings, just audible to the human ear. Some of the shapes were as insubstantial as puffs of smoke but in others he could make out human outlines and here and there an almost perfectly clear head or hand or leg. Some of the fainter shapes seemed to be those of animal-like creatures. Quigley thought he could make out a dog and something like a big cat.

As soon as he spoke, the whispering ceased and the flat was filled with a terrible hush, a hush beyond silence; it was as if the flat had become a vacuum. *Like an empty cathedral,* the priest thought. Goose bumps broke out all over his body as the dim figures froze and seemed to turn and watch him.

He fell to his knees, crossing himself, and caught sight of Law about ten feet away from him, lying in a doorway, half in the bedroom, half in the lounge.

'Dominus vobiscum ...' he intoned as Bahashasda brushed past him. 'In Nomine Patris, et Filii ...'

'God help us,' Bahashasda gasped, gripping the priest's shoulder as if to draw strength from it. 'It's here in all its incarnations.'

'Et Spiritus Sancti,' Quigley said, unzipping his pocket with trembling fingers and taking out the Bible and the cross. He held them out in front of him, threw his head back and began to pray.

'Our Father,

'Who art in Heaven ...'

Beyond the shapes in the lounge (*through them*, he realised, startled, *he could see through them*) he spotted two quite distinct figures in the bedroom, staring at him with a hideous malevolence.

The first was a massive, naked, shaven-headed man with a snake tattooed on his forearm and an ear-ring with a red stone. Beside him squatted a huge woman, six fleshy arms folded over immense, sagging breasts and a mountainous belly. Great putrid sores covered her face and her hair hung in filthy ringlets from beneath a red skullcap containing a flap which fell over her nose.

Bahashasda dropped his attache case and flicked it open. Throwing off his coat, he snatched out a small jar and an ancient Bible, its pages and brown cover brittle with age. Scattering salt from the jar into the four corners of the room, he began to speak, his voice firm, unwavering.

'In the name of Our Father in Heaven and of Jesus who gave His life that we might be saved and of the Holy Spirit, I command and exhort that you depart from this place.'

Some of the shapes dissolved immediately and the others began to move rapidly towards Law, as if being shepherded by an unseen hand. They reached the reclining figure and darted into him one after the other, like early morning mist being sucked into a hollow.

Quigley heard distant groans and grunts, gasps of fear and shrieks now. He knew they were coming from the entities in front of him yet it was as if he was in the countryside and the sounds were being carried to him on the wind from a valley miles away.

Bahashasda's voice became louder, more insistent.

'Depart from this place evil, foul, loathsome thing. Depart from the earth forever. Depart from this home, this Christian city, this Christian land.'

The figure of the woman in the skullcap grew darker, as if a shadow had fallen over her then abruptly she seemed to shrink into herself and vanish.

'Depart evil thing, go back to that place from whence you came. I command and exhort you to depart in the name of all that is holy, in the name of Jesus and of the Heavenly Father and of the Holy Spirit.'

The huge man began to stride forward, the immense folds of flesh that covered his body shaking as he moved.

Bahashasda glanced at Quigley. 'Dacahri the Fifth,' he said. 'King of Didrana.' Then he raised his voice again. 'Return to that vile place from whence you came. I order it.'

The man stepped over Law, his shaven head brushing the top of the doorway, his face twisted with hate and fury.

'I order it in the name of the Blessed Mary, Peter and Paul, in the name of Him who shed his blood that we might have everlasting life.'

Suddenly the man stopped dead. It was as if he was tethered and he had come as far as he could. The anger in his face was joined by a mixture of confusion and naked terror. The flesh on his body began to shake violently then he seemed to shoot backwards as if jerked by an immensely powerful force. His immense bulk diminished like a punctured balloon and he flashed into Law.

Only the head remained in view, alongside Law's, thrashing about like that of a man bound and in pain. The eyes stared at Quigley, defying him.

'Is it almost over?' Quigley breathed, looking over at Bahashasda, no longer caring that the professor might see the depth of his fear.

'Over?' Bahashasda said, striding forward. 'We've hardly begun.'

'I ... I'm sorry.'

The professor stopped about five feet short of Law and made the sign of the cross in the air.

'In the name of Him who died for our sins, in the name of Him who rose from the dead and walks among us still, I command you to depart. Go.'

The head alongside Law's began to gyrate slowly.

Quigley jumped to his feet and hurried after Bahashasda, taking out his bottle of holy water.

'We fear you not,' Bahashasda said, 'and in the name of our Lord we demand you leave. Now.'

The priest dipped his finger into the holy water, crossed himself then began to scatter it about the room and across Law's body.

'In the name of Him who loathes and despises you, I say go,' Bahashasda roared.

From Law's chest, the head of what looked like a handsome young man appeared, lips drawn back from perfect teeth in a silent cry of anguish, bloodshot eyes staring at Bahashasda. It rose in jerky stages, a muscular chest appearing then a hollow stomach and finally the hind quarters of a tiger. As the paws drifted clear of Law's chest, the figure shivered violently then was gone as if it had been an image on a television set that had been switched off.

'Go,' Bahashasda bawled and a thing that looked to Quigley like a huge black bird, its feathers ruffled as if it was trapped in a hurricane, was flung across the room and seemed to disintegrate in the far corner.

'Go,' Bahashasda yelled again.

Suddenly Law's stomach began to jump as if some powerful fist inside him was punching against his skin, trying to force a way out.

His shirt buttons sprang loose and the priest saw the naked, distended flesh erupting three inches, four inches, six inches into the air.

'Poor man,' he groaned, 'my God, poor man.'

Law's body began to convulse and the skin of his face twitched savagely in a hundred places.

Then his eyes snapped open. Quigley had never seen eyes which possessed such utter, indescribable evil.

Its pale blue eyes never left Natalie as it descended from Law's third-floor window.

On the pavement it hovered in the darkest place, its grey

folds hidden in the shadows beside the front entrance as two women walked past and a line of cars trundled through the night.

When the sound of traffic died away, it began to drift forward, heading for the spot where Natalie sat in the Jaguar.

30

Monstrosities in the vague forms of men and women and birds, animals and serpents and indescribably horrible creatures which Quigley thought could not be of the earth continued to shoot out of Law in a flow that seemed endless as Bahashasda intoned the words of exorcism. They disappeared almost instantly, dissolving into the walls like water into a dry sponge or simply exploding silently, fragmenting into pieces so small they were invisible.

Law's eyes remained fixed on the ceiling, staring there as if in a trance, and Quigley found that when he looked at them he felt dizzy. Could these really be *Law's* eyes, he wondered – these heavily-bloodshot oval balls, the brown pupils two minute pinpricks.

The tortured face of the shaven-headed man ducked forward and vanished into Law's shoulder. Then the naked figure of a woman shot out of Law with such force that her long black hair flowed out behind her (it seemed to Quigley that it was almost being torn out by the roots) and her arms were forced violently back in a position of crucifixion. She whipped soundlessly up and away from Law and disappeared through the ceiling as if the wood and plaster were merely an illusion.

As Quigley lowered his gaze to Law again a movement away to his left caught his eye. He spun around and saw a man and a woman cowering near the kitchen door, their faces twisted with anguish and terror, their clothes ragged. As he peered at them he thought they looked like two lost strangers who had just wandered into the wrong room. Then he realised the man looked familiar and after a moment he knew who it was. It was Leo Dempsey. Quigley knew the face from the picture which had been in the newspaper. The woman with him had fuzzy blonde hair. His wife?

The woman reached a hand out towards Quigley, as if begging him to help, and he staggered towards them, aware that his knees were trembling violently.

'Go,' he said, making the sign of the cross in the air above their heads. 'Be at peace. In the name of the Father and the Son and the Holy Spirit, you are free. All your bonds on this earth are cut. Go.'

He peered into the woman's face, into eyes filled with horror.

'Go,' he yelled.

Suddenly it was, as if a great burden had been removed from her, a terrible pain anaesthetised. Her face became tranquil and she smiled up at him as she folded her arms around the man by her side.

As their images began to fade, Quigley swung around and saw that Law's head was turned towards him, the brown pinprick pupils glowing, the teeth bared in a kind of animal fury.

As Law began to sit up, Quigley felt as if acid was trickling down his spine. His knees were trembling so violently now he feared he would fall over.

'Stay away from him,' Bahashasda said, stepping back quickly from Law.

Then it was as if the earth stood still.

The lights in the flat dimmed almost to nothing. There was a grating *keeeerackbang* as the front windows of the flat exploded simultaneously. The roar of a strong wind filled the room (it seemed to be coming from Law, as if he was the centre of a storm, Quigley thought as he was forced back).

The wind dragged at his clothes and hair, whipped into

his eyes, and he saw Law leap to his feet, rush across the room and jerk open the front door with such ferocity that one of the hinges was ripped off.

'After him,' Bahashasda shouted as Law dashed out of sight and Quigley fought against the wind and forced his way through the door.

Law was disappearing down the stairway by the time they started along the corridor.

'We can't let him get away now,' Bahashasda said as they reached the stairs. A floor below them they could see Law's hand flying down the banisters.

'I was close,' Bahashasda puffed, 'I was so close to the core spirit.'

Quigley was covering the stairs three at a time now, leaving Bahashasda behind.

'How do we stop him?' he yelled over his shoulder.

'I don't know … but somehow … we've got to.'

Leaving the first floor, Quigley glanced downwards again and saw Law reach the foyer and sprint down a dark corridor the priest assumed led to the back door.

'I'll go after him, you get the car,' he bawled, jumping over the last five stairs into the foyer.

'Yes …' Bahashasda gasped. 'Yes … all right …'

Natalie was hunched forward in the Jaguar's back seat, her face buried in her hands, when the window of Law's flat exploded. She jerked her head up and saw the street lamps flicker, one of them shattering, sprinkling shards of glass over the pavement.

But why was everything around her so grey and indistinct?

She couldn't clearly make out Lissils Mansions or the cars parked in front or …

It was as if a mist had enveloped the car.

A thick grey mist, its folds spreading, becoming denser.

Then she realised the mist was coming into the car, bleeding in at the top of the driver's door.

It was as she swung her head back towards Lissils

Mansions that she saw the two pale blue eyes watching her from the other side of the window, filled with a wicked amusement.

She covered her face and a scream shrieked out of her larynx.

31

'Go,' Bahashasda yelled. 'In the name of our Lord ... I say go ... base, vile, corrupt thing ... *Go.*'

He had seen the grey shape over the Jaguar from the foyer and rushed, panting, to the car to begin the rites of exorcism. Now, holding his Bible out in front of him, he unleashed his anger and contempt. The grey mist began to contract.

He saw the pale blue eyes begin to gyrate then dart about in the grey mass and shoot up towards him.

He met them with an unwavering gaze, seeing fear in them now.

'Depart from this place and return to the place from whence you came.'

The mist was growing thinner. Bahashasda could see Natalie's face beyond it now, white and fearful. The pale blue eyes drew back quickly as he thrust the Bible up to them and stepped forward.

'I say *GO, GO NOW.*'

His fingers brushed the mist and it felt cold, like a sudden draught wafting into a warm room.

He opened his mouth to speak again but no more words were necessary. The grey folds quivered, contracted to the size of a child's coat and shot away into the night like a rag caught in a strong wind.

Natalie grabbed his arm as he slid into his seat.

'Wh-what was it? Wh-where's Jack? Where's Father Quigley? I ...'

Suddenly a car careered into view from the rear of Lissils Mansions, white smoke belching from the tyres as the car skittered towards the car-park exit, almost out of control.

'It's Jack,' she shouted, snatching at Bahashasda's jacket. 'That's Jack's car.'

Then she saw the priest, sprinting from the back of the building, snatching at Law's door. And missing.

The small red Citroen slewed into the street, bucked, then shot away.

She heard the priest shouting and saw him gesticulating frantically.

'Come on. Hurry up. Come on.'

The Jaguar leapt forward, swung around in a tight circle and screeched to a halt as the priest jumped into the front seat.

'Go. I'm in,' he shouted and Natalie was thrown backwards as the Jaguar jumped into the night.

Roaring up to a road junction, Law flicked on his indicator for a right-hand turn then took a sharp left at the last moment, swinging the car into a four-wheel drift. He wrestled with the steering wheel, brought the car under control and accelerated hard, switching off his lights. He turned left into a narrow side street, then right, then left again, then turned his lights back on, the speedometer wavering around seventy.

He stood on the brakes at the next corner and slipped the Citroen into third, its engine screaming as he lifted his foot off the clutch pedal too quickly.

Too fast, a dull voice in his brain said as he stabbed at the brake again.

The car shot across the road, hit the kerb, bounced onto the pavement and shouldered into a lamp standard. He reversed over the kerb and sent the car bounding away up the street as a man moving out of the darkness shouted after him.

The crash seemed to clear his mind and for about ten seconds his brain filled with questions.

What was he doing? Why was he driving so fast? Where was he going? Why didn't he stop and go back to the scene of the accident?

He struggled for some answers, distantly aware now that his body felt numb. It didn't feel like his own body at all. He looked down at the hands on the steering wheel.

They were his hands.

He glanced at his clothes.

They were his clothes.

He saw that his shirt was open at the waist, his stomach exposed, and felt a cold draught on his flesh.

A new pilot at the controls, a dreamy voice in his head said.

What did that mean?

He was not ... not in control ... of himself.

But he was ... HIM ... Jack Law... ...

They were his hands, his clothes ...

He looked in the rear-vision mirror and two tiny pinpricks of brown looked back at him.

Not his eyes.

Not ...

Then blackness.

'He must know he can't outrun a Jaguar,' Quigley said, as Bahashasda sent the XJ6 smoothly into a bend in the street a hundred yards behind Law's car.

Bahashasda shook his head. 'It knows its only chance of survival is to escape now. The alternative is destruction. It'll push Law to the limit.'

Natalie knew she was in the docklands. She caught glimpses of the Thames, lights glittering on a great moving shape, and saw huge derelict warehouses, the empty windows giving them the impression of blindness. The Jaguar hurtled along narrow streets which glistened after a brief rainshower, between tall, decaying walls topped by barbed wire.

'It's amazing he's only lost control of his car once,' Quigley said, 'considering the speed he's doing.'

'I hope he's not hurt,' Natalie said.

'Even if he breaks a leg or an arm it'll drive him on,' Bahashasda said coldly, lightly caressing the brake pedal as he saw Law's brake lights flick on.

'What are we going to do?' Quigley said.

'Do?' Bahashasda threw a glance at the priest.

'Yes. He isn't going to stop just because we're tailing him.'

Bahashasda sighed. 'The way he's driving I'd been hoping he'd lose control of his car again … but you're right. I'm going to have to try to get my nose in front of him and force him off the road.'

Natalie felt herself nudged backwards by the inertia of the Jaguar's acceleration as Bahashasda stabbed his right foot to the floor.

The Jaguar moved steadily to within fifty yards of Law. Then forty. Then twenty.

'Thank heavens there are no other cars around,' Quigley said as Bahashasda eased the Jaguar onto the right-hand side of the road and sent it kicking forward.

Law accelerated but gradually the Jaguar sliced away the yards.

They reached a bend in the road and Law tried to cut down the Jaguar's space by swinging the Citroen over the white line but Bahashasda manoeuvred his car perfectly with only inches to spare.

'Here we go,' he said, his face taut, as they came out of the corner. He stepped on the accelerator, sent the Jaguar diving forward and edged left.

Natalie caught a glimpse of Law, a dim figure hunched over the steering wheel (was this really her Jack?) as the Jaguar swung to cut the Citroen off.

Then Quigley bawled 'Look out' and she jerked her head around and saw a blaze of headlights straight ahead. They blinded her and she ducked her head away from them.

A car.

Heading straight for them.

Its horn blaring.

Natalie's heart thumped violently in her chest as the professor braked and swept back in behind the Citroen with such savagery that she was thrown onto her side.

She dragged herself back into a sitting position and saw the Citroen bounding away through the night.

'A police car,' she heard Quigley shout.

'What?' Bahashasda said.

'A police car. It was a police car.'

The priest swung around in his seat and Natalie turned and followed his gaze.

Three hundred yards behind she saw a blue light begin to flash.

'We can't stop,' Bahashasda said, 'we'll lose him.'

'Keep going,' a woman's voice screamed and Natalie realised a moment later it had been her.

They had started to gain on the Citroen again when its brake lights winked three times and it disappeared. Bahashasda slowed, assuming Law had turned a corner, but when he reached the point where the Citroen had vanished he saw a huge gate, his headlights picking out a narrow track beyond that ran through a vast wasteland of tall weeds down to the Thames. There was no sign of the Citroen.

Natalie's ears picked up the *eee-aaw eee-aaw* of the police siren as Bahashasda sent the Jaguar bounding along the track.

We're never going to save Jack, she thought suddenly and wondered if she had said the words aloud. *Never. That thing is going to kill him. It is. It is.*

'Watch out,' Quigley yelled as the Thames loomed up in front of them, the Jaguar's headlamps sending a great pillar of light out over the dark back of the river.

Bahashasda jerked the Jaguar left and sent it hurtling through the blackness. Natalie saw they were on a bumpy, rutted wharf.

'He's turned off his lights again,' Bahashasda said, his eyes searching the gloom.

'He can't have,' Quigley said, incredulous. 'No-one could drive here without lights. We must have missed him.'

An instant later, Natalie heard the hideous sound of a car crashing, the thump of impact almost simultaneous with the shriek of violently twisting metal and the rapid tinkling patter of shattered glass.

'There he is,' Quigley said as the Jaguar's headlights picked out the mangled wreckage of the Citroen, folded around the corner of a warehouse.

Natalie gripped the back of the seat as Bahashasda braked the Jaguar to a halt.

'Get the torch,' Natalie heard him yell at Quigley, 'get it … out of the glovebox.'

The Citroen's door fell open and she saw a dim figure emerge and lurch away into the darkness.

Bahashasda jerked his door open, jumped out and turned to Natalie, the flashing blue lights and headlamps of the approaching police car giving his bony face a strange glow. Natalie thought it looked like an ancient skull with almost transparent coloured paper pulled tightly over it.

'Keep the police here,' he said. 'Tell them anything, just keep them here. Tell them we'll explain everything later. Make up any story you like.'

Then he was gone and she saw the huge beam of a powerful torch slicing through the darkness as Quigley ran after him.

She climbed unsteadily out of the car.

Law was vaguely aware he was running, aware of an ache in his chest and a terrible pain in his stomach (it felt like there was blood there, trickling about in his intestines … and something else), aware that a light drizzle had started to fall, dampening his hair, dripping water across his face. He sensed there was something moving about under the skin of his face, like slimy tentacles sliding around the bones and prodding at the back of his eyes.

But he couldn't make sense of anything in this brief

intermission between fantasy and blackness.

Rats scuttled away as he limped into an ancient roofless warehouse.

Limped.

Yes, limped.

He was dragging his right leg.

There was a sharp pain just below the knee and he could feel blood running down into his sock.

How?

The car. He had crashed the car.

He heard men's voices now, behind him, and felt a surge of intense panic.

Panic? Why panic?

Who ...

He kicked through stunted weeds that butted up through the ageing cement floor.

Why was he running? Why was he so afraid?

What ...

The men were getting closer.

Going to destroy him.

Kill him.

End his existence.

He began to pant in terror.

He would be consigned into blackness. Endless nothingness.

There would be no more ...

And a name sprang into his mind.

Not his name. Not any name he had ever heard before. Not a name that belonged on the earth.

It sounded like *Dac-ah-ra-keesh-nah-ram.*

Dacahri. A name like Dacahri.

The men were drawing nearer now, their footfalls echoing off the dank, cold walls of the warehouse, and he ducked into a corridor and ran along it through pools of pallid moonlight.

He found a metal stairway and fled down it. There was a door at the bottom. Padlocked.

Men's voices. Muffled. Not far behind him now.

He touched the wet, mouldy wood of the door. It was rotten, the padlock rusty.

He heaved at the door with his shoulder and it caved in with a damp groan.

Inside, he found a large empty room, the walls covered in green slime, the floor coated in thick dark mud.

He lifted the door back into place and headed for the far corner.

Maybe here in the darkness, he would be safe.

Quigley stopped dead and let the torch's beam play down the metal stairway.

'There,' he said and Bahashasda saw footprints in the accumulated mud and filth on the steps.

'Yes,' the professor breathed.

They descended quietly and found the door.

Quigley reached out and pushed it and it fell in with a muddy splotch.

32

Natalie was aware she had been babbling, not making much sense.

How could she make the policemen understand what was happening when she didn't really understand herself?

The first policeman – a tall thin man with a pale face whose name was Cheevers – had tried to go after Bahashasda and Quigley but she had grabbed the arm of his shirt and held on, shouting at him.

She had tried to explain what was going on without going into the more abnormal circumstances that would undoubtedly have made them think she was some kind of lunatic.

The driver of the red car had been Jack Law, the journalist, she told him. Surely he had heard of Jack Law? Law was a patient (the word had jumped into her mind – it seemed to be the best word she could think of to fit the situation) of the two men had gone after him. They were a Professor Bahashasda and a priest called Father Quigley. Mr Law had had a kind of a breakdown. It was important nobody interfered. The professor and the priest would bring Law back in a minute and the professor would explain everything.

'You've got to stay out of it,' she was saying now, gazing earnestly into Cheevers' eyes, but he was tugging at her fingers, lifting them away from his shirt.

She swung her head around and stared wild-eyed at the second policeman. Constable Allthorp was not as tall as

Cheevers. He was broad-shouldered and square-jawed and had a small mole on his left cheek.

'You must see I'm making sense,' she panted.

Why was she out of breath? Why?

(*Because I'm so scared, that's why*, a shrill voice in her head said.)

'You've got to understand that you can't go after them. You might do something that'll hurt Jack. I'm right ... you see that, don't you? It makes sense.'

(*Sense. You're not making sense. You're coming over as an incoherent hysteric*).

Cheevers had removed her hands from his shirt now and was holding them firmly down in front of her.

'Take her to the car,' he told Allthorp. 'Try to calm her down and find out what's going on. I'll try to get hold of the madman in the Jaguar who almost killed us.'

'Noooooo,' she screamed as Allthorp grabbed her shoulders and Cheevers jogged away through the Jaguar's headlight beams.

Law was squatting in the corner of the room as Bahashasda and Quigley entered. The tiny brown pupils seemed to glow like embers touched by a light wind as Quigley swung the broad torch-beam towards him. Law tried to get up but his legs shook violently and he fell onto his side.

Bahashasda stepped into the middle of the room and faced Law, his hands held out, palms upwards.

He began to speak in a low, resonant voice. 'In the name of Our Lord who cast out evil spirits which cried with loud voices, I come to tell you to go, depart, return to that place from whence you came.'

Law began to thrash about in the black mud that covered the floor, rolling over and over, his body whipping about like a snake in its death throes.

Quigley placed the torch on a grimy, head-high ledge, positioning it so that the beam would shine directly on Law, then knelt down and began to pray, pressing the golden cross against his forehead.

'Hail Mary, full of grace …'

Law was on his back now, quivering from head to foot. His body began to arch, rising higher and higher until the centre of his back was three feet from the ground and his entire weight rested on the back of his head and his heels.

Bahashasda's voice grew louder. 'In the name of Him who cast Gadarene devils into a herd of swine …'

Law began to make loud choking noises. His throat bulged, just above the loosened knot of his tie, then flattened, then bulged again. A tiny black shape, like the head of a snake glimpsed in the darkness, slipped out of his throat and darted about. Quigley saw the pink flesh inside its mouth and rows of yellow pointed teeth. The head shot up and the teeth snapped at Law's face, opening a long gash on his chin which spattered blood over his face and shirt.

The shape grew larger, detached itself from Law, then flopped onto his chest and fell to the floor.

A salamander, Quigley thought. *It looks like a tiny black salamander*.

Bahashasda's voice was a roar now. 'In the name of the Blessed Mary, I demand that you go.'

The black shape began to disintegrate, each tiny chunk melting slowly into the slimy mud on the floor.

'We're near,' Quigley rasped, failing to keep a tremor out of his voice. 'I can feel it. We're near to the core spirit.'

Bahashasda nodded but continued to speak, his voice unfaltering.

It was as Constable Allthorp reached for the back door of the police car that Natalie swung round and clawed her fingernails across his face.

He stumbled backwards, more out of surprise than pain or fear, and she started to run after the other policeman.

She couldn't let Cheevers interrupt whatever it was Bahashasda and Quigley were doing to help Jack.

The priest and the professor might represent Jack's last chance.

Tell the police anything but keep them away. Wasn't that what Bahashasda had said?

In the outer reaches of the Jaguar's headlight beams she saw Cheevers turn into a warehouse.

If Cheevers interfered, Jack might be seriously hurt.

He might DIE.

As she rushed into the warehouse she slipped and fell, one knee slamming painfully into hard, wet concrete, the other sliding in cloying mud filled with soaking, stunted weeds. But she was up in an instant, running again, aware that Allthorp was close behind her.

Don't let him catch me.

Don't let him catch me.

Don't …

The words were like a prayer, a desperate plea for intercession.

Her high heels made sharp clip-clopping sounds as she dashed across the floor of the warehouse, the sounds coming back to her, perfectly reproduced, off the dark walls.

Don't let him catch me.

Jack's last chance might be slipping away.

And it was her fault.

She should have stayed calm.

Should have kept the policemen away.

Should have thought of a better story.

She saw Cheevers' dim outline and glint of yellow moonlight on a chequered cap as he swung to his right and disappeared along a corridor.

'Come back,' she shouted hoarsely. 'Come back.'

Cheevers saw the pool of light outside the door far below him, rushed down the metal stairway and stepped into the room. He hesitated for an instant, his eyes taking in the scene – one man, covered in mud, was lying quite still in the far corner, two others were facing him from the centre of the room, one kneeling in silence, the other speaking aloud.

Like he was delivering a speech.

No. More like a sermon. Or some religious rite.

Bahashasda's voice was low and even now, his eyes heavy-lidded with concentration. 'We who are of the earth, made by our Lord in his image …'

What the hell was going on?

Were they witchcraft freaks or what?

Cheevers paused as if mesmerised by the scene then, annoyed at his hesitation, he marched into the centre of the room. He brushed Bahashasda's shoulder with his hand and said: 'All right, what's going on here? Are you the driver of the Jaguar?'

His brow furrowed as Bahashasda ignored him and continued to speak the words of exorcism.

Quigley stood up quickly.

'I'm a priest,' he said barely above a whisper. 'Please don't interfere.'

'You don't look like a priest. You're all going to have to come with me.'

'*Please*,' Quigley said. 'You don't understand …'

'What's going on … Never mind, you'll get a chance to tell your story later.'

Cheevers half-turned towards Law.

'Is that man injured?'

Instantly Law sat up, sharply, as if he was hinged at the waist. His head hung forward as if it was too heavy for his neck muscles, the tiny brown pupils fixing on Cheevers from the very top of the eye sockets, looking up past heavy eyebrows, through a lock of hair which had fallen forward over his forehead. The skin of his face twisted like putty being kneaded by an invisible hand and a lopsided grin formed.

'I know you.'

The voice came from Law but it was not Law's voice, not like any normal human voice. The harsh, rasping words sounded as if they were being spoken by a man with a serious throat ailment who was talking into a malfunctioning microphone positioned at the far end of a long, rusted iron pipe.

Cheevers saw that the movement of Law's lips was not synchronised with the sounds coming from his mouth.

Bahashasda began to trip over his words. 'W-we beseech, oh Lord, y-your … sup-support … to rid this place of th-this evil spirit …'

'Policeman,' the Law-voice rasped. 'I said … I know you.'

Cheevers stared at Law, his scalp prickling under his hat.

'Do you think I don't know you, policeman?' the voice said and the words were followed by a laugh, a hideous, scraping sound devoid of mirth.

'I know all about you,' the voice said. There was a pause then it added venomously: 'You have a crippled child … a *CRIPPLE.*'

Natalie reached the door and froze, staring into the room, terror stampeding through her veins. Allthorp came up behind her, grabbed her arms, started to say something, then he too stood quite still, his eyes gazing past Natalie, fixed on Law.

'What …' he muttered.

'Please … be quiet,' she whispered and they remained where they were like two statues placed together in a museum storeroom.

Cheevers took a step back, a haunted, trapped look in his yes.

'And you're a thief,' the voice said.

'What … I've never …'

'*A THIEF* … Remember the shop which was broken into. The one where the thieves didn't get all the money. They missed some, didn't they? And you found it and put it in your pocket. You thought nobody knew. But *I* know.'

Another laugh escaped from Law's lips, a hoarse chuckle, the laugh of a psychopath standing over a corpse.

'That's not true,' Cheevers said, looking around wildly.

But it was.

It was.

How …

'Who are you?' Cheevers yelled.

Bahashasda tried to continue the words of exorcism but they were drowned by the voice from Law now.

'Remember when your *cripple* was ill, policeman ... when she was screaming and crying for her daddy and your wife had to get her to hospital. Remember where you were, what you were doing?'

'Stoppit, Shutup.'

'You were with that woman. The fat one whose husband is a seaman ... the one who likes to be tied up and ...'

'Shutup.'

How? How could anyone know?

Who was this man?

It was if he was dreaming, having his guilt thrown into his face in a nightmare.

'You tied her to the bed and ...'

'Shutup. She wanted it. She ...'

Cheevers took an angry step forward.

What happened next was over so quickly Quigley wasn't sure what he had seen.

He thought he saw a tiny dim form shoot out of Law and punch into the policeman's chest. Cheevers screamed, his fingers clawing at his shirt, and began to slide to the floor. Quigley felt his gorge rise as he watched the policeman – it was as if all the bones in his body had been atomised, leaving only flesh and muscle and blood. In a moment all that was left of Cheevers was a small pile made up of crumpled, blood-soaked policeman's uniform, lumps of flesh and a clump of hair. Tiny rivulets of blood began to trickle across the muddy floor.

Law's head turned slowly, mechanically, and the eyes found Quigley.

'And you, priest ... I know you too.'

Quigley fell to his knees, kissed the cross in his hand and began to talk quickly, trying not to listen to the words which flowed from Law's mouth.

'Father Quigley, helper of the poor, man of compassion,'

the voice said contemptuously.

'Oh Lord,' Quigley mumbled, 'let me draw strength from the Holy Spirit in this my moment of need, show me your divine compassion and ...'

'I know about your vanity. *Quigley's so handsome* – isn't that what the women in your congregation say? *What a waste as a priest.* And you like that, don't you? Always combing your hair just so. *Vanity.* And what about your well known self-sacrifice, your love of the poor. Is it self-sacrifice? Love? Or do you just want people to tell you what a good job you're doing. Don't you just want the glory. You ... *hypocrite.* You even despise some of the people who come to you for help. You sit in judgment on them.'

No. It wasn't true. He sat in judgment on no-one. He just did his best for suffering humanity.

'I know the things you think about women when you're alone.'

No-one knew that. Only his confessor.

He was a man after all. Imperfect, like all men. A sinner, yes, but forgiven. And he suffered for ...

'Remember Mrs Linklater.' The voice spat out the words. 'You couldn't get her out of your mind ...'

Thoughts. Just the merest fragments of thoughts he had had, quickly shut out. He was a sinner, yes, but again and again he tried to be perfect. This ... this thing was twisting everything.

'Stop it. Don't say any more,' Quigley yelled and felt Bahashasda's hand on his shoulder.

He bowed his head.

'Our Father,

'Who art in Heaven ...'

Natalie raised her head and looked into Allthorp's eyes, searching for answers but seeing only confusion as deep as her own. He put his arms around her shoulders and held her, trying to comfort her.

The voice changed pitch, grew softer, mocking Quigley. 'You were sorry when Mrs Linklater moved away, weren't you? You were ...'

'Be silent,' Bahashasda roared suddenly. 'I command it in the name of the Father and the Son and the Holy Spirit. You, who are not of this earth ...'

Law's head wobbled like that of a drunken man and swung to face the professor.

'And you, professor ... for you a question. What is the greatest sin of all?'

'Loathsome, vile, abhorrent creature, enemy of our Lord ...'

'To deny God,' the voice rasped. 'And you have.'

'Thing of darkness, beast from the slime ...'

'Remember when your youngest daughter died – she died in hideous pain, didn't she? Remember you asked – where is my God now?'

A sob slipped from Bahashasda's lips and his words began to come between tiny gasps. Quigley saw two large tears run down his dark cheeks.

'Yes,' the voice screeched. 'She died in terrible agony and you asked why your God didn't help. You cursed him, didn't you?'

Bahashasda seemed to shrink into himself, become visibly smaller.

'And you've had other doubts about your God. You only pretend total belief, you ...'

Everyone has whisperings of doubt, Bahashasda told himself, his words faltering. *Brief moments when something mutters in your ear that maybe, just maybe, there is nothing. But ...*

Suddenly Bahashasda seemed to stiffen and stand erect again.

His eyes stared into the tiny brown pinpricks.

'In the name of Him who shed His blood for us,' he bawled at the top of his voice, 'I command and exhort that you return from whence you came, you are consigned to the piiiiiiit.'

Instantly Law whipped backwards into a lying position, his eyes closed, his body entirely rigid. Then all the muscles relaxed and he seemed to be asleep.

Quigley heard a sharp gasp and saw Bahashasda clutching at his chest, his body sagging.

'My heart,' the professor said. 'It's my heart.'

Allthorp snatched his arms away from Natalie, dashed into the room and caught Bahashasda as he fell, lowering him gently to the floor.

'I don't know what's going on here, but this man needs an ambulance,' he said, throwing a glance at Quigley, deliberately not looking at the pile of flesh mingled with policeman's uniform away to his right. The tiny rivulets of blood were still now, beginning to harden into dark-red ridges.

Before Quigley realised what was happening, Allthorp had stood up, hurried over to Law, knelt down and started to search for a pulse.

The priest flung himself at the policeman, grabbed the collar of his shirt, dragged him away from Law and threw him across the room with such strength that Allthorp thudded into the far corner and fell to his knees.

'Never touch a man possessed,' he said. 'Never.'

Natalie was kneeling in the mud now, cradling Bahashasda's head. His eyelids flickered then closed.

'Quigley,' he muttered. 'Quigley. You have to be stronger than it is. You must have more faith than it has.'

Quigley realised he was trembling.

Alone. He couldn't do it alone.

'Do it,' Bahashasda groaned. 'We've reached the core spirit. It's weakening. It's on the run. Do it.'

Quigley held the cross up above his head.

'Creature of another place, beast of evil, loathsome, vile thing … I call on you to go in the name of …'

As he continued to speak, the buttons on Law's shirt began to pop free one by one, spinning away across the room.

'The Father and the Son and the Holy Spirit …'

Law's chest and stomach were exposed now, the flesh twitching.

'I command you to come out of this Christian man …'

A goo, like glittering, hot black tar, began to ooze out of Law's skin, forming into a pool on his belly, dribbling down his sides.

'I exhort and command you to depart, I demand that you …'

The tarry substance seemed to lift off Law and hover in mid-air above his chest. Then it began to grow until it was the size of a man's overcoat.

Like a shapeless piece of sequined black material, Quigley thought.

Then the glitter was gone and all that was left was a blackness like a shadow, as if there was one section of the wall where the torchlight could not reach.

But it was a blackness beyond blackness, Quigley realised.

The blackness of a hole. A bottomless pit.

'Go from this place,' Quigley shouted.

Then he saw two tiny dots of red light, close together near the centre of the blackness.

Eyes?

An ice-cold hand of terror closed over his heart as if trying to rip away the last of his courage and every part of his body shivered.

I'm shaking in my shoes, he thought crazily. *Literally shaking in my shoes.*

'Go,' he yelled.

Around the glowing pinpricks of red, what looked like the outline of a face began to form.

Not a human face, Quigley realised. It was like the head of a jackal.

'Go,' he groaned.

The red pinpricks seemed to stare at Quigley and he felt his vision blurring.

Natalie looked past the blackness and saw that Law had started to turn blue.

'Jack,' she screamed. 'Jack.' Then, to Quigley: 'Hurry,

please hurry.'

Bahashasda breathed some words, swallowed, then repeated them as Natalie put her ear over his mouth.

'He says use its name,' she shrieked at Quigley a moment later.

The priest opened his mouth but found he couldn't speak.

And the black shape had started to come towards him in a series of jerky movements.

He couldn't handle it. He was going to lose. Going to die. Going to let everyone down. Let God down. Again.

Chilled sweat ran down his back.

Then a voice began to whisper in his brain, talking rapidly, hissing out the words.

Lord. Give me strength. Let the Holy Spirit enter me and give me the strength of a lion. Let ...

The jackal face was three feet from him now, then two feet, then a foot. He could see minute black pupils in the centre of the red.

Oh Jesus, let the Holy Spirit come into this receptacle, your humblest of servants ...

Without warning, his fear vanished. A strange glowing calm began in his chest and spread outwards quickly. A certainty, a confidence he had never known before shot through him.

He leaned forward until his eyes were inches from the jackal face.

'Dacahri. I know *you*. Dacahri, master of fear, prince of evil ...'

The red eyes glittered, unwavering.

Quigley thought the thing spoke but there was no sound in the room, only meaningless words in his brain. Challenging him.

He shook his head slowly and smiled.

'*Dacahri* ... I know you, but I do *not* fear you. You *cannot* win. You have lost your place here.'

The eyes quivered.

Doubt?

Was that it?

Doubt?

'Dacahri, here you are not feared ...'

More words came into his mind, words that made no sense, harsh, ugly whisperings that seemed to have travelled across galaxies.

'Dacahri, you're finished, you hold no terrors for us, your power is gone. Without fear you have no power. In the name of Him who is omnipotent, I *COMMAND* you to leave.'

The eyes quivered again.

Not doubt.

Fear.

Blind terror.

Quigley wanted to laugh.

'Go,' he yelled, spitting the word into the jackal face.

The black shape leapt backwards, stopping at the far wall, instantly contracting to half its size.

'You're loathed here, ridiculed, no-one fears you.'

It began to diminish, the edges contracting in trembling jerks.

'Depart, Dacahri, *depart.*'

Instantly, the shape shrank to a tiny black dot.

Natalie screamed and covered her ears as the room was filled with a *crack* like a thunderclap.

Quigley blinked then peered at the wall, searching for the black dot.

But it was gone.

33

Law opened his eyes and tried to smile at Natalie but the
swelling in his face and the medicine he had been given
combined to make it look more like a grimace. His face was
grey against the white sheets of the hospital bed.

'Car crash,' he managed to say, his words slurred, as if
his mouth was full of cotton wool, and Natalie gripped his
hand tighter. 'I remember ... I was in a car crash ... that's
what I'm doing here, isn't it? I can't recall very much.'

'That's right, Jack, you were in a crash,' Natalie said,
fighting back the tears as emotion swelled through her.

'I don't know what's been happening, Natalie. I feel
better now ... I'm in pain ... but I don't feel sick any more
... the nausea has gone.'

His brow furrowed.

'It's like ...'

'Don't think about it now, Jack.'

The nurse moved quietly into the room, white dress
whispering.

'I'm sorry, but Mr Law should sleep now.'

Natalie kissed Jack on the cheek.

'I love you,' she said.

He nodded slowly, a drugged nod.

'I'll be around when you wake up,' she said as she left the
room.

Quigley hurried out of the waiting room when he saw her
walking up the corridor.

'How is he?'

'They say he'll be fine. Cuts here and there, but nothing serious. Apparently he's suffering from exhaustion. How is the professor?'

'Slight heart attack. He'll be OK.'

She ducked her eyes away from the priest's then looked at him again.

'I don't know how I can ever thank you.'

He laughed, a broad grin that made his face more handsome than ever.

'You don't have to thank me.'

'If there was only some way ... something I could do ... or say. After all you and the professor have done ...'

He stroked his jaw with his right index finger in mock thoughtfulness.

'There is one thing,' he said.

'What?'

'Be happy.'

She looked into his eyes and it was as if all eternity was encapsulated in that moment, as if each was totally opened up to the other. Later she could never quite comprehend what she saw in Quigley's face.

Emotion surged through her in a prickly wave and she found she was crying, letting go completely.

He wrapped his arms around her and held her tightly and she wept for a long time.

34

Days later Law remembered the dream. In it he was in pleasant countryside, the air filled with the scent of flowers, the buzz of bees and the smell of ripening fruit. He didn't know where he was but he was aware that something terrible had happened there – perhaps a war or a natural disaster or some kind of mass disease. But something told him everything was going to be all right now; something in his brain was laughing with a healthy chuckle. Around him new grass was growing a shining green and the trees were covered in blossoms and above him fine clouds, the colour of old men's beards, danced across the sky with infinite slowness.

Epilogue

Natalie found herself humming a light-hearted, trivial pop tune and realised she was happy, realised time had done its work, begun to heal the ugly scars of the past, soothe the memories of the time when Dacahri ...

She thrust back the thoughts which threatened to avalanche into her mind. It was almost three weeks now since the exorcism and there was no point in raking up all those things again. That time, and all her yesterdays, were as dead as corpses in a graveyard, she told herself irritatedly. And tomorrows were just dreams that might or might not happen. Today was what mattered. Now. This moment.

'Just be happy and glad of it,' she murmured and began to hum the pop tune again, checking the roast she was cooking in Law's kitchen.

Three days before, Law had taken her to dinner with the Bahashasdas and Quigley, at the professor's house in Putney. Bahashasda had seemed to be recovering rapidly from his heart attack. Quigley had turned out to be quite a humorist and Jack had seemed almost back to his old self again. They had had a nice evening.

She smiled, recollecting it, then swung around when she heard a knock on the door. She strolled across the lounge and opened the door, ready to greet Law with a smile, a kiss and a joking admonishment – 'Forgot your keys did you ... and you're always saying I forget things.'

But it was not Jack. It was another man, slightly shorter,

square-jawed, with a mole on his cheek. And he looked familiar.

'Good morning,' he said. 'Is this Mr Law's flat?'

'Yes,' she said.

The man looked ill. His face was an odd shade of ashen grey and his lips were colourless.

'Is Mr Law in?'

No. I ...'

He looked closely at her, inclining his head, then said: 'Don't you remember me?'

'I'm not ... sure.'

'Allthorp.'

'I'm sorry. Yes, I remember you. The policeman. I didn't recognise you out of uniform.'

(*Liar.* You hardly recognise him because he looks so ill, because he looks ten years older than he did *that* night.)

'When do you expect Mr Law back?' Allthorp said. 'It's important that I talk to him.'

'Not for hours.'

Why had she lied? Again.

Why were alarm bells ringing in her brain?

Was it because of his appearance, the sleepy, drugged look in his bloodshot eyes?

'All right,' Allthorp nodded. 'Could you tell him I called. I must see him. I'll come back later.'

He nodded curtly and was gone, striding along the corridor towards the lift.

She returned to the kitchen, still wondering why she had lied.

Why did he want to see Law? He was out of uniform therefore it was unlikely to be official.

Less than a minute after Allthorp left, she heard a key grate in the front door and Law entered.

'Sorry I'm a bit late. I got held up on crucial business.'

She nodded doubtfully. 'A few pints at the pub.'

'Correct first time,' he said.

He threw down his briefcase, went into the kitchen and

kissed her, locking his hands behind her waist.

'Someone was just here looking for you,' she said as he drew his head back.

'Who?'

'Allthorp. You remember ... the policeman who was there ... in the warehouse. You met him the day after ...'

'Yes. What did he want?'

'I don't know. You must have passed him in the foyer.'

'I came in the back way.'

He turned away from her, strolled to the window and drew the curtains back ...

His eyes picked out Allthorp immediately, getting into a car across the street.

Picked out Allthorp and something else.

The vague outline of a second head protruded from Allthorp's right shoulder. This second head was that of a dark-skinned man, the features of the face almost hidden by huge folds of fat, the skull shaved, an ear-ring with a red stone dangling from the left earlobe.

As Law stared, the indistinct image of the second head grew clearer and it began to turn towards him, two eyes – slits in the puffy flesh – rising towards his third-floor window.

He stepped away from the window, pressing his back against the wall, horror dripping into his heart like molten metal.

'God,' he muttered.

'What is it?' Natalie said, her face suddenly taut, afraid.

He shook his head in brief, jerky motions, unable to speak.

'What's wrong?' she said.

He was breathing hard when she reached him and clasped his face in her hands.

'What is it?' she said again, insistently, her face twisted with apprehension.

'Not ... over ...' he managed to say. 'It's ... not over.' He spun around and lifted the edge of the curtain away from the wall, giving her a tiny slice of window to look through.

Allthorp was seated at the wheel of his car, the image of the shaven-headed man quite distinct now.

And there was something else. Dim shapes and dark forms that seemed to lick around Allthorp like smoky flames from a small campfire.

Natalie's head turned slowly and she looked up into Law's eyes.

'He touched you,' she said simply.

'What do you mean he touched me?'

'During the exorcism ... he touched you. Quigley threw him back but ... Quigley told me at the hospital that if a possessed person is touched during exorcism the spirit can pass through into the second person.'

'But ...'

'If one part of it slipped into Allthorp ...'

'Yes ... go on ...'

His eyes demanded an answer but were afraid what it might be.

'If ...' She hesitated then continued. 'If one part of Dacahri managed to find a body to inhabit then ...'

'Then it's all there, is that what you're saying?'

He swung his head back to the slice of window and saw the shaven-headed man staring directly at him, the head quite still, upturned, the fat face twisted into what looked like a grin.

As he spun away, dropping the curtain back into place, he saw Allthorp starting to get out of the car.

'Get your coat,' he rasped and when Natalie didn't move he shouted: 'Quickly. *Now*. We've got to get out of here.'

As she dived her hands into the arms of her coat, he dragged it roughly onto her shoulders.

They paused for an instant outside the front door, their eyes riveted on the blinking lift lights at the other end of the corridor.

Ground floor.

Second.

'Down the back stairs,' Law said hoarsely. 'Run.'

He grabbed her arm and propelled her along the corridor and down the stairs to a lane at the rear of the building.

'You go that way,' he panted, pointing to his right. 'Get to Quigley. Tell him I'll call him as soon as I can.'

'But ...'

He grabbed her shoulders, drawing her face close up to his. 'You're not safe with me.' His eyes were sharp, angry and afraid at the same time. 'Can't you see? It's *me* it wants. Now go.'

He pushed her away from him and sprinted along the lane, heading towards the front of the building.

From somewhere high above him he could feel cold, malevolent eyes, watching him, boring into his back.

HEYWOOD BOOKS

TODAY'S PAPERBACKS
– AT YESTERDAY'S PRICES!

Heywood Books is a new list of paperback books which will be published every month at unbelievably low prices. It will range from up-to-date contemporary women's novels to exciting romantic thrillers and the best in historical romance, from classic crime to nerve-tingling horror and big adventure thrillers, presenting a superb list of highly readable and top value popular fiction.

Look for this month's new titles:

HAMMERSTRIKE	*Walter Winward*	£1.75
GOD OF A THOUSAND FACES	*Michael Falconer Anderson*	£1.50
MUCKLE ANNIE	*Jan Webster*	£1.75
THE WINDMILL YEARS	*Vicky Martin*	£1.75
QUICKSILVER LADY	*Barbara Whitehead*	£1.50
THE WINNOWING WINDS	*Ann Marlowe*	£1.50

HAMMERSTRIKE
The secret plan for a mass breakout of German POWs

A great war thriller from
Walter Winward

In Skiddaw POW camp, imprisoned Luftwaffe officers
plan their escape. Back across the Channel, the war is
going badly for Germany. In a desperate bid to tip the
scales, Goering has masterminded Hammerstrike, a
daring plan for the mass escape of German POWs in
Britain. But, unexpectedly, the key man in the plot, a
senior Luftwaffe officer, is shot down and interned in
Britain.
To save the plan, an ex-SS officer must do the impossible: before the British can discover their prisoner's
true identity – and the secret plan called Hammerstrike –
he must penetrate British defences and spirit the general
out of Skiddaw or, failing that, make sure the secret dies
with him.

MUCKLE ANNIE
A vivid saga of bitter poverty and hardship – and the
triumph of undying love

Jan Webster

In spite of her family's wealthy past, Annie McIlvanney
has only known deepest poverty. When she is insulted
and cast out of work, she at first loses hope, but is saved
from the depths of despair by her love for Hector, the
laird's son.
Annie follows her Highland love to Canada, enduring
the discomforts of a bride ship. On the dreadful journey
she hand-rears a baby whose father begs her to marry
him. But Annie's heart belongs to Hector and she is
determined to find him, even if it means braving the
dangerous Indians, bitter weather and the grinding
hardship of the goldfields.

QUICKSILVER LADY
Sequel to THE CARETAKER WIFE
Would she make a 'good' marriage or marry for love?

Barbara Whitehead

Arabella was eager to go to London to taste the delights
of fashionable society. Disappointed in love, she hoped
that the distractions of the city would sooth her aching
heart. At the advanced age of twenty-one, she hoped to
find at last the man of her dreams.

London welcomed her with balls, masquerades,
theatres, eligible young men – and trickery. Seeking
fashion, wealth and the advantages of a great match, she
found instead that she too must follow the dictates of her
own heart.

THE WINNOWING WINDS
Death and danger lurk in the snow-clad mountains

Ann Marlowe

Deirdre Sheridan hoped that a teaching post at an expensive school in glamorous jet-setting Gstaad would help her forget a recent tragedy. But there is danger and the threat of death even in the idyllic peace of the Swiss mountains. Among her pupils is the heir to the oil-rich sheikhdom of Qaiman, an obvious target for kidnappers and assassins.

But Deirdre is captivated by Prince Haroun and his two motherless young sisters and when one near-fatal accident follows another, she becomes increasingly worried about their safety. In her anxiety, there are only two people she can turn to: Sadiq, the children's enigmatic but attractive uncle; and the father of another pupil, who has gone out of his way to befriend her. But as the peaceful Alpine resort becomes a setting for violence and conspiracy, she realises she cannot trust even them . . .

THE WINDMILL YEARS
Two sisters, with the world before them
A dazzling saga of contemporary love

Vicky Martin

They were sisters, but no-one would have guessed it. Anna was tall, overweight and terribly shy, a talented artist who was terrified of men. Her sister Linden was a superb professional cook, coolly beautiful, poised, and ruthlessly pursuing her ambition to marry a rich man.
But both Anna and Linden find that life – and love – are infinitely more complicated than they had ever imagined. Anna becomes obsessed with Freddie Munroe, an ambitious art dealer who thinks that she too can be moulded according to his wishes. And Linden chooses James Carroll, cold, successful and rich, ignoring her passionate feelings for a penniless art student . . .

HEYWOOD BOOKS

FICTION

One Little Room	*Jan Webster*	£1.50
The Winnowing Winds	*Ann Marlowe*	£1.50

SAGA

Daneclere	*Pamela Hill*	£1.75
Making Friends	*Cornelia Hale*	£1.75
Muckle Annie	*Jan Webster*	£1.75
The Windmill Years	*Vicky Martin*	£1.75

HISTORICAL ROMANCE

The Caretaker Wife	*Barbara Whitehead*	£1.50
Quicksilver Lady	*Barbara Whitehead*	£1.50

THRILLER

KG 200	*J. D. Gilman & John Clive*	£1.75
Hammerstrike	*Walter Winward*	£1.75

HORROR

The Unholy	*Michael Falconer Anderson*	£1.50
God of a Thousand Faces	*Michael Falconer Anderson*	£1.50

NAME ....

ADDRESS ....

....

Write to Heywood Books Cash Sales, PO Box 11, Falmouth, Cornwall TR10 9EN. Please indicate order and enclose remittance to the value of the cover price plus:
UK: Please allow 60p for the first book, 25p for the second book and 15p for each additional book ordered, to a maximum charge of £1.90.

B.F.P.O. & EIRE: Please allow 60p for the first book, 25p for the second book, 15p per copy for the next 7 books and thereafter 9p per book.

OVERSEAS: Please allow £1.25 for the first book, 75p for the second book and 28p per copy for each additional book.

Whilst every effort is made to keep prices low it is sometimes necessary to increase cover prices and also postage and packing rates at short notice. Heywood Books reserve the right to show new retail prices on covers which may differ from those previously advertised in the text or elsewhere.